CITY OF HOPE

AND RUIN

A FRACTURED WORLD NOVEL

KIT CAMPBELL

SIRI PAULSON

TDP

For Andrew, for always having my best interests at heart.
-K.C.

For my family, who has always believed in me.
-S.P.

CHAPTER ONE
THEOSOPHY

THE CRACK IN THE world was closing, and Theosophy was chasing monsters. She pounded after Astrolabe down the narrow lane to the nearest ladder, wondering where in the City their third partner, Rhetoric, had gotten to. Astrolabe reached the rooftop first, stepped off the ladder, and stopped dead. Coming up behind him, Theosophy could see nothing until her head cleared the edge of the roof.

Three monsters stood together, each twice as big as a skinny City-bred human. She tried to count limbs and failed. Fucking shapeshifters. They bred like rats, too. If she and Astrolabe could just manage to kill them before dawn...

"Look," said Astrolabe quietly.

One monster held Rhetoric's knife.

He'd been just ahead of them, leaping across the gap between two buildings, but a rotten floor had given out beneath him and by the time they'd found a way down, he and the monsters had both vanished.

Theosophy squinted across rooftops in the predawn gloom. At this hour, the sky looked too much like the world's edge. It gave her the creeps. She finally spotted another triad of monsters a few blocks

1

over, heading away and carrying a limp body with a musket dangling off its back.

She swore. Beside her, Astrolabe bent over, keening.

Theosophy cast him an annoyed glance. Brothers they might be, but there was no time for this. The monster with the knife strode across the roof, flanked by the other two.

"Get up," Theosophy snapped.

Astrolabe gave no sign of hearing her.

In a single movement, Theosophy unslung her musket and drove the sword-bayonet into the nearest monster's chest. It fell, but the other two were almost on her.

"Astro!" she yelled.

The limb holding the knife shifted, from tentacle to paw to a great leathery hand that looked almost human but for its size, but the knife never wavered as it rose, then plunged. Theosophy dropped and rolled, hit the corpse of the first monster, and flipped onto her back in its stinking blood. The knife-wielder loomed over her.

It did not raise the knife again. Instead it leaned down, closer, closer, and then collapsed sideways. Astrolabe stood behind it, his expression distorted. He yanked his spear out of the dead monster's back, rolled the creature over, and spat in its face.

"Where's the third one?" Theosophy said.

Astrolabe looked at her, bent almost double, tears running down his cheeks.

"Don't tell me you let it get away?"

"Theo, he was the only brother I had left. And I don't think he's dead. I saw him twitch."

She sat up and grabbed him by the shoulders. "Don't. Just don't. Rhetoric is dead, all right? There's nothing you can do to change that now."

Astrolabe looked away and finally nodded.

Theosophy grunted as she stood. She'd been doing this for ten years, since joining the Militia at fourteen, and her body was starting to feel it. She looked across the rooftops—some flat, others tiled and steeply angled—and spotted the third monster, already into the ruins of the University and moving fast. As she watched, it dropped out of sight. A moment later, she felt the Rift in the center of the world slam shut, leaving just the thinnest trickle of *wrongness*, just as sunlight touched the top of the clock tower.

The City was safe again...until night, and Theosophy's next shift on patrol.

Only then did she turn her attention back to Astrolabe. "You almost lost both your partners instead of just one," she said flatly.

He turned away from her and squatted down on his heels. After a moment, his shoulders began to shake. This time she let it happen.

After all, she'd been like that once, long ago.

BY THE TIME Astrolabe pulled himself together and walked in silence with Theosophy back to Militia HQ, dawn was turning to full morning. The formerly deserted warren of cobblestoned lanes was beginning to fill, reinforced shutters to lift, shops to open. Most buildings had two solidly built stories, but two or three or four levels had been built higgledy-piggledy on top, making the walk at ground level nearly as dark as night—if night had not held such terrors. Crystal-powered lights were coming on in the shopping stalls and front rooms they passed. Above their heads, washing was strung from one side of the lanes to the other, layer on layer, and window boxes full of pale, straggling hydroponic herbs were positioned to grab what sun they could.

Back at the HQ building, they stripped down and showered quickly, both lost in their own thoughts. Astrolabe was quiet and distant, and Theosophy was occupied with getting sticky monster-blood out of her hair. Even though she kept it shorter than finger-length, her hair was so tightly curled that it gripped and held *everything*. Fighters had the luxury of hot-water showers, which helped with the new aches from the last night's patrol, but not the tightness from older scars, white lines crisscrossing her light brown skin.

Once dressed in a fresh jacket and breeches, Theosophy gave Astrolabe one last look before parting ways. His olive skin was paler than usual, but his eyes, when they met hers, held a resolve that they hadn't before.

She sighed. One more kid, hardened to steel; one more true fighter in the making. If he was lucky, he'd survive the angry-and-stupid phase. She'd have to watch both their backs until that passed.

Her quarters were as barren as any new recruit's, though this room had been her home since she had earned the right to move out of the dorm. This building, at least, was secure; they couldn't afford to lose trainees. But it meant no windows on the ground floor, and only narrow slits on the upper floors. Sunlight, she missed. And the day was promising to be a warm one. Even though she needed to sleep, she took her bowl of beet-and-rat soup from the dining hall and headed for the rooftop gardens.

Solvent was already there, eating breakfast, as Theosophy had known she would be. Although Solvent still lived at Militia HQ, she worked the day shift with the Faculty of Hydroponics. Her work was mostly underground, but she hated being indoors and avoided it whenever she could. She even napped up here during the long daylight hours of summer, ignoring Theosophy's nagging about the danger of sleeping into the dusk...but then, she hadn't been caught out yet.

In the distance, all around the City, the nothingness brooded. The HQ building was set midway between the University ruins, at the center of the world, and the wall of darkness and mist that encircled the City, where the world ended. The building faced the Wall, but Solvent was sitting at the back, facing in toward the ruins. Her feet dangled over the four-story drop, and she was chewing rock salts, even though she'd be heading in to work before long. Theosophy wove through the hydroponic flats of sprouts and greens toward her.

"Want some?" Solvent asked as Theosophy dropped down beside her. She'd been at it long enough that her voice was lazy, her pupils dilated so that the blue ring of her irises barely showed.

"Not today." That stuff would kill you, sooner rather than later. She'd taken it before and would again, but not every day like Solvent. Theosophy couldn't blame her for it—it took the edge off without impairing you too much—and sometimes she wondered why she didn't just give up too. But so far she hadn't.

"Aw, c'mon, Theo," Solvent said. "You know it's no fun to do alone."

"You have other friends," said Theosophy.

"'Friends', huh. Is that what we are?"

It was an old argument. They'd been having it for years with varying consequences, as they both cycled through other lovers and, eventually, back to each other. Today Theosophy surrendered herself to its patterns, knowing full well what she was doing. They went through its beats, back and forth, and at last Solvent cried, "That's it, I'm through, I'm going to do my duty to the City and have babies," and Theosophy growled, "Oh, are you?" and kissed her, hands tangled in Solvent's silky blonde hair. Solvent kissed her back, the taste of rock salts strong in her mouth. Theosophy drew Solvent over to the blanket they'd stashed in the rooftop shed for just that purpose, and they fell together. Astrolabe's grief and Rhetoric's face and the rest of the world finally went away.

She woke, sometime later, to one of the new recruits shaking her. Solvent had gone and the sun outside the shed was high and hot. When he saw that she was awake, he stepped back from the blanket and said, "Sir! The dean wants to see you, on the double. Astrolabe's gone!"

DEAN PROSODY WAS pacing in her cramped office when Theosophy arrived. Her bayonet and whetstone lay forgotten on her desk.

Theosophy stopped just inside the door. "Sir?"

"He's not in his quarters, and he took his spear," said the dean, not looking at her.

Theosophy reached into her belt pouch and pulled out her double crystal, tuned to her partners. One side had gone dark, of course, but the other pulsed weakly. She could feel the direction of the pull—toward the ruins—but that meant nothing, surely he wouldn't be such a complete...

"What did you say to him?" Dean Prosody demanded.

Theosophy shrugged.

"Nothing about avenging Rhetoric?"

"I should hope not," she said. "I was a little busy fighting for my life. With one partner gone and the other just standing there..."

The dean gave her a look, blue eyes snapping.

"What? I let him mourn after. But he still let the third one get away, and almost got me killed. I had to say *something*."

The dean sighed.

"There's a reason I'm the longest-serving fighter. And it's not because I'm nice."

"About that, Theosophy...maybe you should consider stepping down."

She opened her mouth, but nothing came out.

"I know you're the reason a lot of these kids are still alive. But you're turning sour. It's not healthy."

Theosophy grimaced. The thing was, staying alive the longest wasn't any kind of mercy. It just meant everyone you used to know was dead.

"What about easing off from active duty and taking over training instead? Or better yet, switching faculties altogether."

Theosophy stared at her commander for a moment. "Fuck. You've been talking to the chancellor again, haven't you?"

"We've chatted," Dean Prosody admitted. "After all, you've done your duty here and then some. And you're the last of your line. The City needs all the bloodlines it can get."

Theosophy shook her head, but the dean stood up and gave her a hard glare. "If I were you, I'd think about it. Hard. Before someone takes the choice away from you."

Before Theosophy could decide how to respond, the young recruit knocked on the door, out of breath. "Sir, someone saw him crossing the barricade."

The dean swore.

Theosophy shook her head slowly. He'd done it—the stupidity phase had gotten him. And there went her other partner. "Fucking idiot."

Dean Prosody sighed. "I hate to do this, but...you'll have to go after him."

Theosophy laughed, but the dean didn't. She felt her jaw drop. "Excuse me? Sir?"

"You'll take backup fighters, but not too many—one trio should do. That way you can still move fast. Hopefully fast enough. I don't have to tell you to be out of there before sunset."

She couldn't believe what she was hearing. "You remember the fate of the last expedition, right?"

"Are you challenging my orders, fighter?"

"No, sir. I'll do it. Just...can I ask why?" She bit her tongue to keep from finishing the sentence: *why we're risking four lives for one?*

"Because with his brother dead, Astrolabe is the only child his parents have left."

That was no kind of answer. Half the people in the City could say the same, and for the same reason. Sure, Astrolabe's father was the Dean of Biology, and Astro had no living cousins. She'd known that the whole point of putting Astro and Rhetoric in the same trio was that she herself was the best qualified to look after both of them. But that didn't mean he was worth four lives.

Still, he'd been her partner. Even if he was probably a dead man like his brother, she owed it to him to try. Besides, she'd always known her death was only a matter of time. Might as well make it count.

BEFORE SHE COULD go into the ruins, she had to choose a trio of young fighters—two teenaged boys and an equally young androgyne, whose names she didn't bother to remember, though she had done training with them all at one point or another. If they survived the mission, she'd ask them again. Then they all had to be properly outfitted, their weapons and crystals checked. By the time they were ready to set out, the sun was already past midday and dropping, too fast for her liking. But if Astro was in the University ruins, alone or with his injured brother, he wouldn't survive the night.

The four of them walked through the main square and into the lanes beyond. She led the others, threading her way through the hot and cramped maze of alleys, past handcarts and goats and chickens and someone's tame flock of pigeons. Every few corners held a tiny shop, just barely big enough for the proprietor to sit in but packed full of an amazing array of bits and bobs, household items, and messages held for others in the proprietor's head. The shops were as close as most people got to addresses—especially here, in the poorest area of the City.

Then the jam-packed buildings fell behind, and she and the trio were facing the ruins.

She had been in here a few times before, but only on the very edges, she and her trio—different partners each time—moving as one among the half-collapsed buildings. The last major foray had been disastrous in ways she didn't like to think about, and Dean Prosody had not ordered another assault since.

No time to hesitate, though. Theosophy strode forward through the no-man's-land of rubble, clambered nimbly up the blockade, saluted the guards manning it, and dropped down on the other side.

Her young trio caught up before she was halfway down the block. Some of the buildings she remembered had collapsed, but as she went, she tried to identify each ruin, to map the paths she was taking, so she could tell the dean later. Some of the structures had been built up by monsters since the Great War, in weird ways that made her brain hurt to look at. But on the whole, there was a lot more sky above her than she'd ever seen at ground level in the City. She could even see the

Wall from here, though she was nearly at the center of the world. A sense of wrongness throbbed through her body from directly ahead. Behind her, one of the trio vomited. It had hit her that way the first time she'd come in here; now she knew what to expect, and could steel herself. She still felt queasy, though, and the longer she stayed the worse it would get. Especially in this heat—she wasn't used to working in daylight.

Astro... If she were Astrolabe, coming in here alone, looking for her brother who'd been carried off, where would she have gone? Her crystal was pinging in resonance with Astro's, but it was hard to follow, with buildings in the way and that wrongness interfering with the signal, possibly bending it around corners and who knew what else.

They'd have to check the buildings. Dangerous, for whatever monsters were still here during the day would be lurking indoors, out of the sun. The ruins were eerily quiet as she led her trio among them. The pinging of the crystal made her wince, even as it sped up. She was uncomfortably aware that the farther in they went, the longer they'd have to run or fight on their way back.

A few blocks in, someone said, "Psst!"

Theosophy halted and looked up.

Astrolabe was at a third-story window, fingers to his lips. He pointed down, toward the floors below him.

Theosophy froze. "Monsters?" she mouthed, and he nodded. The fool had gotten himself trapped upstairs—he should have known better. "How many?"

He flashed three fingers, twice. She swore silently. Outnumbered, and with only tyros to back her up...

Well, here went nothing.

"Hold tight!" she mouthed. "We're coming."

He nodded and dropped down, out of sight of the street.

Theosophy glanced at the trio of fighters behind her and pointed at random to one of the two boys, wishing she were familiar with their strengths. "You, stand guard. The rest of you, with me!" She didn't wait for a response but tilted her bayonet upward and dashed into the building.

The monster triad in the first room was caught off guard. She killed one and yanked her bayonet free of its chest before the second and third could do more than rise, writhing from shape to shape, from the meal they were making of some unlucky Citizen. By then, her backup was inside the room, each headed for one monster. The andro kid speared their target easily—they were fast, and stronger than their wiry body would suggest, she noted—but the boy tripped over a human skull and his bayonet thrust went wild. Fangs sank deep into his shoulder and he screamed. By then Theosophy was there to dispatch the monster, but the damage had been done. She heard snarls from deeper in the building. The other triad knew they were here.

She shook her head once in frustration. The andro knelt over their fallen partner and looked up at her. "It's not good."

"Come on," said Theosophy. "We've got to take them out first."

The andro hesitated, and she could see panic and grief rising in their eyes. Then they seemed to tamp it down with an effort, nodded, and rose.

Theosophy stepped out into the hallway. A dark shape faced her, growling, with two more behind.

"Come get me," she said, and stepped forward—and fell.

She landed with a crunch in a pile of rotten boards and dust, her breath knocked out of her. Above, three shadows leapt over the hole one by one. She heard snarls and the clash of metal on claw; then the fight moved away down the hallway and she could hear nothing more.

She pushed herself to her feet, wincing—her ribs hurt, she'd landed on her musket—still trying to catch her breath but knowing there was no time. She had to get out of here, the poor kid didn't stand a chance alone. But the hole she'd come through was too high, no convenient furniture...there had to be a staircase or a ladder. She stepped gingerly into the next room.

Down here, the air was cool. To her left, light filtered down from a staircase that even seemed reasonably intact. She picked her way through debris toward it and paused. On a long table lay a complex-looking pre-War device, only twice the size of her hand but built around the biggest crystal she had ever seen.

She grabbed it on her way past, thinking *barter*, and started to shove it inside her jacket. Her thumb hit a button. And the world went away.

CHAPTER TWO
BRIONY

THE SOFT MOSS OF the forest floor helped dampen the sound of Briony's footsteps as she crept along behind Poes. The mountain cat occasionally glanced from side to side, his golden eyes scanning the near-dark of the forest for danger, but mostly he stayed focused on their target ahead.

Briony paused next to a beech tree, lowering herself down toward the ground. The forest was silent in the fading afternoon light, except for the occasional trill of a songbird, but Briony had spent too much time among the trees to fall for its seemingly innocent appearance. Still, this spot seemed safe enough.

Poes had noticed she'd stopped and padded back to her side. He sat down on his haunches, flicking his tail as Briony dug into her bag and pulled out her notebook. About twenty feet away from her, a vine twisted up the charred remains of a tree. A deer—or at least what looked like one—wandered nearby, its head lowered among the grass and moss. It hadn't noticed them.

Briony took a deep breath. The deer was a perfect subject, assuming it wasn't a Fracture. She flipped quickly through her book until she found the spell she'd written there. Another spell to try, another attempt to find some magic within her. Magic was her ticket to the Academy in Cynestel, and to getting her family out of here.

She owed them that much.

There wasn't much time. Her brother would expect her home for dinner, and she didn't want him knowing she was out here. "Are you ready, Poes?" she whispered. The mountain cat glanced at her, then lowered himself all the way to the forest floor, eyes locked on the deer.

Briony ran her fingers over the amulet her mother had given her for good luck, then closed her eyes, reaching one hand out toward the deer. She tried to imagine she could feel it across the space between them. She had to open one eye to peek at the spell—gibberish, really, as they all seemed to be—before murmuring it under her breath. In her mind, she pictured the deer coming toward them.

She wrapped her other hand around her amulet. *Hidden power*, her mother had told her, before she died. The amulet grew warm in Briony's hand, and she allowed herself to hope.

But when she opened her eyes, the deer was where it had been. It hadn't even looked up, though if it got much closer to that vine, it would regret it.

Briony sighed and sat down. Poes immediately raised his head and placed it on her lap, looking up at her with those large eyes. Briony scratched him behind the ears. "Well," she said, "I guess we can cross 'animal control' off the list, too." A list that was quickly getting distressingly short. More refugees trickled in from the border every day, sharing whispered stories with her as she tended their wounds.

And those were the lucky ones. The thought of the Scarred marching down from up north, of subjecting her family to the things those stories spoke about...

Briony shook her head. Worrying would accomplish nothing, and she was afraid she was running out of time. She reached around Poes to grab her notebook, but the truth was that she had no idea what she was doing. No one she knew used magic except for Kishan. It would take a miracle to get this to work. But it was the only chance she had.

It was growing late, and the darkness of the forest was deepening. She needed to go before the night creatures came out. "Maybe the spell doesn't work on Fractures. Does that look like a Fracture to you?" It was so hard to tell. The deer looked natural enough, but the Old Ones had been meticulous about their details, the better to lure their enemies into their traps. And Briony wasn't going to get any closer, just in case.

There was a loud crack that echoed through the undergrowth. Briony shrank behind the tree next to her as Poes twisted around toward the sound and bristled his fur. The deer turned and fled, disappearing into the trees.

The forest was silent. Briony strained her ears, but heard nothing more. The tree's bark was rough under her fingers, and she could feel it cutting into her palms.

Silence and stillness was never a good sign. She should get out of here. Briony glanced around her, scanning for choke vines or other Fractured plants that could hinder an escape, but the surrounding area was thankfully clear.

Beside her, Poes bared his teeth and growled low in his throat.

Briony edged out from behind the tree, shuffling slowly backward, making sure she hadn't attracted anything's attention. There was another crack. She took refuge behind a sizeable bush as a large group of something moved out of the dark and mist. Briony put one hand on Poes to calm him and pulled him closer. Poes's light coat sometimes made him painfully obvious.

As the group got closer, Briony could tell they were human. She narrowed her eyes, keeping hold of Poes. People, this deep in the forest? Hardly anyone came in here, especially not this deep. Her mother had made sure she and Jael knew the forest's ways, but their land backed up to it and Briony needed it for her medicinal draughts. Most people in Westenaedre avoided it unless absolutely necessary.

There was something unnatural about their movements. As they got closer, Briony could make out their features through the gathering dusk. Her breath caught in her throat. People they were, yes, but their faces were covered by some sort of horrific mask that hid their features and gave them insect-like appearances. Tubes twisted from the masks into metallic canisters on their backs. Now she could hear their breathing as well, rough and much too loud. Every whispered tale from the refugees flitted through her head. The Scarred. But they shouldn't—couldn't—be here. They were still at the border.

What did it mean that they weren't?

Briony fought down the urge to run. Poes growled again, and she wrapped her arms around him, willing him to be quiet.

The Scarred passed her by, marching in time through the undergrowth. One of them held something in one hand that dripped on the moss at their feet as they went.

Bile rose up Briony's throat. Old Ones, was that...a head? She couldn't tell if it was human or not, and didn't want to.

The refugees said that they came in the night with no warning. That they swept into towns, leveling buildings with people still inside. That they chased down those that tried to flee and cut them down. That they held down people, still alive, and carved symbols into their faces and bodies before carting them off to who knew where, for who knew what purpose. Whole towns were wiped out in a single night. There were never any signs beforehand. There was never anything left, afterward.

The lucky ones were the ones that died.

Briony waited until they disappeared back into the dusk before she fled.

By the time she reached the edge of the forest, she was completely out of breath. She leaned over, resting her hands on her knees, and noticed that she had scratches up both arms, and her cloak was torn. She must have wandered too close to some of the Fractured plants.

So much for her brother not knowing.

Ahead she could see the warm glow of the cottage she shared with Jael and his children. It was almost dark now, and dinner would be ready. She could see the smoke twisting into the sky. Briony swallowed around the anxiety in her throat. This place had been home forever, but if the Scarred were coming—were *here*…

She needed that invitation to the Academy, and nothing was working.

Poes nudged her affectionately, then melted back into the trees. Briony let him go. Jael wasn't wild about the mountain cat as it was.

She brushed herself off as best she could and headed in, weaving through the different fence posts that remained from centuries of various fences. As a child, she'd loved twirling around them, reveling in their differences: tall ones, short ones, square and round, and even one large, flat-ish one with some sort of weird carving on top. In the dark, they tended to trip people up, but Briony knew each one like the back of her hand.

Jael's eldest, Auberon, almost as tall as her these days, looked up from the hearth as she pushed the door open. A frown creased his brow, but all he said was, "Pa! Bree's home!"

Dinner smelled amazing. Briony took her cloak off and hung it by the door, then turned just in time to have her nieces and other nephew—Marcea, Brin, and Leo—almost knock her over with their exuberant greeting. Her brother followed them in, wiping his large hands on his work apron. "Got so late I thought maybe you were eating elsewhere, perhaps with Kishan. Would have been nice to..." He trailed off, giving her appearance a once-over and narrowing his eyes.

"Go and set the table," she told Marcea. Brin, who followed her sister everywhere, went with her. Leo stuck his thumb in his mouth and blinked up at Briony before running after his sisters, shouting, "I get to do the forks! I get to do the forks!" the whole way. Briony smiled after them, then straightened, absently brushing at her clothes as if that would help anything. Jael waited. Briony finally looked up into his eyes.

"Bree," he started.

"Don't take that tone with me, Jay, I'm not one of your children." She sighed, running one hand through her hair. "I was in the forest." Jael's face darkened, and she held up a hand to forestall his lecture. "Listen to me, this is important. There were—" she trailed off, eyeing Auberon. The boy was still stirring dinner, but he wasn't even trying to look like he wasn't listening in. Briony inched closer to her brother, lowering her voice. "There were *Scarred* there, Jay."

Jael crossed his arms over his chest. "There were not." Briony gave him a look, and after a moment the annoyance dropped off her brother's face, replaced with worry. "It doesn't matter."

"It doesn't matter?" Briony realized her voice was rising and fought it back down to a whisper. "We can't stay here—we've got to go, get the children away from here. If they're already this far into Aelduende—what if the rumors are true?"

Jael waved one hand dismissively. "It'd be one thing if they were, but they're not. Everyone exaggerates, Bree. If you're forced out of your home, why not make it because of metal, poison-breathing monsters?" Despite his words, he pulled on his white-blond beard and looked away.

Briony laid a hand on his arm. "Jay, we can't stay here. Not if the Scarred are crossing the border."

But Jael was already shaking his head, just like he always did. "This is our home, Bree. It has been for generations, and we need to stay here. I will not be run off by rumors. It's as much family as you or me."

"Jay," Briony started, but her brother pulled out of her grasp and headed toward dinner. Briony glared at his back. Well, it was back to the magic plan, though that was quickly proving useless. But she had to do something. She wouldn't sit here, defending a piece of land, waiting for the Scarred to come and carve up the people she loved.

DAY DAWNED without any new answers. Briony slipped a sheet of paper out from underneath her pillow, staring at it. It was in a sad state, folded and worn from overuse. On it, she'd listed every type of magic she could think of: fire, water, air, earth, light, control of plants, control of animals, healing. With her failure of the day before, there was only one option left.

With that in mind, she dressed and went to see Kishan.

He wasn't hard to find. Briony could see the bright red of his healer's robe from several buildings away. Westenaedre was calm and quiet in the early morning, its orderly wooden and stone buildings sitting in their straight lines. Sometimes it bothered Briony, but she thought that might have to do with their family's land, where the handful of buildings seemed to be placed with no thought of logic. She could just see the start of the forest off to the east. In the morning sunshine, it was hard to believe the events of the evening before hadn't been a bad dream.

Kishan was outside their shop near the center of town, surveying a pot that'd been knocked over in the night. Briony silently joined him in cleaning it up, her heart dropping at the state of the plant within. Its stem was bent, its leaves ripped. She could maybe save some of the roots and regrow it, but more likely she'd have to venture into the forest to find some more to try and cultivate.

Kishan, tall, dark-haired Kishan, wiped his hands off on his robe and shook his head. "Some animal, come out of the forest," he said.

"Maybe," Briony said. Once—just once!—she wished he would go instead of her, that he would volunteer to take on something himself. But he wouldn't, and it was too early in the day to fight about it now. Instead, she busied herself by patting the dirt back into place as if that would help anything, and tried to think about how to ask what she wanted to ask.

"Kishan," she said finally, "how did you know you could heal?"

"What, no 'good morning'?"

Briony rolled her eyes, but she stretched up on her toes, wrapped both arms around his neck, and kissed him. "Good morning, dear one. Now answer the question."

"Why?" he asked, brushing a lock of white-blonde hair out of Briony's face. He looked her up and down. "Did you find something?"

"Find something? What does that mean?"

"Never mind." Kishan wiped his hands again, no doubt annoyed about the nonexistent dirt staining his palms. "Don't worry about healing magic, dear one. Healing is a rare gift, you know. Runs in the family."

Nothing ran in her family except that stupid cottage. Well—her hand closed around her amulet again—she'd gotten this from her mother, as well as the healing skills she used to earn her keep. Not magic, not like Kishan, but enough to get by. Not every injury needed that extra touch, after all.

"Don't be sad, Bree," Kishan said. "You knew your magic idea was a long shot."

Briony felt what little hope she'd mustered that morning die. "What am I going to do? I've got to have a good reason to get Jael to move the children away from this death trap."

"Bree, look at me." Kishan took her hands. "Is this about Nerys? Because that wasn't your fault, and it's not your job to look after the children for her. You can't save everyone every time."

It was an old argument, but no matter how many times they went over it, it didn't change how she felt. "There must have been something I could have done."

"I wish you wouldn't blame yourself, dear one. Jael doesn't. The children don't."

"Someone's got to look after them."

Kishan gave her hands a squeeze, then released them. "They're Jael's children, Bree. Like it or not, he gets to make those decisions." He pulled the door to the shop open and disappeared inside. "I don't know why you're worrying so much as it is. The Scarred will never breach the border. The government will hold them there, and we'll be perfectly safe here. There's nothing wrong with wanting to stay where one's roots are."

"There's nothing wrong with wanting to move someplace safer, either." Briony took a deep breath, closing her eyes. Why wasn't anyone else worried about this? The Scarred were getting bolder, if they were here in the forest. Briony had been raised on stories of the Great War between Aelduende and the Scarred, and the atrocities they'd committed then. That had been before they were Scarred, and the rumors from the border only seemed to make them sound worse now.

If one group was in the forest, why couldn't there be more? And they'd been so organized, so unafraid of the dangers that lurked inside. Surely that said something, and Briony didn't think it was anything good.

Kishan reappeared at the door. "You're still worrying," he said. "I promise you that we're safe here. If, on some off chance, the Scarred do make it here, I'll protect you, and Jael can protect the children." He took one hand, patted it, then raised it to his lips. Briony appreciated the sentiment, but what protection would he be, when he wouldn't even venture into the forest when they needed more supplies?

She was being unfair, and she knew it. She'd been raised on the edge of the woods and had had their dangers and secrets shared with her from the time she'd been a child. He'd been raised pampered and privileged, a healer in a long line of healers. He didn't know any better.

Jael might actually be some protection. But why couldn't they just go where they wouldn't need protection at all?

"Come inside," Kishan said. "We've got to make some more burn balm, and we should do it before the day gets too hot."

IT WAS SWELTERING by midday. Briony tried to get her hair off the back of her neck, but a few strands always seemed to escape and cling.

Kishan had discarded his robe, even though it marked him as town healer and he generally hated to go without it. Briony eyed it where it hung next to her tattered cloak. According to Kishan, the robe had been in his family for at least five generations, but it still looked practically new.

"Blast this weather," Kishan murmured. He'd laid his head down on the counter some time ago and Briony had assumed he was asleep.

No one had been in all day, which was aggravating. Briony had been hoping to be able to observe Kishan, to pick up a spell or two to try later, but no luck. She'd have to ask him for one straight out, which she'd been avoiding doing.

What would she do if healing didn't work either? She pulled her paper out of her pocket and smoothed it out against the wood grain of the counter. The Academy would never take her if she couldn't get some magic to show up somewhere, and she couldn't think of any other reason to pack the family up for the safety of Cynestel, at least not that Jael would go for.

They'd left the door open in an attempt to keep the shop cooler, and hence there was no warning when someone came in.

"Hello, Kishan," said Yara. She didn't acknowledge Briony's presence as she sauntered across the shop while Kishan hurriedly lifted his head. Briony leaned her head on one hand and watched, bemused, as the petite woman practically draped herself across the counter in front of Kishan. "I came for more of your delightful sleeping draught."

"Of course," said Kishan, all smiles again, "Briony just brewed a new batch this morning."

"Oh," said Yara. She firmly avoided looking in Briony's direction, though she recovered after a moment and leaned forward again. "Well, surely you have a little older batch that *you* made.

Nothing against Briony's work, of course, but I would really rather have some of yours."

If she leaned forward any more, she'd probably topple over the counter into Kishan's lap.

The smile on Kishan's face drooped a little. "I'm dreadfully sorry, but Bree makes all the draughts." He brightened again. "Brilliant, aren't they? I don't know what I would do without them."

"Oh, oh." Yara pulled back, drumming her fingers on the counter. She looked around the shop, probably looking for inspiration, but Briony made most of their physical wares. "Well...oh. I just remembered that I have some left at home. I guess I just wanted to spend some time with you." She smiled, just enough to seem shy.

Briony was impressed by her persistence, but the scene was starting to wear on her. She stood, not sure what exactly she was going to do. There was only so much blatant—

Another woman ran into the store, panting loud enough to draw everyone's attention. "Please," she gasped, "it's Fen. He's fallen out of a tree."

Kishan was up immediately and out the door, leaving Yara in his wake. Briony paused long enough to grab the pouch she always kept stocked. "Which way?" she asked the woman, whom she recognized as being one of the first refugees who had trickled in, though she could not recall her name.

The woman pointed and Briony took off in that direction. She could see Kishan ahead of her, not as obvious as usual without the red of his robe, and slowly overtook him. Briony was used to running; Kishan, not so much.

They reached the orchards on the southern end of town. The trees were thick with leaves, and some branches hung heavy with fruit. Fen was easy to find by the crowd that had gathered around him. Briony and Kishan pushed through, reaching the boy where he lay on the ground. He was conscious, but seemed stunned, and one arm lay at an unnatural angle.

"Move back," Briony ordered as Kishan knelt beside the boy. She watched as her partner leaned over him, hovering his hands over the boy's chest and murmuring under his breath.

Confusion, then horror, crossed Kishan's face. He stared at his hands, then his arms, and Briony realized that his magic wasn't working.

But why? There wasn't time to linger, however. The crowd would notice soon enough and then the whispers would start. Briony dropped to her knees on the other side of the boy and said, "I'll stabilize his arm, and then we can take him back to the shop where you'll be able to examine him."

Kishan shot her a grateful look and pushed himself back to his feet. He turned to the woman, who had followed them, and was probably the boy's mother. "I think he'll be fine. I'll be able to do a more thorough look back at the shop. I've got a table in the back just for such an activity."

Briony tuned him out. "Can you hear me?" she asked the boy quietly. "I need you to move your fingers and toes. Just wiggle them."

It took a long moment, but just before she started to think there might be more damage than was originally obvious, the boy complied. The movement looked natural, unforced, except on his bad arm. Briony ran her hands around his head and down his neck, gently, checking for breakage, but everything seemed fine. Kishan was still talking to the crowd, though what he could possibly be going on about was beyond her. At least he wasn't hovering, watching her and saying things like, "Speedy as we can, Bree," which always made her want to hit him.

25

She pulled a splint and bandage out of her bag. "This will probably hurt," she warned the boy. "Relax as best you can."

The break was bad, but not as bad as she'd seen. Nothing had broken the skin, and it seemed like only one forearm bone was out of place. Briony set the splint underneath the arm, placed her hands carefully, and twisted.

The boy, to his credit, only let out a whimper. "There, that's the bad part," she murmured. Taking the bandage, she wrapped it around both arm and splint, then used some extra to secure the arm across the boy's chest. "You did great."

Patting his shoulder, she stood. "All ready, Kishan."

"Thank you, Bree. Excellent work, as always." He kissed her on the cheek, then recruited a few men to help carry Fen back to the shop. Briony took her time repacking her supplies before following. Why had Kishan's magic failed him? Was magic something that could desert you? Surely not.

Fen had already been set on the table back at the shop when she arrived. Kishan had replaced his red healer's robe and was politely, though firmly, shooing away potential spectators, including, against the odds, Yara, who must have waited for him to come back. Briony pushed her way through and took Fen's good hand.

Finally they were alone, except for Fen's mother. Kishan took a deep breath, closing his eyes, then let it out slowly before opening his eyes and moving back to the table. His shoulders were tense. He held his hands out over the boy again, breathed again, and murmured under his breath.

Not loud enough for Briony to hear, of course.

Kishan almost immediately relaxed, as did Fen. Briony frowned as Kishan's hands and mouth moved in their usual, practiced manner.

Why was it working now when it hadn't before? Nothing seemed different.

After a few minutes, Kishan dropped his hands and smiled at the woman. "I'm pleased to say that the arm is the worst of it. Everything else seems to be mostly bumps and bruises. I've got the bone started on healing, but it'll be best if he keeps it wrapped the way Briony's done it for a few weeks. Limited movement, and please come back if you need help with that or anything else."

The woman gazed at Kishan with the same awed look that Briony had seen on others' faces her whole life. She'd heard—didn't know, certainly, as she'd never had the chance to investigate—that many villages didn't have magical healers. Kishan might be the only one in this part of the country.

Briony helped Fen up and off the table while his mother enthused at Kishan and tried to squash the envy that wound its way through her chest. She should be used to this by now. Kishan always got the recognition while her more practical skills were ignored. It had always been this way, even before they'd decided to join their work together five years ago.

But it still hurt.

Kishan saw Fen and his mother to the door, then shut it firmly behind them. He leaned his back up against it. "Maybe we should close up for the day."

The door handle jiggled behind him, and Yara's voice floated through the door. "Kishan?"

"Old Ones," he murmured, "why does she persist?" He locked the door.

"Because until you and I are official, there's still hope," Briony answered. "And who wouldn't want to be partnered with our prized healer?" A little bit of her bitterness slipped into her voice, but Kishan

27

didn't seem to notice. There were other reasons as well—whispered rumors about why she lived with her brother, why she ventured into the forest, but Kishan was probably unaware of these, and she did not need his sympathy.

"I have made my choice," he said, moving away from the door, "and I will not change it." He reached for her. "You're amazing, Bree. I would never be so successful without you."

"What happened back there?" she asked, and Kishan's arms dropped. "The magic didn't come."

"No, it didn't." Kishan seemed pale. "I didn't know what to do." He looked up, smiling at her. That warm, loving smile that somehow made her feel both special and annoyed. "Yet another reason that you remain the right choice."

Briony took a deep breath. "What if it happens again?"

"It won't. I did something wrong."

"Something wrong? You could do that spell in your sleep."

"You're right." Kishan sat down heavily on his stool behind the counter. "But I'll be more careful from now on."

Briony placed a hand on his shoulder. "Maybe," she said slowly, "you should try to teach me a spell so I can help out in the future, if need be."

Kishan drew back. "What? It won't work. You don't have what's necessary, Bree."

Anger flared, but Briony forced it back down. She knew as much if not more about healing, magical or not, but bringing that up right now wouldn't help. "But, Kishan, if your magic is failing—"

"It is not failing!"

"—then perhaps it would be good to have some sort of back-up, wouldn't it? For the good of the partnership."

"Bree," Kishan said, "this is insane. You've no magic of your own, and you've never shown signs of having any. You're just trying to have some reason to get away."

"Kishan—"

"No, listen to me. Magic is not something you can just dredge up when you think you need it. We are *fine* here. The Scarred are not waiting outside our doors to steal our children and dig out our eyes. They'll never get through the forest. So you need to calm down and focus on what's important and stop trying to force something that's never going to happen!"

Kishan stopped, breathing hard. Briony blinked, feeling tears well at the corners of her eyes. She stepped back from Kishan, turning away.

"Bree," he said softer, holding out a hand, "please don't."

Without answering, she went through the shop to the back door, and shut it behind her.

SHE FORCED HERSELF to walk calmly through town, though inside the hurt roiled. What was worse was that she suspected Kishan was right, and then what would she do?

Briony reached the edge of the forest and kept walking. Kishan hadn't come after her. That hurt too, though in a different way.

Was she wrong? Were they really safe here like Kishan claimed? She wanted to believe that, but she couldn't, not with the rumors drifting in with the refugees from the border. Not when she'd seen the Scarred *here*, not when even the forest hadn't seemed to slow them down. Maybe they'd all walked into a choke vine and perished shortly after, but that seemed like a remote chance. They'd never had made it so far in the first place if they didn't know what they were looking for.

Who knew? Maybe they had forests back home where the same Fractures and dangers lurked. The Scarred would have learned to adapt too, maybe even better than Aelduende had. And if all the signs pointed to invasion, like Briony thought they did, what would those adaptations mean for her country when the Scarred came?

And then there was Jael. She could see the worry in his eyes. So why wouldn't he go?

She paused mid-step, realizing the forest was too quiet. Her heart jumped into her throat and she turned, expecting to find the masks of the Scarred lurking behind her, but all that was there was a deer.

Briony stared at it for a long moment, wondering at the dread that wormed its way through her. Then it hit her. The deer was much too close. A wild animal, especially a prey animal, would have given her a wide berth.

The deer blinked its wide eyes at her and flicked an ear, the perfect picture of innocence. Too perfect.

Briony took a slow step backward. The deer flicked the other ear. It seemed to tense. Briony took another step.

The deer laid both ears back and opened its chest, revealing two rows of finger-length sharp teeth. It roared, then charged.

"Oh, shit," Briony said. She stumbled backward, turning to flee. But one leg didn't move. She'd gotten too close to the nearest tree, and a tendril of vine had wrapped itself around her ankle.

It was only one tendril. Briony threw herself to one side, wrenching her ankle free just as the Fracture went through the space she'd just been in and smashed into the tree. Briony scrambled to her feet and ran. The Fracture righted itself and came crashing after her before the vine got its hold on it.

Old Ones, this was why she didn't come into the forest without Poes. Now she was going to die out here because no one knew where she was, or even where to look, and she would just disappear, just like her mother.

Briony darted as close to the trees as she dared, hoping another vine would be able to grab the Fracture, but luck didn't seem to be on her side. The creature bellowed behind her, never seeming to lose track of her no matter how she ducked and dodged.

This was not how she wanted to go. Her mother had warned her a million times to be aware of her surroundings when in the forest, that any Fracture could hide itself innocuously enough if one wasn't looking. Is that what had happened to her? Had she gone into the forest that day and missed a warning that would have saved her life?

Briony slipped and fell, sliding under a bush. The Fracture soared by above, taking the bush with it. Briony pushed herself to her feet and took off the other way. There was another roar from behind her, and a second later the sound of hoofed feet followed after her again.

Jael and the children would never go if she couldn't convince them to. She needed to stay alive for them.

The forest was a blur around her. She had no idea where she was, how far she'd come, and the Fracture was still back there. Why couldn't the wretched thing tire out?

Ahead, the ground suddenly dropped out of sight. Briony couldn't stop—wasn't sure she wanted to if she could—and managed to throw herself across the gulley that had come out of nowhere.

She rolled on the other side and managed to regain her footing. She kept running, dodging and changing directions, blood pounding in her ears.

Nothing followed. Briony slowed hesitantly down, but the forest behind her was silent. She froze, not wanting to draw the Fracture's attention back to her if it had lost her. Long minutes, perhaps forever, passed. Eventually a bird overhead starting singing, and Briony let herself relax.

Where was she? She turned in a circle, but nothing looked familiar. Briony took a deep breath. No panicking, not now. She might not know where she was, but she knew where she'd entered the forest and could read directions from the trees and the sky. That was something. Once she got west of the forest she would be in open land, even if she missed the town.

However, now that she'd stopped moving, one of her ankles had started to throb. From the choke vine, or at some point during her escape? It didn't much matter now. She'd probably have to splint it either way.

Ahead, the trees thinned out. That would be a good place to try and get her bearings. Briony limped forward and discovered the shores of a massive lake that she'd never seen before.

That figured. Briony took one more look around, but the forest sounded normal and she was nowhere near any trees, so she risked taking off one boot. She sat down. The cold water of the lake helped soothe her ankle. For a long moment, she rested, letting the lake lap at her ankle and listening to the breeze.

Across the lake, there almost seemed to be the hint of something—a large building? A city?—but when Briony tried to focus on it, it faded away. She shook her head. Probably some sort of illusion caused by the water.

It was growing late and she would need to get out of the forest. She didn't like to be out here after dark, especially without Poes. Reluctantly she replaced her boot and stood, testing her ankle. It would probably hold, for now.

What a mess. And she had no spells to try out any potential healing magic. And what if Kishan was right and it didn't work? What then?

She closed her eyes. *Please*, she prayed to the Old Ones, as bad an idea as that might be, *please, I just need some magic to save my family.*

"What the fuck?" said a voice from behind her. There was an accent to it. When Briony turned, she found herself looking at a strange, ethereal woman who glowed blue in the fading sunlight. Briony's breath caught in her throat. A spirit, Old Ones, a spirit. She hadn't even considered spirit talking in her magic list—it was said the spirits couldn't be trusted, and that people who consorted with them sought forbidden knowledge to sow evil and mayhem—but it was a sign of magic within her somewhere, and maybe she could use that to transition to something the Academy would accept.

The spirit was beautiful, a tall, statuesque woman who had a hard glint in her eyes. Her hair was short, indigo blue through the glow and tightly curled, her skin a lighter shade over wiry muscles. One hand clenched a smallish item made of metal, the other a long tube with some kind of blade on the end. Briony had never seen anyone like her. Though she glanced around and held her body like someone expecting danger, her bearing was proud and strong, and every inch of her spoke of power and competency. A warrior. Briony had heard stories of them, left over from the Great War, but had never seen one herself.

Was that when this woman was from? The War?

"The trio—the monsters—where am I?"

Briony realized she hadn't responded, and that perhaps this spirit had been looking for someone to talk to for a very long time, and maybe she would assume Briony couldn't see or hear her either. "Don't be afraid," she said.

The spirit's eyebrows rose. "That's a...never mind. What is this place?"

"Well," Briony started, taking a step forward. But her ankle buckled and she stumbled, managing to catch herself before she fell.

"You're injured," said the spirit. "Were you attacked?"

"Yes—you see, there was a Fracture back there, and—" Confusion crossed the spirit's face. Maybe she was even older; maybe she didn't know about the War. "There was a war, many generations ago, and the Old Ones, though I don't know if it was ours or theirs or both, created creatures and plants that looked normal but weren't. Fractures. Because they...fractured some part of the creature. I don't know." Briony was aware she was not being clear, though the woman just watched her intently. "Anyway. There were these people—they were supposed to save us. But they abandoned us and left us on our own. And we drove off the other side—the Scarred—eventually, but we couldn't get rid of the Fractures. If that makes any sense."

"A Fracture is...a monster?" the spirit asked. The idea seemed to mean something to her, though Briony could not imagine what.

"Yes, you could say that."

The spirit raised the long tube with the blade, glancing around with hard eyes. "Is it still here?"

"No, no. I outran it. We're safe now."

The spirit gave her an odd look. "Safe," she echoed.

Briony ran one hand through her hair, feeling useless and plain next to the spirit's poise. "I'm Briony, by the way, or Bree, if you like. I live in a town nearby. Westenaedre. Do you live here, in the forest?"

The spirit's gaze softened as she took in the trees, staring as if she'd never seen them before. The lake also seemed to be something of interest. "It's so peaceful," she said, so low Briony was not sure she heard correctly.

"I'm sorry?"

The woman looked at her again, apparently coming to some decision. "I'm Theosophy," she said after a moment. "You may call me Theo."

"Theosophy," Briony echoed, rolling the name over her tongue. It sounded strange and beautiful, just like the spirit. "I'd like to help you, if I can. Is there something you need?"

The spirit seemed surprised. For a long moment, she stared at Briony. Then she lifted the hand with the smallish piece of metal, as if to offer it to Briony. "Yes, you could tell me what this—"

And just like that, she was gone.

The gathering darkness was more obvious without her glow. Briony felt oddly bereft at her loss, but also jittery. She had spoken with a spirit! And without a spell or anything. Maybe there was hope for this magic plan yet.

As long as no one caught wind of the fact she was spirit talking. Not even Jael or Kishan would be able to save her then.

CHAPTER THREE
THEOSOPHY

THEOSOPHY STARED around wildly. Half-ruined basement room, staircase, long table. The mysterious device was in her hand, just like before. But only a moment ago, she'd been standing...where? A place like nothing she'd ever seen before. Plants as tall as buildings, and loose water the size of a market square...and that beautiful woman, delicate and nearly white-haired, blue-eyed though her skin was golden, standing with confidence amid all that strangeness, as if she understood it, as if she belonged there. Everything had been bathed in a weird blue light—untouchable, odorless, and distant, as if seen through glass. A place she wouldn't have believed possible. And all of it summoned, and then banished, with the touch of a button.

"What just happened?" she said out loud.

The sound of combat penetrated her confusion. Fuck, there was a skirmish still happening upstairs.

This was no time to stand there, just *thinking*. What had gotten into her? She raised her musket and charged out of the room and up the stairs. The young andro stood in the hallway among dead monsters, yanking their spear out of the last one. A quick glance showed her that both their trio-mates were dead as well.

She realized that the device was still in her other hand, and shoved it hastily inside her jacket. "Watch my back," she said, and waited just long enough for the kid's nod before turning to the second-floor stairs. She took them two at a time and turned out of the stairwell.

And there he was, slumped against the wall below the front window.

His right arm was a mangled mess, and even in the dim indoor light she could see how pale his face was. Blood was matted in his mop of black hair.

"Astro," she said roughly.

He stirred and looked up at her. "He's dead, Theo. I saw his body. I thought I didn't care if I died then, but when they found me...turns out I did care after all. But I couldn't get away. I fought them off, but..."

"I should have been there," Theosophy said.

He laughed a little. "No. It was a stupid idea."

"You're right. What were you thinking, dumbass?"

"Probably the same thing you were when you decided to mount a rescue party. That's not like you."

She winced and shook her head. "Don't worry about that now. Can you walk?"

"Maybe, but I for fucking sure can't fight. And I've lost a lot of blood."

She groped under her jacket for her shirt, tore a strip off the bottom, and knelt to tie it around his arm as tightly as she could. He let her work in silence. There wasn't much left of the arm—he was going to lose it, even if they somehow got him back to HQ—but she wasn't sure what would happen if she lopped it off right then and there, so she just bound it to his chest.

Astrolabe didn't stir until she was tying off the knot. "What are you doing, exactly?" he said.

"I have to get you out of here."

He met her eyes, and she saw no fear of death there, just a bone-tired resignation that she understood all too well. "There's no point. You're an able-bodied fighter, and I'm not. The City needs you."

"But..." She didn't know how to put her thoughts into words. She wasn't supposed to be the one walking away from here. She had been content to die rescuing him, knowing she'd saved a life, and a useful life at that. But to rescue him and let him live like that...

Still, she had a job to do. Dean's orders, and the dean had said nothing about leaving him behind. "I'm bringing you back and there's nothing you can do about it. Ready?"

He argued, but she slipped an arm under his good shoulder and heaved. He staggered to his feet. Most of his weight was on her—they'd never get far that way. She nudged upward, just a little, and he stood, wavering, on his own two feet.

"Good lad," she said.

A slithering and a scuffling, as of many large creatures, came to her ears. Night had fallen. And then a howl. They'd smelled the humans.

"Sir?" The kid's voice, from downstairs.

Astrolabe met Theosophy's eyes, and she saw terror.

"Time to go," she said cheerfully. Hefting her musket, she led the way downstairs.

SAFELY OUT OF the ruins and on the other side of the blockade, Theosophy eased Astrolabe to the ground, then dropped down to a crouch, panting. This wasn't a good spot to rest for long, not after sunset when the blockade was left unmanned, but the monsters would be roaming deeper in the City by now; she could at least catch her breath. A moment later, the kid dropped down beside her.

It had been a nasty business, getting the three of them out. The kid had proven to be better than she expected from such a tyro—sharp-eyed, light on their feet, and quick. She would never have made it back without them. Astrolabe had managed to walk under his own power for the most part, but the best he could do was hide while she and the kid scouted or fought their way forward a few buildings' worth of distance. They'd done that over and over again until Astrolabe passed out. By then they were almost within sight of the blockade, and fucked if she was going to give up then.

She stirred to glance at her new companion. The young fighter's eyes were blank and staring. Theosophy studied their beardless face and slender, unscarred hands, wondering if this was the first time they'd been inside the ruins, or just...no, dumbass.

"Sorry about your partners," she said awkwardly. "They died well."

After a moment, during which she wondered if the kid was worse off than she'd thought, they stirred. In a light tenor she hadn't noticed before, they said quietly, "No such thing."

Theosophy snorted. Couldn't argue with that. She stood up, scanning the area for danger. "Come on."

They looked up at her, wordless but pleading.

"We can't stay here," she said. "Unless you want to get yourself killed too."

"Wouldn't mind," they mumbled.

Here we go again. What was it about young kids that made them so ready to die for nothing? She herself expected to go down fighting, but she was going to do it for a good fucking reason. But this one reminded her a little too much of herself, years ago. Theosophy sighed. "What's your name, kid?"

"Lever," they said.

"So, Lever, you wait for one of the monster triads to find you. What then? You take out one, maybe two, before they get you? Won't bring your partners back."

"If you stayed..."

Theosophy shook her head. "Nuh-uh. I'm not fighting with just one partner. Especially one I haven't even worked with yet."

The kid stood up slowly. "Yet?"

"You're going to need a new trio. So am I. You're fast and quick-thinking—a better fighter than your partners were." The kid frowned, but she ignored them. "You'll need a lot more training, but you've got guts, and I like that. And you do what you're told. In other words, you're trainable. Are you in?"

Lever's gaze cleared for the first time, and they gave a firm nod. "Yes, sir!"

"Good. Let's get out of here."

With Lever's help, Theosophy dragged Astrolabe back through the darkened City, tagging along with other trios as much as she could. The other fighters recognized her, offered to see her safely to HQ, but she refused. They had a job to do. She was supposed to be on duty too—maybe the dean didn't think so, since she'd already run a mission, but Theosophy did—but with most of two trios gone, there was nothing she could do until the next shift. In the meantime, the best she could do was get Astro back to HQ.

Besides, there was the device. Last night she'd had two partners; today she had half of one, and the device, and the intriguing woman it had shown her. No way was she going to lose it now.

THE THREE OF THEM made HQ without incident. Dean Prosody took one look at Astrolabe and had him whisked away to Medical, leaving Theosophy sitting awkwardly in the dean's office next to Lever.

The kid stared off into thin air and didn't talk, which suited Theosophy just fine, as this was the first chance she'd had to think about the mysterious woman with the captivating blue eyes. She'd seen fighters hallucinating after too much exposure to monsters or the ruins. It was the most likely explanation, but it didn't *feel* right. And she hadn't survived this long by ignoring her gut. She closed her eyes, trying to reconstruct what had happened. She'd touched something on the device and it had started the...vision...and then accidentally touched it again and everything had gone away. That seemed oddly specific to be a hallucination. Pre-War devices sometimes did weird things, but she'd never heard of anything this weird.

Well, there had to be an explanation, and she would find it.

She opened her eyes and glanced at Lever, who seemed to have fallen asleep. Her hand crept into her jacket and she pulled out the device. Finders keepers, that was the rule: a perk for the dangerous life of a fighter. The dean had no claim to it, but she felt a little guilty keeping it to herself, for its value in trade far outweighed anything else she'd ever found. The crystal alone was worth a lot, never mind all the other parts...but if she kept it intact, she could barter it to the Dean of Engineering, maybe even the chancellor.

She fiddled with the device, trying to remember exactly what she had done before, to get to that strange place with the fascinating woman. Yes, that was it. Hold *that* button down, and hit the other at the same time...

Nothing happened.

She tried again. Still nothing. The device lay inert in her hands. She remembered an empty, echoing feeling from the first time, and that wasn't there now. The thing was dead.

Dean Prosody's confident stride sounded outside the office, and Theosophy shoved the device back inside her jacket and nudged Lever awake.

A moment later, the dean came in. She looked Lever up and down and ordered them to bed, "maybe with a couple of beers first." Theosophy privately thought the dean could stand to be off-duty too—she didn't seem to have slept since the news of Astrolabe's disappearance—but that wasn't her business.

"Well?" said the dean, after Lever had gone.

Theosophy suddenly felt weariness hit her, right down to the bones; she hadn't had a full day's sleep, either. She shrugged.

The dean gave her a long look, then closed her office door, went to her cabinets, and pulled out a bottle of watered vodka and two glasses.

Theosophy shook her head. "I don't drink, sir. Dulls the senses and fucks up the reflexes."

The dean poured anyway. "You'll be off duty at least until tomorrow. You'll be fine by then."

Theosophy accepted the glass and took a swig. It burned a little as it went down, but two breaths later, she felt much better. The sight of Astro's crushed arm and the defeat in his face, still hovering behind her eyes, started to go fuzzy around the edges.

The dean watched her and nodded. "Report."

"Rhetoric is dead, sir. As are two of the trio you sent with me." She gave a concise description of the mission—the layout of the ruins, the monsters they had encountered, the combat and Lever's good showing, their dangerous progress back with Astrolabe. She did not mention the device. It wasn't any of the dean's business.

"What about Astrolabe?" the dean said.

"Sir?"

"You haven't asked how he is."

Theosophy swallowed and looked away. "He'll never fight again. What more is there to know?"

"It looks like he'll live, for starters. But without the arm."

"That's good for the bloodline, then," Theosophy said tonelessly. She didn't want to think about Astro, living like that. Or Rhetoric either, but at least he was cleanly dead, easier to put out of her mind.

The dean frowned. "When was the last time you took a day off, Theosophy?"

"Fuck that, pardon my language, sir. We can't afford days off, and you know it."

"Let me worry about that. I'm the dean, in case you've forgotten."

"Sorry, sir," Theosophy muttered.

"You've been under a lot of strain lately, with your trio dissolving. And then there's the way the ruins play with a person's mind. You wouldn't be the first good fighter to have a breakdown after something like that."

"Sir, after all I've done, can't you trust me to do my job?"

The dean waited, and when Theosophy mumbled her apologies again, she went on. "You will sleep tonight, relax with your lover— you're back on with Solvent, right?—or whatever you like. Tomorrow, report to me for your new trio."

Theosophy swallowed down her objections. "About that, sir...I'm taking Lever."

The dean gave her a level-headed stare. "Do you mean you'd like to request Lever?"

Theosophy looked away, embarrassed. "I mean I already told Lever I'd like them on my team."

"Be very careful, Theosophy. I don't want to lose you on the front lines, but if you continue overstepping, I'm moving you elsewhere."

"Yes, sir."

"Fine. Take Lever for training and I'll think about your third trio-mate. Unless you've already promised that position, too?"

Theosophy looked carefully and saw a hint of a smile. "No, sir."

"Good. And...I'll be keeping a close eye on your mental state. I suggest you do the same."

"Yes sir," said Theosophy, and escaped.

CHAPTER FOUR
BRIONY

IT WAS SURPRISINGLY hard to find someplace to herself. There were only a few buildings on their family's land. The house had children everywhere, and there was no guarantee that, even if a room was empty when you started something, it would stay that way. And Jael often moved between the other buildings, caring for their animals and working on other projects.

Since the shop definitely afforded no privacy, Briony ended up locking herself in her room by shoving a table in front of the door. The children might still be able to get in eventually, but at least she'd have some forewarning.

The first thing she needed to do was write to the Academy. There'd been a boy, when she was young, who'd gone, and it had taken weeks for him to hear back. The trickle of refugees from the border was still slow, but it'd been increasing, and Briony couldn't say how much time they had left before the Scarred—all of them, not the ones lurking in the forest—came. She didn't have time to waste.

She hated to do it with only spirit talking to show—that was not a course she wanted to follow—but the spirit talking proved she *did* have magic, no matter what Kishan thought, and she would just have to figure out something else she could do before the Academy got back to her.

So she'd send the letter in as quickly as possible—though she'd worry how to do that discreetly later—so that hopefully she'd get good news and would finally be able to convince Jael to go. But how to word it?

She got out a sheet of paper and stared at it. She had to say enough to garner their interest, but not be too specific since disclosing the spirit talking would be a bad idea. It wouldn't be a good idea to leave rough drafts about for the children or worse, Jael, to find, so she would have one chance at this.

It took a while, but she finally settled on a short, quick message.

Have recently discovered some magical aptitude. Would like to request a place at your academy to expand my skills. Please send reply to Briony Ealadgast, Westenaedre.

That would have to do. She didn't know what else to say.

There was a knock on the door. "Bree?" Kishan. Briony carefully folded the letter and slid it into her trouser pocket. "Bree? Are you in there?"

Lovely. Why was he here? Was she late to the shop? Kishan could mind it just as well by himself for a bit, if he'd bother, but now he was wandering around as well, and no one was there.

There was really no way to subtly move a table. Kishan occasionally called her name while she maneuvered it back into its normal place, no doubt wondering what by the spirits she was doing, but she ignored him. She was still somewhat hurt from what he'd said yesterday, and she wasn't sure whether or not he'd be able to sense her new magic, and, if so, what kind it was.

He'd probably talked to Jael on the way in. Nothing good would come of that. It'd been hard enough to sneak into the house so her brother didn't notice the aftereffects of her expedition into the forest.

But she couldn't avoid him forever. She straightened her clothes, hoping there were no obvious scratches showing, and limped over to the door.

Kishan brightened as she opened it. "Bree! Good morning. I wanted to—what happened to your leg?"

"Nothing," Briony said. "Who's minding the shop?"

Kishan frowned at her. "I wanted to apologize," he said. "I was feeling out of sorts and I took it out on you. That wasn't fair. Now sit down so I can take a look."

Briony let him lead her over to her bed. His healing magic tingled a bit, like it always did. She'd hoped it would seem different, now that she'd done some magic too, but there was nothing new.

She still needed to give healing magic a try. Since Kishan was going to be no help, she made a mental note to steal one of his books later. It was still her best option, aside from spirit talking, since everything else had been a failure.

But her ankle did feel better.

"Part of it was me being selfish," Kishan said. "I need you here, so the thought of you running off to the Academy, well, I don't like it."

"You could come too," Briony said. "Why haven't you gone? I'm sure they'd love to have someone of your caliber there."

"I'm needed here," Kishan said, a little too brusquely. "There, that should do it." He stood, holding a hand out to her. "Will you forgive me?"

Why wouldn't he want to go to the Academy? Surely, if healing magic was as rare as she'd heard, he could do more good there than here.

Something to think about.

"Yes," she said, and, when Kishan pulled her closer, she wrapped her arms around his neck and laid her head against his.

"Let's go to the shop."

"I need to do something first," Briony said, feeling the letter as a heavy weight in her pocket. She hated to go behind Kishan's back on this when she was already going behind Jael's, but he obviously didn't approve.

"I'll come with you."

"No," Briony said, then pulled back, laying a hand on his shoulder. "Someone should be at the shop in case someone's sick or hurt. This will only take a moment, I promise."

Kishan looked at her, then nodded once. "Okay. If you're sure."

"I am."

He went without further protest. Briony took a moment to twist her hair up, then headed out. Hopefully Kishan was far enough away that he wouldn't see which way she went.

Leo latched onto her leg on her way out, but luckily Auberon was nearby, practicing carving on a scrap of wood Jael had given him, and the promise of sharp objects lured the little boy away easily enough. Jael was nowhere to be seen. Thanking the Old Ones for little blessings, she hurried to the edge of town, to the Sender's.

Briony rarely had a reason to visit the Sender. She knew no one outside of town and had no reason to converse with anyone, though she had occasionally come when Jael needed supplies. Luckily no one else was there.

The Sender, a middle-aged woman named Rissa, looked up as Briony came in and shut the door behind her. "Good morning, Briony. Are you expecting a message?"

"No, Rissa, I came to send one." Before she could lose her nerve or think better of it, she took the letter out of her pocket and handed it over. "I need it sent to the Academy in Cynestel, please."

"The Academy?" Rissa echoed. "Something for Kishan, no doubt. Well, I won't ask. Come into the back."

Briony followed Rissa into a back room with no windows. A lone lamp, glowing faintly yellow, lit the room. Rissa shrugged into her official Sender robe, long and blue with elaborate embroidery across the bottom, and placed the letter on a featureless square box in the middle of the room. She held her hands over it, palms flat and facing downward, and murmured under her breath.

The letter flashed blue and was gone.

Rissa smiled at her. "There we go! I'll let you know if we get a reply."

"Thank you." Did Sending count as magic? Briony pondered that as she made her way toward the shop. Probably, but not the same way. She was pretty sure the magic was in the box, not in the Sender themselves.

Kishan was not at the shop when she arrived. His robe was gone as well, so perhaps he'd been called away, which suited her needs perfectly. Briony let herself into the back room and headed for where Kishan kept his books. They were ancient, predating the War, and she'd have to handle them carefully. He'd never let her look inside, but she just needed one spell to try out.

She reached for a book, then paused, listening closely. It was quiet in the shop. She'd be quick, and then Kishan would never know she'd touched them.

Briony chose one at random and flipped it open. Inside were detailed illustrations of various parts of the body and diagrams of internal systems. Interspersed were definitions and explanations, but there was nothing that was obviously a spell. She put the book back and took out another one, but it was much the same. Crap. What was she going to do? Kishan would never give her a spell to try.

He could be back at any time. Briony scanned through the books. One was different than the others, newer yet more worn. She pulled it out and flipped it open. It was a diary of sorts, a jumble of thoughts and healing cases and more personal notes, all written in Kishan's own handwriting.

The door to the shop opened. Briony jumped and almost dropped the book. She ran as quietly as she could manage across the room to her workbench and stuffed the book under her own journal, where she kept her base of knowledge. This she flipped to a random draught just as Kishan came into the back room.

"Old Ones, what a mess," he said, running a hand through his hair. "Entire family ate rotten fruit."

He sat down heavily in a chair. Briony made appropriately sympathetic noises while she gathered her supplies—apparently today she was making stomach-calming draughts—and tried not to drop anything. How long would she have before Kishan noticed the book missing? She wasn't sure she'd ever seen him write in it. But admittedly she never really paid attention to what he was doing while she was working.

Her luck continued to hold, however, as he paid the books no mind. "Honestly, if something smells as bad as this fruit did, common sense says not to eat it. I worry about this town, sometimes."

It was a perfect opening to bring up the Academy again, but she bit her tongue. She didn't want to draw attention to magic in case it reminded him of the books. Instead she murmured, "Ridiculous," and finished laying out her tools. She was hyperaware of Kishan's book and was sure any moment he would notice that she was acting weird—she felt like she was acting weird—and call her out on it.

She needed to get out of here. She'd take the book, look through it, try out a spell or two, and then slip it back in here, hopefully without Kishan being any wiser. "I need to go gather some supplies," she said. She took a shoulder bag down from the wall and shoved both her and Kishan's books inside in one hopefully inconspicuous motion. "I'll need to head into the forest for a bit."

Kishan sat up, frowning. "Didn't you just do that a few days ago?"

"Yes, but apparently I missed something. Don't worry; I won't need to go in very far, and if you like, I'll take Poes with me."

"Well, don't take too long. I feel like I've barely seen you today, and I still need to make up for yesterday."

Did taking his book and going through it make up for him speaking her fears aloud? "I won't be long," she said, then forced herself to cross the room and give him a kiss on the cheek. "If Yara shows up while I'm gone, light her on fire."

Kishan chuckled. "Yes, dear one."

Briony felt she bolted out the rear door a little too fast, but she didn't wait to see if Kishan would notice. His book knocked against her leg every step of the way.

POES MELTED OUT OF the forest as Briony approached. She scratched him affectionately behind the ears as he wrapped around her legs. "Where were you when that Fracture tried to eat me?" she asked.

The mountain cat merely butted his head against her hand and purred.

"Fine, you're forgiven," she said.

Today she stuck to familiar paths, just in case. If Jael or, more improbably, Kishan came after her, she'd be easy to find, but she'd take that chance. Logically, Fractures could strike here as well, but there was something comforting about sticking to the same parts she'd traveled with her mother as a child.

The forest was mostly quiet now, with faint trills from birds floating on the light breeze. Briony had left her cloak back at the house, but it was warm enough that she didn't need it. There was no sign of any Fractures, thankfully, and even the choke vines seemed less numerous than usual.

Poes padded along beside her as she made her way to a clearing. She often came here because it was one of the few places where some of the flowers she used in her healing draughts could grow, because there was just enough sunlight that managed to break through the cover of the trees. She knelt in the middle of the clearing and placed her bag on the ground. Taking a deep breath, she pulled Kishan's book out and flipped it open to a random page.

She was immediately rewarded. Among notes of various patients he'd worked on, Kishan had made notes of the spells he'd used. The most common seemed to be the spell he used to see what was wrong with someone. That would be easy enough—Briony could try it on Poes, or even herself.

She had the big cat lie down before she hovered her hands over him like Kishan always did. Closing her eyes, she murmured the incantation under her breath and waited.

There was nothing, not even a tingle.

Briony tried again, then repeated the process, using herself for the focus instead. But the result was the same. Nothing. If her amulet did have anything to do with magic, it was doing nothing now. Briony could feel it hanging heavily against her sternum.

With a sinking heart, she tried a few more spells from Kishan's book. Nothing worked, and it seemed like if the basic spells didn't, then she'd have no hope with his more complicated ones.

She sank down into the moss, fighting back tears. There was a reason magical healers were so rare. Healing magic had always been a long shot, which is why she'd put it on the bottom of her list.

Briony fished her amulet out of her blouse. It was blue crystal cut into a triangle, about the length of half her thumb. A thin line of metal twisted around the outer edges. Her mother had given it to her right before she'd disappeared into the forest ten years ago, never to return, had made her promise to keep it and pass it on to her children, or Jael's if she had none of her own. Her mother had told her that it held some hidden power, though she hadn't elaborated.

Briony had hoped that it would help with her magic, but it seemed she was wrong. Maybe the 'hidden power' had just been something to comfort a young girl. Maybe Mother had sensed that something was going to happen, that she'd be gone, that Briony would need something to keep her going. Jael had taken her in easily enough, though he'd already had a family of his own, but Mother's loss had hit him hard as well.

Shaking her head to clear the memories, Briony let the amulet drop and pulled her own notebook out of the bag. Aside from the recipes she used for the draughts and other things her mother had taught her, she'd written down the various spells she'd tried for the other magic affinities.

One of them had to work now, right? It had to. Magic had come when she'd asked for it, and she needed to get her family to safety.

Briony went through each spell carefully, making sure to pronounce everything correctly and do the proper hand motions. But each spell, one after another, yielded nothing.

Poes watched her for a while, but eventually he curled up in a sunbeam and went to sleep.

Briony pitched her journal across the clearing, then went to retrieve it. What had she expected, honestly? She'd cobbled these spells together. She knew nothing about how magic worked. She could be doing everything completely wrong, if she even had useable spells at all.

Kishan's words echoed—that this was all for something that would never happen. But something *had* happened. She'd spirit talked. Just for a moment, yes, but she had seen that other woman as clearly as if she'd been standing next to her. And what a woman—calm, beautiful, strong. Briony could have looked at her forever. She'd never seen someone like that before.

Too bad she was just a spirit. Briony rubbed her temples. What had she been thinking, offering the spirit help? That was probably how they got you, how they lured you into their evil ways. But there had been something so open, so vulnerable in the spirit's—Theo's—expression. Something that said that she was in pain.

And Briony had wanted to ease that pain.

Well, if spirit talking was all she could do, then she would have to accept that. The Academy would probably still take her. It was magic, after all. She would just have to hope that the Academy was a little more open about the skill. And if Briony got to see her spirit woman more…well, she wouldn't complain about that.

Briony packed both books back into her bag and stood. Maybe she should try spirit talking again now, so she could be sure she understood how to do it. And it would be nice to have some company, and to know that she wasn't a giant failure.

She closed her eyes, took a deep breath, and realized she had no idea how to go on. Most magic required incantations or rituals of some sort, but she hadn't done either to reach the spirit woman. Briony had just prayed, and her prayers had been answered.

Eyes still closed, Briony reached for her amulet. *I'd like to talk to the spirit woman again*, she thought, picturing the woman in her head. Picturing that fire in her eyes, that protective and confident bearing. Her amulet grew warm in her hand, but then it gave an audible spark. Briony opened her eyes—it had never done that before—and looked down just in time to see it glow brightly and go out just as quickly.

What, by the Old Ones, did that mean? For a terrible second, Briony feared the worst—that whatever she'd done she'd done just the one time, that the amulet and whatever powers it had had died. But she swallowed that feeling. No. She *needed* this magic to get her family out of here, and she needed the Academy to offer her acceptance so she had a reason to leave, and so failure was not an option. She had done this. And she would do it again.

But she'd been gone a long time, and Kishan would be getting worried. It seemed like she never had enough time. Rousing Poes, she shouldered her bag and headed back along the forest paths toward safety, or at least as much as could be expected with the Scarred getting ever closer.

Poes gave her hand an affectionate nudge before leaving her. Briony watched him go, disappearing into the trees. How she sometimes wished she could fade into the forest as well. But what would happen to her family if she did?

Kishan was still at the shop when Briony returned. Still in the back too, so she couldn't put his book back, but at least he didn't seem to have missed it yet.

Belatedly, she realized she had forgotten to pick any supplies to justify her trip.

"Find everything you needed?" Kishan asked. "It was nice today, wasn't it? Probably a perfect time to pick flowers in the forest. Speaking of which, I think we can dedicate a little more space to drying, so you can have supplies through the winter."

That would be helpful, though she didn't intend to still be here once the snows started to fall. "Have you ever heard of anyone spirit talking?" she asked, partially to change the subject, and partially because if someone else knew something, maybe they could help her.

Kishan went still. "What?"

"Spirit talking—you know, where—"

"I know what it is. Bree, you couldn't possibly be considering even trying—"

"Of course not!" Great, now she was actively lying to people. But what was one more on top of everything else? Jael didn't even know she was trying magic in the forest. "I was just wondering."

Kishan stood and crossed the room. He gripped her by her shoulders. "Bree, I'm serious—spirit talking is not something you want to get mixed up in. I mean, look what happened to Carys."

"Who?"

"Exactly. If memory serves me, she got run out of town. Lives somewhere north these days, last I heard. But she's not welcome here. We don't mess with the spirits, Bree. Promise me you won't try that. Whatever your plans, nothing's worth what will come with that."

Kishan didn't understand. Briony shook her head.

His grip tightened. "Promise me."

"I never intended to spirit talk," Briony said. That was true enough. "It was just a question." She knocked his hands off and stalked over to her side of the room, putting her bag on the counter. She could feel Kishan watching her, but after a moment, he turned and walked out into the front room.

Briony pulled his book out and put it back while she could. She would stay until closing, because if she left now Kishan would know where she'd gone, and she couldn't risk that. But tonight, afterward, or maybe tomorrow, she'd see if she could find this Carys.

What would Briony do if spirit talking was all she could manage? Even if the Academy would accept her for it, her home would disown her. She shook her head slightly. Well, if all went well, they'd never come back here again, and it wouldn't matter.

She had to follow this for now. As she went to work, the image of the spirit woman lingered in the back of her mind.

CHAPTER FIVE
THEOSOPHY

THE ROOFTOP WAS OUT of bounds at night; monsters weren't attracted to vegetables, so the garden could stay undefended, but if they smelled a human not locked away behind heavy shutters, they'd be on her in no time. So Theosophy went to her quarters, stashed the device under her cot, and tried to sleep. She wasn't used to sleeping when it was dark outside, though, and all she accomplished was tossing and turning, with way too much time to think. She thought about the woman, Briony, how there'd been something about her expression, something she couldn't put her finger on. An openness, an innocence. Briony didn't live—if she even lived at all; Theosophy hadn't decided—in a place where monsters came every night, and suddenly Theosophy wanted that too, wanted it so bad her chest hurt. Even if it was just a hallucination.

She carefully did not think about Astro as she'd last seen him, unconscious, right arm crushed, now just a civilian in need of defending...that shook her worse than Rhetoric's death. Finally she couldn't keep him out of her head anymore; his face hovered behind her closed eyelids. At last she threw back her blanket and got up.

It was still the middle of the night; the dean was still on duty and Solvent was presumably asleep in her own quarters. Theosophy, remembering that she'd missed the evening meal, scrounged some leftovers and took them back to her quarters, where she forced herself to eat. To help with the not thinking about Astro, she pulled the device out from under the cot and glared at it.

"Why didn't you work?" she muttered, trying the various buttons again and poking the huge crystal inside the device. It remained stubbornly dead. "Why there, and not here?" No combination of buttons made a difference. She even waved her locator crystal at it, thinking of harmonic resonances; nothing. For all she knew, it would only operate in the room where she'd found it. If that was true, she was out of luck—she could never get there on her own, nor ask her new trio to go with her, nor ask the dean for permission. And it wouldn't be worth nearly as much in trade if it was dead.

What she needed was information. Her mind went first to the rooms she'd left behind when she joined the Militia, but she shrugged off the idea. Granddad wouldn't want the memories that a visit would awaken, any more than she did. Maybe she could find answers closer to home. Thank fuck he'd insisted that she learn how to read, and well. Most people didn't, and she'd never seen the point herself. Until now.

In the downstairs corridor, next to the dining hall, Theosophy checked carefully for unwanted observers, then opened a door and slipped inside. HQ archives were housed in a cramped, windowless room, so she had brought a small crystal-powered lamp.

The archives were a mess; Dean Prosody and her predecessors had better ways to spend manpower than organizing records. Theosophy could identify the older shelves mainly because they held actual books, with leather covers and impossibly thin pages that had been written on only once, or not even written but made of lettertype, that technology now long lost. The newer shelves had sheaves of parchment bound together with thread, and seemed to consist mainly of the logs kept by the previous deans, palimpsests in tiny handwriting, from before parchment had been deemed too precious for such uses. All knowledge about the Militia since that time was contained in the heads of the dean and a select few others. An interesting resource, those parchment logs, but not what she was after just now.

The older books were jumbled up. Some were dated in the 300s, 200s, even in the upper two digits; others bore four-digit dates from before the War. None were close to the year zero, but Theosophy hadn't expected any. Whatever had happened to reset the counting 534 years ago, it was lost to the centuries between, known only as the Dark Time. There had been a terrible, cataclysmic war; that was all she knew.

Well, that was old history now. She pulled out pre-zero books at random, turning pages carefully. None of them said anything useful about strange crystal devices or why they might stop working. She went through a dozen of the ancient books and, conscious of time passing, reluctantly decided to give up. *One last try.* She lifted one more book down from the shelf. The spine came apart in her hands, the pages split into sections, and a folded paper fell out.

Theosophy picked it up. It took her a moment to understand what she was looking at. A map of buildings and streets, to be sure, in something like the City's layout. But the configuration was so strange, and so many things missing and others present where nothing but empty lots remained, and...

The City occupied a rough oblong in the center of the map. Around it, outside where the Wall ought to be, were what looked like more parts of the City where none existed. The main streets ran straight off the edge of the page. Between them were a web of smaller streets with unfamiliar names, and labels that looked like they ought to be for neighborhoods, only the neighborhoods were surrounded by empty space. How could there be so much emptiness in the world?

There was only one answer. The map encompassed more than the entire world.

Could the mysterious woman—Briony—be out there somewhere? *Outside?*

The monsters came from another dimension, everyone knew that. It leaked into the City at night and closed during the day. So...what if the City and the Rift were not the only two dimensions that existed? What if there was another place, where giant plants and free water and young women could exist without fear?

She looked more closely at the map. The neighborhoods surrounded by empty spaces had labels, like the street names but in bigger writing. On the far side of a clump of mysterious upside-down V's with vertical lines through them, she spotted a label that read "Westenaedre."

It existed! Somewhere beyond the boundaries of the world, past the impenetrable Wall, Briony lived in a place called Westenaedre. She was real, not a hallucination after all. This place had existed before the War—when the map was made—and still did. Somewhere. But how had the mapmaker known?

So absorbed was she that she didn't notice the passage of time until the lamp began to run down and grow dimmer. When she finally realized that she'd been squinting more and more, she jerked her head up to look at the lamp—the *crystal-powered* lamp—and began to laugh.

"WHAT DO YOU know about crystal power?"

Solvent stared off over the morning cityscape, squinting against the pale grey clouds and absentmindedly playing with her tin of rock salts. One hand came up to twist off the lid.

Theosophy took the tin away, fielding the glare that earned her. "Come on, Solvent, this is important."

"I don't know where to start with that question," said Solvent, flopping onto her back. "Give me some context here."

"Well, suppose you had a...device with a dead crystal that needed to be powered up. But it wasn't a common device. How would you know how to power it?"

Solvent blinked up at Theosophy. "There's a limited number of devices in the world, Theo. How can it not be common?"

"Just pretend it isn't."

"This makes no sense. Either it's something you've seen a hundred times, or..."

"Or?"

"You've found something, haven't you?"

Theosophy looked away. "Even if I had, I couldn't tell you. Security and all that."

"Goatshit. You may be the dean's top fighter, but you're not exactly part of the privileged in-circle."

"How do you know? I don't tell you everything."

"Yeah, fucking right you don't."

"What's that supposed to mean?" Theosophy demanded.

"You didn't warn me before you went into the ruins, dumbass. And I've been waiting for you to talk about losing your trio."

"Who told you?"

"Dean Prosody. She's worried about you, Theo."

Theosophy felt a flicker of guilt, but shoved it down. Solvent should know better than to waste energy worrying about people's safety or mental state. "Well, you can just keep waiting. I don't talk about stuff like that. You should know that by now."

"Maybe that's your problem," said Solvent.

"What?"

"You don't tell anybody anything. Not poor Astrolabe, not the dean, not me. You're one big bundle of pent-up hurt, is what you are. Have you even been to see him?"

"No. He won't want to see me. Why would I go?"

"Because he's your *partner*, dumbass. Even I stopped by before I came up here. He's in a bad way, you know."

"I don't have time for this."

"Then tell me what you found."

Theosophy swore. Solvent grinned.

Theosophy gave Solvent the short version of what she'd told the dean, then explained about the device, though she was vague about what she'd seen. She especially didn't want to tell Solvent about Briony, though she wasn't prepared to think too much about her reasons.

When she was done, Solvent shook her head. "They had some crazy stuff back then, didn't they? What would be the point of something like that?"

Theosophy tried for casual. "Who knows. I'm just curious."

Solvent studied her for a little too long. "Can I see it?"

Theosophy hurried down to her quarters, grabbed the device and her bedroll, and got back without running into anyone who wanted to ask inconvenient questions. When she regained the rooftop, Solvent was just closing her tin of rock salts. Theosophy, deciding she'd pushed her lover far enough, refrained from commenting. Ignoring her,

Solvent headed for the cache of bricks that she'd built onto the chimney, where she kept her stuff at night. She squatted down and rummaged through it, and finally waved Theosophy over.

"Let me see that."

Theosophy forced herself to hand the device over, hoping that Solvent hadn't sensed her hesitation.

Solvent turned it this way and that, humming to herself; the rock salts must be kicking in. "Fascinating, isn't it," she said. "Look at all this extra shit they stuck on here. They could've made this work with a lot less material."

Theosophy shrugged. "Everybody knows they were wasteful, pre-War."

"No, no, that's not it at all. They just didn't have to *think* like that. They had access to all this stuff we can only dream of."

"But how?" Even as she said it, Theosophy remembered the giant plants. All those leaves would have made an awful lot of salads, not to mention all the uses that the stalks could be put to if the entire plant were harvested. Briony lived in such a place. Was that why she looked so very young?

Solvent snorted, bringing Theosophy back to the rooftop. "If we knew that, we wouldn't be using our muskets like spears. They weren't made for that, did you know? They were made to throw things, kind of like really powerful slingshots. I think the dean still keeps some of the things that were meant to go inside and get shot out, but there are so few left, they're essentially useless."

Theosophy felt her hands clench into fists. Solvent got loose-tongued when she was salted up. Theosophy was willing to bet the dean didn't realize Solvent had even learned about those things before she'd washed out of the Militia, let alone that she was blabbing about them.

Solvent pulled out a much smaller spare crystal and some wire, and started fiddling with the device. Theosophy let her work, while wondering again at the size of the crystal. Was it so large just because of its age, having been neither cut down for multiple uses or worn down by the years? Or was it vastly more powerful than most?

At last the two crystals flickered in unison. Theosophy held her breath. The light steadied and grew brighter and did not fade.

"There," said Solvent. "That should do it. Now...what did you say it did?"

Theosophy thought of introducing Solvent to Briony, and felt her insides knot. "I'm afraid that will have to wait," she said.

"What? But—"

"It's so late already, you've got to go to work, and I was up half of yesterday..." She rubbed her eyes and let out a feigned yawn that turned into a real one halfway through. "If I don't sleep now, I'm going to do a shitty job with whoever my new trio is."

"Surely you're just going to be training tonight." Solvent's hands crept closer to the buttons.

"No such thing as *just* training." Theosophy snatched the device away, got up, and began to lay out her bedroll. "I'm going to sleep, and if you touch this while I'm dreaming—or out working—I'll have your hide."

"All right, all right, no need to be so pissy." Solvent got up, still grumbling, and punched her in the arm. "I'm glad you made it back from the ruins."

Theosophy looked away, not wanting to see what was in her lover's eyes. "Not as glad as I am," she mumbled.

Solvent's laughter followed her. "Goodnight, grumpy."

DESPITE HER exhaustion, Theosophy woke with a start well before her usual hour. The clouds still obscured the sun, but she guessed it to be late afternoon. She lay there in her bedroll among the plants for a moment before she remembered. This was almost the same time as when she had spoken to her mysterious woman yesterday. Maybe the hour would prove auspicious, the boundaries between dimensions thinner, if she tried again now.

The device sat where she had left it, tucked close to her boots. She pulled on the boots and took the device. Looked over her shoulder, nipped around the far side of the chimney, then leaped to the next rooftop. This one was tiled and peaked, like most in the City. She half-ran, half-climbed one-handed to the top, then inched carefully down the tiles on the other side until she was out of sight of the HQ gardens.

From here she had a good vantage point of the Wall, roiling mist and darkness where the world ended. She could even see one of the roads from the map, running through the City and into the mist. Briony seemed so close...but Theosophy knew better than to try walking straight through. Animals wouldn't go near the mist, and people had tried in the past, with horrendous results. The mist was impenetrable—except, apparently, for the thing she held in her hand.

Theosophy held up the device and closed her eyes, expecting the world to fade around her and make her queasy again. This time she didn't want to watch. She wanted to just *be there*.

She took a deep breath and depressed first one button, then the other. The world seemed to shift a little, with the same echoing hollowness that she remembered from last time.

Then she opened her eyes and her breath caught.

Rooftops. City. Wall. No Briony. "Briony?" she said aloud. "Are you there?" But she knew the answer.

Had the crystal drained again? No, for it still glowed faintly, and there was the hollow feeling, unmistakeable. Maybe she had pushed the buttons in the wrong order or too quickly, or not exactly the way she'd done it the first time? Holding her breath, she tried again, and again, but every combination produced the same result: absolutely nothing.

Disappointment washed over her. It wasn't because of Briony, exactly, she told herself. It was because of the device and what it might represent, that whole other world that existed...somewhere...alongside her own. She had to get back there, had to see her—*it*—again.

She hadn't felt anything so deeply in years. Having a need like that shook her more than she wanted to admit.

CHAPTER SIX
BRIONY

BRIONY RAISED HER cloak hood as she left the shop. Kishan had wanted her to come with him to dinner, which had been tempting, but she'd lied and said Jael needed her home. It'd been a few days since she'd brought up spirit talking with Kishan. If she had any luck, he would have forgotten the conversation by now.

She was doing a lot of lying this week.

North of town was free of forest, at least for some distance. Briony had never had a reason to leave Westenaedre, so her knowledge was mostly theoretical. Still, in the late afternoon light, the road was visible, winding across the plains. The forest echoed the curves of the road to the east, though with a decent-sized buffer.

Hopefully this Carys would be easy to find. She could be anywhere. Why hadn't she moved to another town instead of lurking just outside theirs, as Kishan had implied? Surely one would learn their lesson and keep their mouth shut. There must be something to keep her here.

As Briony went, she passed small groups of refugees streaming south, ragged and worn out. A few stopped her and asked the distance to the next town. Westenaedre had room for them, for now, especially with the harvest coming, but what would they do once the snows began to fall? They were hemmed in on the east and the south by forest and the dangers within, and the plains were not the most reliable for water. Sometimes they could barely support the families they already had.

Another reason to leave.

Hopefully none of the refugees would mention that they'd seen her going this way. The white-blonde hair that was the mark of her family was fairly obvious, but her hood should cover it. She reached up to make sure. She didn't want this trip getting back to, well, anyone.

Westenaedre disappeared behind her and the sun began to set. Maybe this was a bad idea, but she had to try. Why hadn't she been able to talk to her spirit woman again? Why had her amulet made such a weird noise? She needed answers, for her family and—though she would not admit it out loud, not yet—for herself.

The darkness of smoke appeared against the sky, and Briony followed it to its source, which proved to be a small, somewhat decrepit cottage just off the path. It wasn't close enough to be welcoming to travelers, but it was obvious enough that it wasn't trying in any way to hide.

Briony trudged through the tall grasses and knocked on the front door. If Carys wasn't here, perhaps whoever did live here would know where to find her, if Kishan's information was at all accurate. She checked her hood again to make sure her face was in shadow.

She could hear someone moving around, but they were a long time in coming. Briony shifted her weight from foot to foot. Maybe she should knock again. Didn't the unknown person inside realize how important this was?

This waiting was doing terrible things to her nerves. Briony knocked again.

The door swung open almost immediately, revealing a woman who was about the age her mother would have been, were she still alive. "For the love of the Old Ones, child," the woman said, "what do you want?"

Briony hadn't been called a child in many years. "I'm looking for someone named Carys."

The woman heaved a heavy sigh. "Let me guess—your lover died, and you want me to contact him on the other side. I don't know how many times I have to tell you people. It doesn't work like that."

Briony felt hope bloom in her chest. Kishan had been right after all. "No, no, nothing like that. Can I come in, please? I would feel better not discussing this out in the open."

Carys stood silent for a long moment, one dark hand still on the door, but she eventually nodded and stood to one side and motioned for Briony to come inside. The inside of the cottage was the complete opposite of its outside appearance. It was warm and well-lit, and decently furnished. Maybe the outside was an added layer to scare people off.

"Why do you stay?" Briony found herself asking as she lowered the hood of her cloak.

Carys stared at her, surprisingly green eyes looking out of skin as dark as mahogany. "Let's start with why you're here, child."

"Yes, of course." Briony fumbled with her amulet. "I spirit talked. I'm sure of it. But now I can't do it again, and I *need* to." The image of her spirit woman came back into her mind, and Briony could feel her cheeks heat up. "They said you were a spirit talker."

The other woman crossed the room, pulling a kettle off the fireplace. "Sit down. You do know that spirit talking comes at a

70

terrible price? They would not have me in town, yet they still come to me when they want something." She gathered two cups out of a slightly lopsided cupboard.

Briony sat. Carys put a cup in front of her, then poured from the kettle into it. Whatever it was smelled flowery and earthy. "Chamomile?"

"Partly." Carys poured her own cup and then sat down across the table from Briony. "I am not surprised to see you, honestly." She reached out, running a strand of Briony's hair down her fingers. "Spirit talking has long run in your family."

Briony looked up from her cup in surprise. "It has?"

"Oh yes. Your mother and I used to go together."

Briony went back to staring at her cup, as it was easier than meeting Carys's piercing gaze. Her *mother* had been a spirit talker? Her hand went back to her amulet.

"She was more discreet about it, of course." Carys reached across the table, taking Briony's hand. "Tell me, young Briony, why it is so important for you to pursue this course."

Briony found herself telling the older woman everything—from her fears for her family to the Scarred, and even about her spirit woman. She could feel the heat in her cheeks rising again, but she couldn't help it. Theo had been completely different from anyone she'd ever met, and she couldn't help but feel cheated by how short their conversation had been.

"Ah," said Carys when she had finished. She patted Briony's hand then leaned back. "You will not be able to pursue spirit talking at the Academy, I'm afraid. It is too far away."

"Too far—?"

Carys leaned forward again, lowering her voice. "You see, Briony, the spirit world that we can reach is not that of the dead. And the threshold to it is only here, by the lake. The farther away you get, the harder it will be to reach that other realm."

"But, I've already contacted the Academy."

Carys shrugged. "The Academy will not care. They can teach new magic to those that have shown aptitude."

"How do you know?"

"I know." Carys stood, returning the kettle to the fireplace. "If it is your wish to go, the Academy will take you, but you will not be able to talk to your spirit woman any longer."

Briony wrapped her hands around her cup. It was a little rough, giving her fingers something to do. The thought of leaving Theo felt worse than she would expect and she found that she didn't really want to. But she would, of course she would, to protect Jael and the children.

"But why didn't it work?"

Carys shrugged. "There are rules. Things that have to be in effect for the connection to be made."

"Like what?"

"I'm not sure. Your mother always seemed to know, but she never told me."

Mother had apparently kept a lot of things to herself. "Thank you," Briony said, standing. "I'd better get back."

She pulled her hood back up and headed for the door. Carys opened it for her, and Briony stepped out into the fading light.

"Briony," Carys said, drawing her attention back to the well-lit cottage. Briony wished she could stay, ask a million questions, but Jael would eventually get worried and seek out Kishan, and then her cover would be ruined. "Two things. One is that the spirit world has knowledge that we need, and if you know how to ask, you can access that."

A chill crept down Briony's spine. "About the Scarred?"

"Perhaps."

"And the second?"

It was hard to make out Carys's features against the glow from inside. "Beware the Academy, if you decide not to go."

"I don't understand."

"Let us just say that the Academy does not like knowledge to be denied it. These are things your mother would have told you, had she lived longer."

"But—"

"I can say no more. Go, Briony, and good luck to you. You will need it." Carys shut the door firmly, cutting off both light and answers.

Briony stared at the door, but it remained closed, and she forced herself to move back to the path, retracing her steps back to Westenaedre.

Jael was waiting for her when she returned home. "Where have you been?"

She frowned at him, partially because he was using his parenting tone on her again, and partially because she had absolutely no idea what to say. So she made a big show of hanging her cloak up on its peg. When she turned back around, her gaze fell on a sheet of paper folded on the table. "What's this?"

"That came for you while you were out. Now, I'm serious, Bree, you've been completely unreliable lately! Think of what the children are learning…"

Briony tuned him out as she picked the paper up and unfolded it.

Dear Miss Ealadgast,

We would be pleased to offer you a position at our academy. We welcome all students, regardless of skills or level of talent. You may start immediately if you are so inclined. Please report to...

Briony's hand shook slightly. Carys had been right. To respond before even a week had passed—Briony had never expected them to move so fast, nor for them to offer her a position without knowing what she could do.

"Are you even listening to me, Bree?"

Briony thrust the letter at him. "Look at this, Jay. We can go!"

Her brother frowned, but he took the letter and read over it himself. His eyebrows shot up into his own white-blond hair. "The Academy? Magic? Are you mad?"

"We can go anytime, Jay. We'll pack the children up, find a nice house in Cynestel, and then we won't have to worry about the Scarred or the Fractures, and the children can go to a real school and Auberon can be apprenticed to an actual trade, and—"

"Bree." Jael rubbed the bridge of his nose. "We won't go."

"But Jay..." Briony could hear the wobble in her voice and stopped, taking a deep breath. "Look at this opportunity. This could keep us safe. Keep the *children* safe. Think of them. Don't they deserve better?"

"This is our *home*, Bree." Jael swept his arm in a broad gesture meant to take in the house, their land, the town. "It's our family duty to stay here."

"Family duty? Jay, I *saw* the Scarred in the forest!"

"We will not leave this land and this house." Jael set his jaw, staring down at Briony. "You are welcome to go to this Academy if that is what you want, but I and my children will stay here where we belong. Where *you* belong too, Bree, no matter what you think. Think of what you have here! You have your shop, you have Kishan, you have a whole, happy future ahead of you. Why would you want to leave?"

Briony stared at him. She had been so sure—but she could see now that Jael would not leave, that even the promise of better things and safety would not sway him.

She swallowed around the lump in her throat and blinked away the moisture in her eyes. If they would not go, she would need a different way to protect them.

One is that the spirit world has knowledge that we need, and if you know how to ask, you can access that.

Her spirit woman was a warrior. Maybe it was time for Briony to become a warrior as well.

She turned on her heel, snatching her cloak off its peg.

"Bree!" Jael caught her by the arm. "Where are you going? It's late. Have you even eaten?"

Briony's stomach rumbled in response. Jael gave her a look, but she pulled her arm loose. She grabbed a stray hunk of bread off the dining room table, tossed her cloak over her shoulder, and turned back to the door.

Jael planted himself in front of it, crossing his arms. "Whatever you're doing, you can do it in the morning."

"Move out of my way, Jay. I need to do this." On some level she was aware that this was utter madness, that it was almost dusk and venturing into the forest now was potentially suicide. But she'd been working so hard on getting into the Academy, and now the whole thing had fallen apart—she needed to redirect her energies. And if her spirit woman could help protect her family, well, then maybe this whole magic debacle wouldn't be for naught.

Her brother watched her, but after a moment he moved out of the way without further argument. "Take that stupid mountain cat with you," he mumbled, "and I expect to see you back here for breakfast."

"Yeah, yeah, love you too." Briony stretched up to kiss Jael on his cheek and then was out in the fading light, whistling for Poes as she went.

She'd go back to the lake. Carys had said that was the focus, right? And why the other woman stayed, despite the ridicule she'd received. So Briony would go back, and maybe this time whatever rules Carys had mentioned would be met, and her spirit woman would be waiting for her. She wrapped one hand around her amulet again as she hurried, Poes melting into his place beside her, his light coat glowing in the last rays of the sun.

Now all she had to do was find her way back to a place she'd only found by accident, with night falling, without getting eaten by a Fracture or a choke vine or running into the Scarred on the way.

Just a walk in the woods, right?

CHAPTER SEVEN
THEOSOPHY

THEOSOPHY DODGED the punch, ducked under the kick that followed, grabbed the leg, and upended her adversary. Lever hit the ground with a *huff* as the air went out of them. Theosophy reached down and offered a hand, but Lever just lay there gasping.

Dean Prosody's voice rang across the practice room. "Now, Theo, let's try not to injure your new partners before they even get out of training."

"It's not like the monsters will go easy on them," Theosophy muttered, but she felt a pang of guilt. She hadn't meant to slam Lever into the ground quite that hard. They were wiry and strong, not unlike Theosophy herself, but as Theosophy knew well, bony limbs did not make for a soft landing. Her fault for being distracted. Stupid mysterious, gorgeous women from other planes of existence.

Lever rose with a grunt and settled into a ready crouch. "Again?" they said.

Theosophy grinned.

"Hold off a moment, fighter," the dean said, striding across the room. Behind her slouched a young man. "Theosophy, here's your third, Synthesis."

Theosophy glanced from her to the fellow. She remembered taking her turn to train him; he'd been cocky then, and judging from his body language, he was still cocky now. Great, just great. She stepped closer to the dean and spoke quietly. "He was in a trio, wasn't he? Are they both..."

"No," said Dean Prosody. "I've split them up to fill out other trios. None of the tyros in training are ready yet."

Theosophy caught the dean's unspoken message: that trio had not been working well together. "Understood," she said.

"I'm sure you can handle it."

"Yes, sir," said Theosophy. She'd pushed to get Lever; best not to push back on this too. Best fighter or not, she didn't want to try the dean's patience too far.

"I'd love to give you a week to get used to each other before I send you out," the dean went on, "but I don't have the luxury. You will spend the next three days in intensive training, starting in midafternoon."

Theosophy dropped her gaze. *Briony...*

"Is there a problem, Theosophy?"

"No sir," she said crisply.

"Good," said the dean, and raised her voice. "Have fun getting to know each other."

Theosophy waited, listening to the dean's footsteps die away behind her.

As the door closed, Synthesis said, "So you're the one who's going to bully me into shape. The greatest fighter who—"

"First, I'm only the greatest because I happen to have lived the longest. It wasn't all luck, I'll grant you, but a good part of it was. Second, I need partners who are going to obey my orders and have my back. Otherwise we're going to go out on patrol and get slaughtered, and I won't be the longest-serving fighter anymore. If you can't bring yourself to do that, you'd better walk away now. Understand?"

Synthesis looked away and mumbled, "Yes, sir."

Theosophy turned on Lever, who flinched. "And you," she said. "If I hit you too hard again, I want you to get right back up and hit me back. Understand?"

Lever smiled a little. "Yes, sir."

"Good. Now let's see what you both can do."

She put them through the same drills they had done as young tyros: first working solo, then against each other, then with all three together. Unarmed first, then with dulled weapons.

Lever was fast, faster than Theosophy herself, but lacked stamina; Synthesis had the advantage of strength and reach, but lacked speed. And of course, all three of them would need to work hard to become an effective fighting team. That part she didn't mind, as she'd done it several times before—one of the many disadvantages of outliving one's trio. The part that bothered her was how hard she had to work to keep up with her new partners. Both were years younger than her, and it showed. She might be the one throwing them to the ground, but she bet she'd be equally sore tomorrow.

Still, the hard work had one major advantage: it kept Astro's injury away from the back of her mind. She ran the practice until all three of them were sweat-soaked and gasping, then ordered them to wipe down and reconvene for a seated session on strategy and the habits of monsters. When that was done, she armed them—spear again for Lever, muskets for Synthesis and herself, though she'd change that up over the course of their training—and led them out onto the streets in the fading night so she could see how they moved through the City. She was careful to keep them out in the open, in well-patrolled areas; they weren't ready to fight together yet. On their next shift that afternoon, Theosophy decided, she would start them with a run across the rooftops before dusk and danger set in.

She led them back to HQ as dawn was breaking, and dismissed them. Synthesis gave her a baleful glare before he ducked his head. She wasn't worried about that—he'd come around when he realized her methods kept him alive, and repeated nights of combat would forge the three of them into a team. Lever, though...Lever lacked spirit, and that worried her more. Anger was easy to work with; despair was much harder.

She ought to know.

OVER THE NEXT TWO days, Theosophy tried the device as often as she could sneak away, at different times and places. Each time, only the echo came back. She was starting to worry that she'd have to go back into the ruins, somehow. But before that...one last try.

She sent Synthesis and Lever to patrol the perimeter of the City, where the buildings stopped and the Wall began. It was the farthest they could possibly get from the ruins; they would be safe without her until full night. At first she followed and watched. They were making good progress toward becoming a cohesive team, watching each other's backs and being cautious about ambushes. She could track their general direction with their double crystals now tuned to hers; she would have to hope that she caught up with them before dark, or that they would keep up their caution until she reached them.

She turned tail and ran. Up one rooftop and down the next, the device thudding against her chest under her jacket. The patrols here were thin, for the same reason she'd felt all right letting her new partners go off alone—the streets closest to the Wall were the safest, and therefore richest, area of the City. She let the next fighter trio pass. Had there been a noise, just then? No, she was imagining things. She clambered up the brick wall of an abandoned mansion she knew of. Its defenses had been breached not long ago, and it hadn't yet been claimed by another family: the taint of death was still too new, at least for the sort of people who had the luxury to live in these houses.

The top floor was where the monsters had entered; they had smashed through a weak point, an upper window poorly reinforced. Idiots thought they were safe here, but the nearest patrol had been busy with another monster triad, and the whole family had died. She slithered into the nearest window, keeping her weight on the sill until she had tested the floorboards at the edge of the room. The boards had given way completely in the center, where the monsters had smashed through to the floor below, following the scent of human. From the looks of it, this room had been the parents', with the children's just below—and she cut off that line of thought right there.

She edged along the wall until she reached the wider patch in the corner. It seemed all right, and the floor below was unoccupied aside from overturned furniture and probably rats. She'd be safe here, as far as anyone was safe anywhere at night.

Theosophy pulled the device out of her jacket and took a deep breath.

Keeping her eyes open this time, she depressed both buttons. The hollow feeling came back. For a long moment nothing happened.

Then the walls faded around her and dissolved into nothing. The momentary darkness resolved into giant plants, loose water, weird blue

81

light, and standing just in front of her, Briony. Smooth tan skin, nearly-white hair, even more beautiful than she remembered.

"Hi," said Theosophy, suddenly shy.

"Oh, you're here!" said Briony. "I was afraid you wouldn't be."

Theosophy blinked. "Me too," she admitted.

Something by Briony's side made a noise. Theosophy glanced down and saw a cat the size of a large goat, its golden eyes gleaming in the dimness. This place Briony lived in was looking stranger all the time. "What is that?"

"Don't be afraid. It's just Poes; he's a mountain cat, and my friend."

Afraid. She'd said that the last time. Fear was a luxury or a constant, or maybe both. What kind of place was this anyway? She opened her mouth to ask, but the other woman was talking again.

"Look, I can't stay long, but I need your help. What can you tell me about the Scarred?"

"What?"

"The Scarred." Briony huffed. "I told you about the War, right?"

"The War," said Theosophy. "We had one of those, too. Before it happened, the world was different—nobody knows exactly how, but they had much better technology. Ever since then, we've been living in the ruin of what once was. But go on about your Scarred."

Briony had been listening intently. Now she stirred. "That's who we were fighting against back then, and I think they're going to start a new war soon, if they haven't already. But we don't have any real defenses, and my family's in danger. I need to get them out of here—I even have a way out—but my brother won't listen to me. You know how to fight them, don't you?"

Theosophy frowned, trying to make sense of Briony's words. "A way out? Out *where*?"

"Away from Westenaedre. There's the Academy, see, in Cynestel, and—"

"Wait," said Theosophy. She thought back to the map. Westenaedre had been in the middle of a lot of empty space, with roads running long distances. Briony's world had once been bigger than the City, but now... "Do you mean to say you can walk for days in one direction?"

"Of course," said Briony.

"But what happens when you come to the edge of the world?"

Briony looked confused. "The world doesn't have an edge. It just keeps going, farther than anyone has ever been."

Theosophy felt her mind reeling with excitement and—yes, fear. But there was no time for that. She had to focus. "How about this. What's east of Westenaedre?"

"Just this forest. The one I'm standing in. And the lake." Theosophy must have looked blank, for she pointed at the loose water. "Lake. And these are trees. Don't you have those in your realm?"

Theosophy shook her head, more out of confusion than anything. "Listen, I found a pre-War map. My world—the City—should be right where you're standing."

Briony blinked, then looked around at the lake. "I think I've seen it." She was almost whispering. "Across the lake."

"What I'm trying to say is, I think we used to be part of the same world," said Theosophy. "Somehow."

"The same...?" Briony trailed off. "If we were—that's it! If we were once, we can be again." Then her face fell. "Oh—oh. The ones who abandoned us during the War."

"Wait, what?"

"Never mind. I need your help to fight these things. You're a warrior, right?"

Theosophy was startled into laughter. "Yes, but...I'm needed here. You've got Scarred? We've got monsters, too. I've spent my whole life—the whole City revolves around fighting them. They come every night looking for people to take, and—" A thought hit her, so hard she gasped. "And," she went on more slowly, "we've got nowhere to run. Except...if we could find a way through to you..."

Briony was staring at her with the same intensity she felt. "You're all warriors, then?"

"Well, sort of. A lot of us are."

"So if we could get your people out, you could help us fight..."

"...and we could get away from the..." Theosophy trailed off. She couldn't even conceive of it. Not to wake in terror every night of her childhood until she was old enough to sign up with the fighters. Not to spend every sunset waiting for the monsters to come. Not to barricade oneself inside and hope desperately to see the morning. Of course, Briony's world had monsters of a sort, but they were clearly not omnipresent, because there were places to run.

If she could get everyone through the Wall and out, she could die fighting Briony's Scarred for her, while her own people fled to someplace truly safe. That would be a fine death. A death with a purpose, not like every fucking death she'd ever witnessed. And there it was, her mind was dragging out what she'd been trying to avoid, a night long ago, shutters smashing and blood and screaming, and when it was over, only her and Granddad left—

"Theo?" Briony reached a hand out for her. "Are you all right?"

Theosophy pulled herself back to the present with an effort and lifted her own hand. It went right through Briony's, with no sensation at all. Of course; she hadn't felt the wind that rustled the—trees—and the water on the lake, either. She wasn't really there in Briony's world.

Yet.

"Yes," she said fiercely. "Yes. Let's do this."

CHAPTER EIGHT
BRIONY

BRIONY WAS NEVER quite sure how she made it home that night. Poes must have helped her every step of the way. But—a whole people of warriors! If Theo was right, if she had a map that put her right where the lake was now, then Briony had a new way to protect her family. A better way, because they could stay where they were, on their family's land, and Jael would be happy.

Maybe that's why their family had always stayed, because of the proximity to the lake. If Carys was right, maybe they'd been communicating with Theo's people for the whole time. But why had no one ever said anything? Why did no one seem to know, either on Briony's side or Theo's?

Except—Carys knew. Briony would stake her life on it. And maybe she would need to. Spirit talking...if it got out, the best she could hope for was an enforced exile like the older woman. At worst, she could lose everything.

But she would need to tell Jael. Maybe he knew something, something their mother had told him, or something he had seen. But she couldn't keep this from him. Look at how the whole magic thing had gone. And this would be easier with help. Kishan—no, he wouldn't understand.

It was past midnight when she got home. The cottage was quiet. Briony hung her cloak on its peg and snuck into her room, listening to the creak of the house and the sound of the children's steady breathing. It was so quiet, nothing like the forest. And it had always seemed safe, despite its proximity to the forest and the things that lurked within. Maybe that was part of why Jael wanted to stay.

She undressed and climbed into bed, hoping to drop off to sleep after her long day, but sleep did not come. She could still see Theo in her mind's eye, glowing ethereally in the dark of the night forest. Were all her people like her? Beautiful, determined, made of sterner stuff than the people Briony interacted with on a daily basis? Or was Theo special?

She felt special, but Briony suspected she might be biased.

She wanted to see more of her. If Briony's realm was connected to Theo's spirit realm, somehow, if Theo was right and they could reconnect the two, then besides a potential way to protect her family, it was also an excuse to talk to Theo more. And Briony found she liked that idea.

She liked the idea of being able to reach out and actually touch Theo quite a bit as well. But she'd dwell on that later.

They'd made plans to investigate separately and meet again in a few days, but that already seemed too far away.

It was near dawn—Briony could see it seeping in around her window blinds—before sleep finally came.

She was awakened what felt like no time later by Brin and Marcea having a screaming match right outside her door. After she'd scared them straight, she forced herself to get dressed and head into the kitchen for breakfast, which Auberon had already made. Thank the

Old Ones for the boy. Briony, despite her medicinal potions, was not much of a cook, and the entire family had eaten much better since Auberon had taken over the duty.

She was starving since she'd skipped dinner the night before. She tuned out her nieces, who were now fighting about whatever in whispers at the other end of the table, and helped herself to seconds of everything. Her stomach might ache later, but right now it felt amazing.

Jael came in as she finished. "Good morning," he said. No doubt he wanted to talk, but he wouldn't, not while the children were there.

She'd tell him everything, she really would, but the idea seemed harder in the daylight. But surely her own brother wouldn't disown her. He hadn't yet, after all.

"Good morning," she said. "Told you I'd be fine." Briony gathered her cloak up as Jael sat down and frowned up at her. "We can have a good long talk later, I promise. But I have something else I need to do now. Head Kishan off if he comes looking for me."

Jael's frown deepened. "I don't like it, Bree," he said.

"I know." She tossed him an apple. "But I think it's all good news."

Her brother's frown remained, but he shook his head and turned to his breakfast, and Briony escaped into the crisp early morning.

To avoid her fellow townspeople, Briony hiked to the edge of the forest and whistled for Poes. It only took a few moments for him to appear and Briony wondered, once again, what he did in the forest when she wasn't with him. She'd often gotten the impression that he watched over the cottage at night, or maybe he just knew where she was likely to call him. They trekked through the forest until they were north of Westenaedre.

Briony put her hood up again as she emerged back onto the path, but in the light of day she felt more conspicuous. No one else that she passed was wearing theirs. But she didn't want Kishan to hear about this, though he heard about everything. Maybe he wouldn't make the connection. Or so she would hope.

There was no smoke coming from Carys's house this morning. Had she really only been here last night? It felt like forever. Everything had changed since then.

Did the refugees passing her know who this cottage belonged to? Briony felt exposed, despite her hood. But she needed more information. She knocked, though not as loudly as she would have liked, and tried not to fidget suspiciously.

Carys was again a long time coming, but when she opened the door, she did not seem surprised to see Briony. "It's a little early," she said, though she held the door open and closed it behind Briony. As Briony passed her, the older woman leaned out around her, scanning the cottage's surroundings, before ducking back inside.

"The realm," Briony said as soon as the door clicked shut, "where is it, really?"

Carys crossed back across the room to her table. A breakfast of sliced meat and cheese was set out there, waiting. Carys motioned for Briony to sit, though she did not offer to share. "I thought you'd be back, though this is sooner than I expected."

Briony forced herself to take a deep breath before sitting down opposite the older woman. "They are warriors, Carys. The whole lot of them."

"I suppose they must be."

Briony wasn't sure what that meant. "She said she had a map, a map that put where she was right where the forest is now. She said she thought we used to be in the same place. And if we could bring them

89

back, they could help protect us from the Scarred. Surely a whole realm of warriors would keep us safe."

"Ah, yes." Carys seemed much more interested in her food than Briony's news.

"You already knew all this."

Carys shrugged. "I can't say that I did, specifically. The issue with spirit talking is that there must be someone on the other end willing to talk, and it has seemed, as time has passed, that that is no longer true. I rarely even attempt it, anymore. No one answers."

"But Theo—"

"Who knows how long she will answer, Briony? Something must have happened inside, to diminish contact. But perhaps it is just as well."

"Just as well? Carys, they can protect us, they can teach us to fight! If we can reach them—"

"Briony." Carys sighed and folded her hands on the table, staring across at Briony. Briony found herself shrinking away from that brilliant green gaze. "I know you're excited. But the City might not be the answer you hope it is."

Briony set her jaw. Why was Carys being so difficult? Didn't she understand what Theo was offering here? There had been no contact between her country and the Scarred since the Great War. The tales from the border the refugees brought told of terrible things, of horrid deaths and worse tortures. Briony's people were not equipped to fight. After the War, they'd tried to drive off the Fractures, but they couldn't even manage that. When the Scarred got tired of the border, would anyone be able to slow them down?

"You called it the City," she said carefully.

"Yes," said Carys. "It is what they call themselves."

"And it was once here? How is it that we can talk to them? Surely, if that connection still exists, others might as well."

"I doubt it." Carys rose, crossing to the fireplace. She prodded at the ashes until the remaining coals started to glow again. She straightened, as if listening, then retrieved her tea kettle and hung it. "Do you know why spirit talking is frowned upon?"

Of course Briony did. Everybody did. "Yes."

"Enlighten me."

"Because the spirits cannot be trusted. Because they seek to manipulate the living. Because only those who would dare mess with the knowledge of the Old Ones would attempt to speak with them, and that knowledge caused terrible things."

Carys nodded absently.

Briony frowned at her back. "So what?" Theo wasn't trying to manipulate her. Briony would swear on it. There was something so noble in the other woman. Briony couldn't imagine her doing anything dishonest.

"Think about what you just said," Carys said.

Briony thought over her answer, but still couldn't see Carys's point. She shook her head.

Carys sighed again. "The general belief is that spirit talkers try to access the knowledge of the Old Ones. Evil knowledge. Knowledge that caused the Fractures and the War and the Scarred."

"Yes…?"

"All beliefs have an ounce of truth to them."

Oh. Briony could see what she was trying to say, though she wasn't sure why the older woman needed to be so opaque about it. "You're saying that spirit talkers do talk to the Old Ones, and since Theo lives in the realm that the spirit talkers can access, she's…she's an Old One."

"Or what's left of them, at least." Carys leaned against the wall. "Who knows what they've been up to for the last five hundred years in there? What other horrors have they thought up?"

Briony pushed herself up, rattling the table, and stalked about the room. No! Theo couldn't—wouldn't be involved in that sort of thing. She hadn't even known what a Fracture was when Briony had explained them to her. She was a *warrior*, from a group of warriors. The Old Ones had been great sorcerers who could warp the very fabric of a creature. There had to be some mistake.

"How can you say that?" she asked, aware that she didn't sound as calm as she wanted to. "You've talked to them yourself."

"I have," Carys replied. Her glance was indistinct, though, off in the direction of the forest. "But I only know what they said. I have no idea how true any of it is. How do I know if what they said was the truth? How do I know they weren't trying to manipulate me the way the stories say they do?"

"Why keep going back, then?"

Carys smiled wryly. "Oh, the stories they told. If you could have heard them, you'd go back too."

Briony huffed and pressed her hands against the side of her head. This isn't what she wanted from this visit. She needed information. She needed to know if Theo's realm really had been here, what had happened to send it away, and how to get it back. She didn't need all this talk of Old Ones messing with things. Nothing had changed. She needed to protect her family from the Scarred, and Theo was a means to an end.

Even if that meant potentially unleashing the Old Ones on the world again?

Briony felt Carys's hand on her shoulder. "I'm sorry," she said. "I know this is hard to hear. Your mother was supposed to tell you all this. She had centuries of family experience about this sort of thing, things she never told me. Maybe she could have told you one way or another if your Theo could be trusted. But I'm afraid I can't."

"But where can I look?"

"I don't know. I'm sorry." Carys steered her toward the door in a firm manner. "I can't help you."

Was Carys trying to get rid of her? Had she said something wrong? "The Academy offered me a position. Without knowing what I could do."

"That doesn't surprise me. Beware of them, Briony."

"I don't understand why."

They'd reached the door. "Let's just say that the Old Ones are at the heart of the Academy, and some things never change."

More riddles. Carys pulled open the door and practically shoved Briony out of it. Briony raised her hood back up over her hair, confused by the abrupt end of her visit. The sun had risen farther into the sky, and the chill of the early morning was gone. Now her hood and cloak would really stick out.

"If the Academy comes looking," Carys said from behind her, "please don't tell them where I am."

Briony spun, a million new questions battling for supremacy, but Carys had already closed the door. Briony stared at it, strongly tempted to knock anew, but she doubted the older woman would suddenly become more talkative.

Poes was waiting for her on the edge of the forest. Briony scratched him behind the ears, and the mountain cat rumbled low in his throat. Should she go to the lake, see if she could find that hint of Theo's realm that she'd thought she'd seen that one time, see if Theo answered? Briony fingered the amulet at her throat. She wished she knew what the process for spirit talking was. Perhaps Theo knew. She should have asked, but she'd been so excited about the idea of getting warriors of her very own.

Carys wasn't right, was she? Was Theo an Old One, just trying to manipulate Briony into setting them free?

Briony shook her head violently to clear it of the thought. She couldn't be. Briony wouldn't believe it. Not of Theo.

Though she didn't really know anything about her. And if the City was the Old Ones, and the Old Ones had disappeared during the last war, could Briony really trust them—and Theo—not to do so again?

Poes must have sensed her confusion, as the mountain cat butted his soft head against Briony's hand. "This is the right thing to do, Poes," she murmured. "It has to be."

The forest was silent this morning, but not in a Fracture-lurking-immediately-behind-you sort of way. Still, Briony tried to move as quietly as she could, matching Poes's silent passage through the undergrowth. Maybe she should pick some supplies, while she was out here. She didn't really need any, but it might help clear her mind, and it would give her an excuse for being late to the shop.

She'd noticed a patch of dog-bur nearby the week before, and it wouldn't hurt to gather some. Several of the refugees had open wounds, and it would help to have more cleaning salve on hand as they continued to arrive. Briony changed direction, keeping one hand on Poes's head.

The patch was easily found. Briony had to gather the plants, roots and all, into her cloak, as she hadn't brought anything else along. Kishan probably wouldn't notice.

She was almost done with the dog-bur when she tensed. It took a moment to determine what had caught her interest, but then she heard it: a low, constant sound, not unlike the sound of several people moving together. And it probably was—the image of the Scarred moving through the forest without a care for Fractures or choke vines instantly sprung into mind. Briony held perfectly still, but the sound was far to the east, and if it was the Scarred, they wouldn't be able to see her.

Was it the Scarred again? And if it was, why did they stay to the forest, when there were villages to the west? Why not attack like they did at the border?

A terrible thought occurred to Briony. If Theo's realm really was full of Old Ones and their knowledge, maybe Briony wasn't the only one looking for them.

CHAPTER NINE
THEOSOPHY

INFORMATION, that was what she needed, hard facts to bring back to Briony next time they met. What had happened to cut the City off from Briony's dimension, and how could it be reversed? Maybe the answer lay in the history of the map, or maybe in other documents from the Dark Time or earlier. She'd already been through the archives at HQ; she didn't have access to any archives belonging to the other faculties or the chancellor. That left only a few options, none of which she liked.

She tried the most direct route first.

"Permission to lead an expedition into the ruins, sir."

Dean Prosody sat forward in her chair and scrutinized Theosophy through eyes that gave away nothing. "For what purpose?" she asked.

Theosophy swallowed. "I...think there might be something we could learn there."

"We've tried that," the dean rapped out. "You were there for the most recent attempt." Theosophy remembered fire and screams and dark shadows all around her, and winced. "Why are you coming to me now?"

Theosophy had meant to confess about the device, but she found she couldn't. "I've...just been thinking a lot," she said.

"Does this have anything to do with Rhetoric? A misguided attempt at making his death mean something, perhaps?"

She looked away. It didn't, not really, but...perhaps better to let the dean think it did? She shouldn't lie to her superior, even by omission. But she was long past searching for meaning in death, the dean ought to know that about her by now. If not, it wasn't her fault the dean was wilfully ignorant.

Dean Prosody shook her head. "A better way to do that? Being a good leader to your new trio. How are they coming along, by the way?"

"Not bad. Sir. Synthesis has too much spirit and Lever too little, but they'll do. They've both been in fights before, in their old trios; in a couple of weeks we might even be competent as a team."

"Less, I hope. I can't afford to keep *you* away from the front lines that long, but I won't put you in danger by sending you out with incompetent backup."

Work harder, she meant. "Yes, sir," said Theosophy. "About that expedition..."

"Permission denied," the dean said.

"Sir—"

"Theosophy, you know I need you, but if you keep talking like this, I have half a mind to pull you off active duty and put you on full-time training. I shouldn't have to tell you how dangerous those ruins are. Last time...maybe you didn't realize this then, but I'm telling you now: when I ordered that assault eight years ago, we came terribly close to being overrun. Not just the Militia, but the whole City. I won't risk our ability to defend ourselves like that again."

"Of course not, sir." She hadn't known, not exactly, but a number of little pieces fell into place—things overheard, strategies used in the months afterward, a feeling around HQ more than anything else. If they really had come that close to...she couldn't even think it, but a coldness crept over her, and stayed as she bowed her way out of the office.

No, she couldn't ask the dean to risk so many resources. Not even for the chance of freedom. But without that power behind her, she didn't dare go into the ruins again, nor ask her inexperienced trio to follow her there. She would have to find another way to learn what she needed to know.

"FASTER!" Theosophy yelled at Lever, chasing them up the rickety ladder, rungs slick from the steady drizzle. She grabbed at Lever's ankle, and the young fighter yelled and kicked out. Theosophy snatched her hand back, grinning. She tried to grab at the other foot, but Lever was already up the last few rungs and over the edge of the roof. Theosophy followed to find Lever and Synthesis standing together, facing the ladder, bayonet and spear lowered. She swung out one-handed over the edge and landed behind them, grabbing Synthesis by the shoulders. He kicked backward, she dodged, he dropped, and Lever thrust their bayonet. Theosophy danced backward, up the slope of the roof. She had to take care with her footing on the slippery tiles. Lever overbalanced and tripped over Synthesis, going down in a tangle of limbs and nearly spilling both of them off the edge. Synthesis's spear went clattering off down the tiles and ended up in the rain gutter.

Theosophy sighed and perched on the peak of the roof to wait while the two of them sorted themselves out. They had certainly improved, but not enough. She wouldn't trust either one of them at her back yet, and she couldn't take them on patrol until that changed. Synthesis was strong, Lever quick, but they were seriously lacking in awareness of their surroundings. Growing up in the City had taught them how to navigate the buildings; their initial training had taught them to fight and their early patrol experience had shown them caution and fear. What they lacked was seasoning. The best cure for that was time, and that they did not have.

"All right," she yelled. They both finished scrambling to their feet and stood at attention, muskets slung across their backs again. "Go for a run along the rooftops. Five-block square. Back here as fast as you can. Go!"

They took off in the rain. She waited for them to get a few blocks away, then headed in the opposite direction. Just because they thought this was a speed test didn't mean it couldn't also be something else.

A short while later, she was lying in wait behind a chimney. Here they came, feet pounding against the roof tiles, up one side and down the other, leap across to the next, repeat. They looked pretty disciplined, but...

Theosophy stood and, as quietly as she could, launched herself off the roof. One foot scraped on the tiles as she jumped. Lever's head came up and their running slowed, while Synthesis pounded on ahead. Theosophy landed just behind Lever, who yelled and tried to spin around. Theosophy yanked the musket on their back, pulling them off balance. Lever tried to fight, but only ended up flat on their back again.

"If I'd been a monster," Theosophy said, "you'd be dead right now."

Lever wheezed, too out of breath to speak, but glared up at her. Good. Anger was fire, all she had to do was direct—

99

Crunch of tiles behind her, upslope. Theosophy dropped and rolled. It was still daylight and Lever was still down and winded, so that left Synthesis. He rushed her, skipping out of the way when she bounced to her feet, then circling.

"Why are you picking on them?" he said.

"Excuse me?"

"You always start with Lever. Why is that? Because they're smaller? Because I'm stronger?"

"Don't you wish," she growled.

"You just don't want to lose."

Theosophy rushed him. He stepped to the side and she couldn't stop, but she grabbed his arm on the way down and flipped him, then let go and scrambled to her feet again. "Listen, asshole, I warned you about this. I'm your superior."

"Sure," Synthesis said, panting as he rose. "But we're also a team."

"We have to be hard. It's the only way we're going to survive. And it's in my own best interest, and the City's, to make both of you harder." She aimed a kick at his groin.

He jumped backward, then closed in while she was still recovering her balance. "I get that," he said, nose to nose. "But you don't have to be mean about it."

"Hey," said Lever's voice. They spun Synthesis around, and Theosophy stepped back. "I don't need protecting. At least not from our boss. Got that?" And they punched him in the gut.

Theosophy took a deep breath. "No in-fighting!" she hollered. Both of them jumped. "Lever, just for that, you're going to run another lap. Synthesis, since you're so worried I'm picking on Lever, you'll run two. Go!"

They both glared daggers at her behind their dripping hair, but they went.

Theosophy shook her head, spraying droplets. Dealing with people's issues had never been her strongest skill. Physical training she could do, even strategy, but emotions? Argh. Making them hate her, she had that part down, but she'd have to work on focusing their anger. She found herself missing Astrolabe and Rhetoric. They'd never hated her; the three of them had been a good unit from the beginning. It had been easy.

She'd forgotten that life wasn't supposed to be easy. She wouldn't make that mistake again.

∘─◉◯◉─∘

THEOSOPHY DRAGGED herself up the last set of steep stairs to the rooftop gardens. Solvent was already there, waiting out the rain in her shed, and sat up when Theosophy came into view. "Hey! I thought you'd forgotten about me."

"Dean's been working us hard," said Theosophy, dropping down beside her with a wince.

"You all right?"

Theosophy's whole body ached from the combination of drills and practice fights. "Sure," she said.

"What happened with that artifact you brought back?"

"Oh. Nothing. It's a dud." Theosophy looked away.

"I could look at it again. Maybe—"

"No, it's fine."

"You sure? I could—"

"Don't worry about it. I already stripped it down for parts."

"What?" Solvent punched her lightly. "And you didn't split with me?"

Oops. "Hey, I was the one who found it, and nearly got myself killed."

"Sure, but you wouldn't have known what to do with it unless..."

"Fine." Theosophy grimaced. Better to keep Solvent in the dark, even if it meant she had to forfeit something. "I'll bring you some dumplings tomorrow, how about that?"

"How about bringing some rock salts to share instead?"

"Solvent, you know I don't like that stuff."

"You used to do it with me. You've changed."

Theosophy started guiltily, as Briony's face flashed across her vision. "What? No, I haven't."

"You're driven now, in a way you never used to be. What's up with that?"

"Look, give me some of that stuff then."

Solvent laughed. "What, now? It's still early."

What Theosophy really wanted was sleep, or maybe a good fuck and then sleep. "Come on," she said instead. "Give it up."

Solvent didn't need any more convincing. She dug around in a pouch and produced two good-sized lumps. "Here," she said, handing Theosophy the bigger one.

Theosophy swallowed. She hadn't done more than a pinch of the stuff in ages.

"You're not going to back out now?"

"Course not." Theosophy smiled and popped the lump in her mouth.

"That's a girl." Solvent crunched her own lump and smiled back. "I missed doing this with you."

Theosophy felt the fizzing begin to spread through her body. She couldn't deny it felt good. Too good. There was a reason she'd been avoiding it. Her aching and bruised muscles felt lighter already, and the omnipresent dark edge had gone from her thoughts.

"Fine, be that way," said Solvent.

Theosophy pulled her thoughts back to the present with an effort; her mind was losing its grip on logic and sequences of thought. "I'm here now, aren't I?" She reached out a hand. The weight of her arm felt funny and she misjudged the distance. She'd been aiming for Solvent's shoulder, but the hand ended up on Solvent's breast instead. She giggled and left it there.

"Asshole," said Solvent fondly. "Here, have another one." She pressed the rock salts against Theosophy's lips. Theosophy shook her head, keeping her mouth closed. Solvent rolled her eyes and popped the lump into her own mouth, then leaned forward to initiate a kiss. Theosophy's lips opened of their own accord and Solvent pushed the lump into Theosophy's mouth with her tongue as she deepened the kiss. Theosophy tried to pull away, but the second dose was already working, and she gave in and let herself fall.

She was flying over the jumbled buildings, toward the black, roiling mist of the Wall. She tried to turn aside, but the wings or wind that bore her would not heed her. The Wall loomed closer and closer. She wanted to close her eyes, but if she was to die, she wanted to see it happen. The Wall rushed up to her. Darkness surrounded her, and coldness, and a sense of disorientation, of her body stretching and time warping. Then sunshine burst over her again. Below was greenery, stretching as far as she could see, such an intense color that it took her breath away. She recognized the—trees—and the—lake—and beside the lake someone stood, lithe and slender, head tilted up to watch as

she came in for a landing. She alit softly and took the other woman in
her arms. It felt wonderful. She leaned in—

"Hey!" Someone shoved her.

Theosophy opened her eyes. Solvent leaned over her. Theosophy groaned, head spinning with aftereffects.

"Who were you smiling at?" Solvent demanded. "Because it sure wasn't me."

"How do you know?" Theosophy said, stalling while she groped after the scattered remnants of her—vision?

"You never looked at me that way. Not even the first time we fucked."

"Huh," Theosophy said.

"Is there someone else? Not that I mind if there is, just...I'd like to know, you know?"

Theosophy's gaze slid away from Solvent's face. "No," she said.

"Fine. Be that way. Just don't complain if I go off and do my own thing, too." She got to her feet.

"Solvent..."

Solvent froze. "See, right there," she said softly. "That's not like you. Before, you wouldn't have cared if I left. You *have* changed."

This time, Theosophy let her walk away into the rain. It was true, something had shifted inside her. Was it because of Briony? She was getting soft, letting herself feel more. "Bad idea, Theo," she muttered. But if she really was changing, she might as well do it right. After all, she owed Astrolabe a visit.

CHAPTER TEN
BRIONY

IT WAS ALMOST NOON before Briony made it to the store. Kishan was seated behind the counter, head leaning on one hand, though he straightened immediately when the door opened. When he saw it was her, he relaxed, though he frowned as Poes followed her inside.

"Where have you been?" he asked. "I went by your house this morning and Jael said you'd left early."

Briony thought the presence of Poes might be evidence enough, but since it apparently wasn't, she also considered throwing the dog-bur she'd gathered, and was currently holding in one hand, at his face.

Instead, she laid it on the counter near the door to the workroom and went to hang up her cloak.

She heard the scrape of Kishan's stool on the floor as he stood. Poes wrapped around Briony's legs as the healer came over, bristling his fur. Briony curled her fingers in his light coat. Poes wasn't terribly fond of the healer—the opinion was mutual—and Briony had always figured that the mountain cat was jealous.

"Bree," Kishan said in a low voice, though there was no one else there to hear, "I'm really concerned about you. You've been in and out of the forest all week. We can't possibly be that low on supplies. Is this about your magic plan?" He lowered his voice even further. "You haven't been trying to spirit talk, have you?"

Yes. "Kishan, give me some credit, please." Briony pulled her hair back over one shoulder and started braiding it, though she made sure she met Kishan's eyes. His warm, brown eyes met her own blue ones. She'd loved those eyes, once, but they didn't seem to do as much for her as they once had. What did that mean? She'd think about that later, once she got settled for the day. "I'm done with the magic plan. Jael won't go."

Kishan smiled. "Excellent! I'm glad to hear it." Then he seemed to rethink being so enthusiastic about something that she'd been trying so hard on, dropping the smile off his face. He was a dear thing, when he wasn't being selfish, and Briony softened a little. It wasn't his fault the Scarred were lurking, after all. He was just doing what his family had always done. "I am sorry, though," he continued, "I know it meant a lot to you."

"Mmm," said Briony noncommittally. "But now I've got to figure out something else. Do you know if there's any place nearby that has old records or books? Maps, maybe, or history. Stuff from before the Great War?"

The relief that had been written across Kishan's features disappeared. "What?"

Briony went to retrieve her dog-bur. Poes followed her into the backroom, with Kishan behind him, though the healer kept a healthy distance from the mountain cat. Once, he would have asked her to keep him outside—would probably again, some day. "Just some old books, Kishan. Some reading."

"You're not still worried about the Scarred, are you? Old Ones, Bree, they're ages away. They'll never make it this far inside."

"Best to be prepared," she murmured. She started hanging the dog-bur in the new space Kishan had cleared for her. But would it really hurt to be honest with him? Briony dropped her hands down, looking over her shoulder at Kishan. She'd known him forever, had played with him as a child. They'd been partners and more for years. He still accepted her despite the things others found weird, such as her forays into the forest and her friendship with the mountain cat. Would it really hurt to open up to him, to tell him her fears?

There was a knock in the front room. Kishan headed out immediately; Briony finished tying up her current bunch of dog-bur and had Poes lie down next to it before she followed. No one ever wanted to talk to her anyway.

It turned out to be Rissa. "No, no," she was saying to whatever Kishan's question had been, "I have a message for Briony."

A heavy feeling settled into Briony's stomach. "A message?"

"From the Academy." Rissa crossed the shop and delivered the paper into Briony's hand. "Very specifically for you." She shot a curious glance over at Kishan, but thankfully didn't say anything. "Thought I'd better deliver it here, in case it was important. Two messages in a day, after all."

"Yes, of course. Thank you, Rissa."

The Sender inclined her head and left, though she lingered, almost as if she hoped Briony would offer more details if she were slow about it.

The paper was rough under Briony's fingers. Avoiding Kishan's look, she turned and headed back into the back room, setting the paper down in the middle of her workspace and rubbing the top of Poes's head. She took a deep breath and dropped her shoulders, hearing Carys's warnings about the Academy echoing in her head. What could they possibly want?

Did she want to know?

Was there anything involved in her magic plan that wouldn't come back to bite her in the end? She sighed and ran a hand through her hair, forgetting she had braided it.

"Bree." Kishan had followed her back. Briony tightened her grip on Poes's fur, trying to steal courage from the mountain cat. "Aren't you going to open that?" There was an odd tightness to his voice.

"I don't know."

"Why is the Academy sending you a message?"

"I don't know."

"Bree," he said, sounding uncomfortably like Jael's parenting voice, and Briony felt her hackles automatically rise.

"Look, Kishan, I *don't know*. You pushing me is not making this easier!"

Kishan put his hands up. "See? This is what I've been talking about. You've been all secretive and aggressive lately. It's not like you. When you're done messing around and are ready to tell me what's going on, you know where to find me." He shot the letter a look and then flounced into the front of the shop, shutting the door unnecessarily hard behind him.

Briony resisted the urge to throw something after him. Instead, she took another deep breath and reached for the message.

Dear Miss Ealadgast,

Please advise us as to when we can expect your arrival here at the academy.

Sincerely,
Mardu Bodere

Wow. They really wasted no time, did they? Briony would have to write them and let them know that she wasn't planning on attending. With Carys—and to some extent, Kishan—being so nervous about the Academy, it would be best to be decisively done with it.

She tore a page out of a blank notebook and sat back down, staring at the paper. Short seemed to be the preferred manner.

Dear Master Bodere,

Thank you for your note. I have decided not to attend the academy at this time. Thank you very much for the offer.

Briony Ealadgast

She went out the back, Poes going with her, and headed over to the Sender's. Poes left her part of the way for the forest, which was just as well, because he tended to attract unwanted attention in town, and Briony already felt too exposed. No doubt it wouldn't be long until the whole town knew she'd been communicating with the Academy, which would just be another in a long line of things that made her different.

Rissa was thankfully professional when Briony dropped the message off and didn't ask, and Briony escaped as quickly as possible.

When had her life gone so mad?

As she neared the shop again, there was a large group of people out front. Whomever was in the middle was shrieking, and Briony caught a flash of Kishan's red robe through the throng. What was going on? Briony didn't have her supplies, but she pushed through the crowd anyway. The people murmured around her, but it was too hard to make out what they were saying. Still, couldn't they back off if someone was hurt? Why did they always have to stand around and gawk?

She finally reached the center. An older man, bedraggled and too thin, was there, clinging to Kishan's robe. He was too pale and continued shrieking through Kishan's attempts to extricate himself and figure out what was wrong. Kishan looked up as she appeared and sent her a desperate glance.

Briony set her shoulders and marched up. She took the old man's hands gently and firmly removed them from Kishan's robe, all the while murmuring comforting noises. The man didn't stop his horrible shrieks, but at least Kishan could use his spell to see what was wrong. Briony wrapped her arms around the man's to keep him still while Kishan worked. Nothing wrong with his magic today either.

Kishan finished the spell and said something, but Briony couldn't hear him over the shrieks. He turned and disappeared through the crowd, abandoning Briony and her charge, but before she could decide whether or not she should be mad about that, he returned with one of her calming draughts.

It took both of them—Briony manhandling him into position and Kishan forcing his mouth open—to get him to take it. As the man quieted, the crowd started to drift away, their interest apparently lost.

By the time they'd gotten him inside and onto one of the beds, he was asleep.

"Old Ones," said Briony, wiping her brow, "what was that about?"

"I've no idea." Kishan brushed at a muddy smear on his robe, frowning. "They brought him over like that. Refugee, and new, so no one knows who he is or if he tends toward loud bursts of incomprehensibility."

"But nothing physically wrong?"

"He's had some sort of a shock, but nothing beyond that. Hopefully he'll be calm when he wakes up."

"Maybe his last town kicked him out because he was too loud."

Kishan didn't even pretend to smile at her joke. "They just keep coming. How are we going to take them all?"

Briony was tempted to say something about the Scarred, and how they were likely to get even more—or less, if some of the rumors proved to be true, and they hadn't really shown their true might or intentions yet—but Kishan wouldn't appreciate that. He hadn't thus far, and she was tired of trying to get him and Jael to take this seriously.

"I read your message while you were out."

Briony's head snapped up. "What?"

"You're not telling me anything, Bree."

"So that gives you the right to just look at my things without permission?" Briony closed her eyes. She should have known better than to leave it on her workstation. Kishan had never been particularly good with boundaries.

"Well, what am I supposed to think? And now I find you're going to go to the Academy? With what magic, Bree? I thought you said your magic plan was over."

Briony opened her eyes again. "It *is* over, Kishan. I told the Academy I wouldn't be coming."

"Why would they even accept you in the first place when you don't have any magic?"

"It's over, Kishan. Leave it alone." She turned away from him. She didn't have *time* for this. She needed to find some information about Theo's realm, and she had no leads.

"Bree." She hadn't heard him get closer. Kishan reached out and laid a gentle hand on Briony's arm. "Bree. We're supposed to be partners, remember? We're promised to each other. There can't be secrets like this. Please, talk to me." He opened his eyes in that wide, innocent way he always did when he was trying to be earnest.

Briony found herself thinking about Theo's eyes instead. What color were they really, when not enveloped in that blue glow?

"Kishan…"

There was a sharp inhale of breath from the bed, and then the old man bolted upright and started his shrieking again. Old Ones, the lungs on him. Kishan was gone immediately, and Briony followed, frowning. Her calming draughts were normally more effective. A bad batch of one of her ingredients?

She'd need to look at her notes.

Kishan had his hands out in a non-threatening manner, though Briony couldn't hear what he was saying. The old man didn't even seem to see him. He just stared at the wall blankly, occasionally pausing for breath before continuing his ruckus.

This was ridiculous. They couldn't have him shrieking all day long, and no one else would take him either. Eventually someone would turn him out of town, and then he'd be easy prey for the Fractures. It was a miracle he'd made it this far.

With that in mind, she clamped her hand over his mouth. "Quiet!" she shouted, hopefully loud enough that he'd hear her over his own noise. "You're not helping anything, so just be quiet!"

Kishan stared at her, looking horrified, though honestly he should be used to her by now. The old man's eyes widened, but they did turn and finally lock on to Briony. He gave one last aborted shriek, then quieted, staring at her with eyes that were too deep.

Briony tentatively removed her hand from his mouth. He blinked, then looked around, seemingly taking in his surroundings. "Where…where am I?"

"You're in Westenaedre," Kishan said, talking slow and low, as if he were afraid to startle the man.

"Westenaedre?" the man echoed. He frowned, staring down at his hands on his lap. "But—oh, Old Ones." Faster than Briony would have guessed possible, he was up, clutching at Kishan's robe again. "Oh, it was horrible! They were everywhere. Not fast, no, but always there, no matter where you turned, and there would be a friend next to you, and then gone!" He tried to shake Kishan, but the healer was taller and much better fed. "My daughter—they took her, or killed her, or—"

Kishan took his hands firmly in his. "You're safe here."

"No!" The old man looked about wildly, settling his gaze on Briony. "Not safe! I thought—we all thought—that if we got away from the border, but…" He trailed off, shaking his head. "To have them between us and what we thought would be safety!"

"What are you talking about?" Kishan frowned. "The Scarred? They're nowhere close to here."

The old man shook his head furiously. "That's what we thought! That's what we all thought! But then, today—there they were." He paused, chewing on his lower lip. "I don't remember anything else. But Westenaedre—" He looked up at the ceiling, and then around, like he didn't quite believe what he was seeing. "It's still here. How is that possible?"

A cold chill seeped down and wrapped itself around Briony's heart. "You saw the Scarred here?" she whispered.

The man looked at her and nodded. "Yes, yes, just as Westenaedre came into view. A dozen at least." He furrowed his brow. "But Westenaedre is still here. How—how?"

Briony swallowed around the lump in her throat. The Scarred here—not in the forest, but *here*.

"I think you must be confused," Kishan said. "There's been no Scarred here."

He was wrong. The Scarred were in the forest. Doing something. Briony's suspicions that they were looking for something grew. And if they were—

She grabbed the old man by the upper arm. "What direction did you come from?"

"From the north."

Briony sucked in her breath. "Carys."

"What did you say?" said Kishan, eyes narrowing.

But Briony was already out the door.

CHAPTER ELEVEN
THEOSOPHY

ON HER NEXT DAY OFF, Theosophy stood in the doorway to Medical, watching Astrolabe sleep. He looked awfully thin under the covers. The stump of his right arm, still swaddled in greying bandages, drew her eye until she forced herself to look away, at his face. They'd been lovers for a while before her last bout with Solvent, and partners for longer.

"I'm sorry," she whispered. Heat prickled in her eyes, surprising her. When was the last time she'd cried?

Astrolabe stirred. By the time he woke fully, she was inside the room with the door shut, leaning against the wall, her face blank. "Report, fighter," she said.

His eyes went wide and he sat up, more easily than she'd expected. "Theo! I...I thought you weren't coming."

Theosophy shrugged. "Just wanted to see you before you disappear into the civilian world."

He gave her a sardonic look, and she realized that he'd seen the way she kept trying not to look at his arm. But he said only, "I'm going into Hydroponics."

"That's good," said Theosophy, thinking that she'd rather be dead.

"I guess it's where people like me go. Enough danger to keep our hearts pumping, but not so much we can't handle it. That's your job, now."

Theosophy swallowed. "I'll do you proud. I'll kill a monster for you, and one for Rhetoric." And she'd yell their names as she did, just like she had for every other lost fighter she'd known.

"Thanks, but it won't make any difference. It won't bring him back." He paused. "I've seen a lot of people die. I don't know why I thought he would be any different, but I did. You know, my first memory is of the two of us play-fighting with sticks. I won, even though he was a head taller than me back then. I guess I thought I'd always be able to protect him."

Astrolabe closed his eyes, and Theosophy saw tears glisten on his cheeks. Quickly she said, "I think my new trio is going to work out. It's Lever—who helped me rescue you—and Synthesis. They're young and stupid, but they've got potential. They just lack seasoning. All I have to do is keep them alive until they get it."

"Hope it works out this time."

Theosophy winced at his tone. "It must be fucking awful for you," she said before she could stop herself. Fuck. There was a reason she didn't do people, or have friends besides Solvent.

"You don't know a fucking thing about it."

"But it's the worst..." She trailed off, realizing how it was going to sound.

"Thing that can happen to a fighter? Yeah, I know people think that way. I know why you didn't come sooner. Is it the worst? Maybe." He was angry now. "But here I am, and I've got to find something to do with my time before I go stark raving bonkers thinking about him, and about you and everyone else out there every night. That can't be the only way there is to serve the City. If there's something else, I've got to find it."

Theosophy closed her eyes as a memory washed over her, the argument she'd had with Granddad when she joined the Militia. She'd been going bonkers, as Astro had put it, for eight years, every fucking night since her parents had shoved her into a cupboard, clutching a kitchen knife and sobbing, and let her listen to them die. Nothing would let her rest, nothing but fighting to defend the City as soon as she was old enough to talk her way in. She'd tried to explain that to Granddad, but couldn't find the words. He had said more or less what Astro had, and she'd said the most scathing thing she could think of before rushing out. They'd barely spoken since.

Astro was talking again. "Speaking of leaving the Militia..." He reached to the little table beside the bed. "Here."

She took the object he was holding out, and only then realized what it was—his double crystal, one side tuned to Rhetoric's double crystal, the other to her own.

Her stomach clenched. "No. Keep it as a memento." She reached to put it back on the table.

"I'd rather not," he said, blocking her hand. "Clean break and all that."

Forget and move on. She'd been doing that her whole life, and suddenly it didn't feel so great. "Listen," she blurted, "I'm sorry."

"For me being stupid? Theo, it wasn't your fault."

"But if I'd just—"

"I don't need your guilt. I don't need your pity, either. I don't need you looking at me and imagining it happening to you. If that's all you've got, then we have nothing more to say to each other."

"Astro..."

"Have a good life, Theo."

And somehow she was standing outside the door, staring into space. If it had been her in that bed...she would have reacted just like that, would have pushed her old trio-mates away and shut them out. Because she'd been doing the same thing her whole life.

She knew what she had to do next. Had known for days, in fact, just hadn't wanted to admit it.

THE STREETS WERE humid after all the rain they'd had, and with each turn into smaller and smaller lanes, she felt the heat more. Right turn at the little store she remembered so well, with the old lady in the headscarf who used to give her sweets, especially after...but the old lady was dead now, and the new shopkeeper squinted suspiciously until Theosophy moved on. Down the block, second ladder on the left. The ladder was more rickety than she remembered; they'd always tried to keep it at least half mended, no more than every other rung missing, but now it was barely navigable even for her. She wondered how often the inhabitants of this tier left their rooms—but it was none of her concern anymore.

Three floors up, she stepped off the ladder and onto the tiny platform lined with hydroponic window boxes. Granny had grown edible flowers every summer along with her herbs and vegetables, and she was unreasonably glad to see that Granddad had kept up the tradition. There was so little beauty in these lanes.

The rooms were smaller and darker than she remembered. No wonder Solvent hated the indoors so; the rooms in these quarters were bad enough without seeing your family dying in them every time you walked into one. At least, unlike Solvent's, her own family had mostly died out of her sight. Mostly.

"Who's there?" Granddad's voice came quavering through the open door.

Theosophy swallowed and stepped over the threshold.

Ten minutes later, hugs and apologies done with and a cup of mint tea steaming in her hands despite the stuffy heat in the room, Theosophy said, "Do you still have your library?"

"Some of it, yes. These past ten years have not been easy, you know."

There was no way to apologize; she could not have faced him and these rooms before, could barely do so now, echoingly empty as they were. Instead she said, "Can I see it?"

"*May* I, child. We must not lose our niceties."

She grimaced. This was one of the major spots where they had clashed—what good were niceties, in a world like this?—but she had no appetite for old arguments. "May I, Granddad?"

He sighed as he rose. He moved slower now, she noted, and his tightly curled hair had finished going white. "I should have known your visit would not be for my sake, nor because you missed me."

He wasn't wrong. She felt a flicker of discomfort, and dismissed it. "There's a need."

"And what need would that be, child?"

"I can't talk about it," she said automatically.

"Can't, or won't? Surely there's no matter of secrecy."

"The Militia does have its secrets, you know," she said, knowing that this was not one of them.

"So you come not to see me, but for my books, and you will not grace me with the knowledge of why."

"Pretty much," she said, knowing the language would distract him.

Instead he only sighed again. "Come."

Her grandparents' bedroom had once been lined with books on two sides, with barely room for the bed in between. Now only one wall of shelves remained; the other was naked, with even the shelves gone, torn down for defenses or fuel. She'd been expecting something of the sort, but still it made her flinch.

She stepped to the last wall of books, and hesitated, her hand hovering over the nearest. "May I?"

"They are all yours," Granddad answered, and eased himself down on the bed.

She froze. Must she do her research under his watchful eye? Apparently the answer was yes. His gaze was fixed on her, as if daring her to object.

She looked away, and bent to her task.

The library she remembered was sadly depleted. Books were valuable: the pages could be written over again and again until they were illegible. The leather bindings had once been much valued for their stoutness as shoe soles, she knew, but now the bindings were all too dry and cracked. If nothing else, they burned well.

She supposed that Granddad had carefully chosen which books to barter away, but the ones that were left looked like a dreadful jumble of subjects and eras, authors and schools of thought. *His* grandfather had been quite adamant about keeping a curated library of only certain areas of scholarship, or so Granddad had told her, but much of that had been lost before her birth.

Though she hadn't been in this room in years, she saw only a few books she did not recognize. She wondered, but did not ask, if he had traded some of the books from his collection to obtain the new ones, and how he had decided whether a potential new acquisition was valuable enough to give up the old.

Behind one of the new books, another had fallen to the back of the shelf. She pulled it out, intending to put it back properly, and a sheaf of paper fell out.

Theosophy picked it up. It took her a moment to understand what she was looking at. A map of buildings and streets, to be sure, in something like the layout of the University ruins. But the configuration was so strange, and so many things sketched in where she was pretty sure nothing lay now. Other things were missing, and one big thing: the Rift.

The buildings were labelled, she saw now. Military College; Biology; Philosophy. She knew the faculties had come from the University, of course, but she'd never seen them mapped. One of the buildings was circled in a different color. She brought the map closer to her face to read it: the Academy of Theoretical Dimensionary Science and Philosophy.

An image flashed before her eyes: a tall glass cup from her parents' kitchen, stamped with measurements on the side and a label on the bottom. *Academy TDSP*. The same cup, shattered—she flinched away from the memory.

She flipped open the book that had held the papers. On the flyleaf, the same stamp, and a strange word written by hand: Farhan.

Theosophy looked up. Granddad was watching her intently.

"This was our faculty," she said. "Fuck."

He nodded.

She paused, then realized she was waiting for him to criticize her language, and the fact that he didn't say a word bothered her more than anything else. "What happened to it? There's no dean..."

"Look at where the building was," he said.

Her gaze fell to the paper again. The defenses that the second dean of the Militia had built were missing, but the clock tower was *there*, and...

"The Rift," she whispered. "It's right on the edge of the Rift."

"Or, more precisely, when the Rift was created, our faculty was right in the thick of it," said Granddad. "If anyone knew how it came into being, it was them."

She laid the book and papers on the bed, and sat down hard beside them. "What *happened*?"

"That I do not know. I've been searching my whole life for answers." He nodded at the books. "I read every one of them, you know, until my eyesight started to fail. Some of them speak of a crystal device, larger than any other, that is somehow related to the Rift, but I have never been able to learn how. They call it a 'dimensional modulator.' If it once existed, it has long since been destroyed, for it lay somewhere deep in the University, underground. Perhaps it fell into the Rift."

"Were you going to tell me about all this?"

"How could I have? You left."

"It wasn't like the monsters got me, Granddad."

He shook his head. "You transferred faculties. The Militia is everything to the City, I know, but their priorities and allegiances are not mine."

"What *allegiances*? I'm trying to keep the City alive, that's all. That's all there *is*." She swallowed. "I've been fighting my whole adult life to keep the monsters at bay."

"Has it been working?"

She stared at him. "What?"

"You've sacrificed everything—family, love, your ability to experience a full range of emotions—oh yes, I know. I can see it in your eyes. And you didn't even know about this." He tapped the map. "Now that you do...what does that change?"

Theosophy picked up the map, staring at the faded ink. "Nothing. And everything."

If she could only learn how the Rift had come into being, maybe she could figure out how to undo it. That meant she would have to enter the ruins again. But first, she had to plan.

HE WAS WRONG about her, Theosophy decided on her way back to HQ. She could *feel* just fine, especially now. That was the problem. If she could just give up trying, like Solvent, things would be so much easier. Too bad it didn't seem to work that way. She still cared—she knew that because she bothered getting angry. Angry at Astro, at the dean, at Solvent, at her useless trio-mates, at the monsters, at herself.

Only Briony didn't make her angry. That was peculiar; there was *something* happening inside her, when she talked to Briony or thought of her or, fuck, even dreamed of her, and it wasn't quite the same as the lust she felt for Solvent, either. But she couldn't put a name to it, and couldn't stop worrying at it. Like running your fingers over a new scar, getting used to the shape of it and how it affected everything else.

Like now. She couldn't just charge blindly into the ruins without a plan again—that had already cost Lever their trio-mates. If she got Lever or Synthesis or both of them killed just when they were starting to work together, the dean was bound to do something drastic, like put her on training tyros full-time for months. She would not command her trio-mates to come with her, and couldn't count on them volunteering, not with the way she was treating them. She had no other options for back-up. But she'd have to make sure that, whenever she went, her next shift was covered, so her absence wouldn't leave a corner of the City vulnerable—all without tipping off the dean.

This was going to take some work.

CHAPTER TWELVE
BRIONY

A SMOKING CRATER was all that was left of the cottage. Even the trees surrounding it were twisted and charred, bent away from where the cottage had been. Briony slid to a stop in front of it, covering her mouth with her hands. "Oh, Old Ones."

There was no sign of Carys. Had the Scarred taken her? Or had she met the same fate as her home?

Old Ones, Briony had just been here. If she'd lingered...

There were others here, mostly refugees that she didn't recognize, but there were some townspeople as well. Briony turned, found them watching her. Of course. She swallowed, then set her shoulders. She was allowed to come and look as much as anyone else.

More, maybe.

She turned to the nearest person she recognized. "What happened here?" she asked. "Is anyone hurt?"

The suspicious look immediately vanished off the woman's face. "Oh!" she said, "I'm not sure. Will Healer Kishan be coming as well?"

"Maybe." Briony looked around. "It might depend on the number of injured. I'm supposed to take stock."

Kishan probably would follow along in due time. He wasn't stupid, and he would make connections. At least he probably wouldn't make a scene in public.

Briony checked with each of the townspeople, but they had all come after the fact, attracted by noise or smoke, and had no idea what had happened. The refugees, however, were gathered close together, as if seeking safety in numbers.

She approached them slowly, afraid of a repeat of the old man, except several times over, but they just watched her, staring silently. "Are any of you hurt?"

Most of them shook their heads, though some continued just looking at her. Briony frowned. She certainly didn't see any injuries. So what? The Scarred had showed up just for Carys?

But why—to secure her knowledge, or suppress a potential competitor?

Briony needed more information about Theo's realm, and she needed to move faster than she was. If the Scarred got there first—she should at least warn Theo. Briony glanced off in the direction of the lake. She still wasn't quite sure how talking to the warrior woman worked. Could she just go anytime? Did Theo need to be in a certain place? This whole thing was a mess.

And maybe she should avoid the forest for a few days until Kishan got less suspicious about what she was up to.

Theo's people were warriors. They would probably be okay if the Scarred got to them first.

But would Briony's family?

Leo was just five. Briony cursed the Old Ones for creating the Scarred and abandoning them instead of finishing what they started.

She turned back to the refugees. "Did you see what happened?" she asked, though obviously they had. Why else would they be stuck together like a flock of sheep confronted with a wolf? She felt a momentary pang of pity for them. Had they seen their villages and families burn again?

"They came out of the forest," one man whispered.

"They went straight for the cottage," said another.

The assembled refugees nodded and managed to huddle even closer together. One child, so dirty and haggard that Briony wasn't sure whether it was a boy or a girl, started to cry.

"You don't have to tell me if it's too hard," Briony said, even though she desperately wanted to know. "Just tell me if I need to go look for injured in..." She faltered, looking back at the remains, if they could be called that, of the cottage. A few charred pieces of wood marked the corners of where the building had stood, but the rest was just a blackened, molten lump. If anyone had been inside—if Carys had been inside—she was gone.

One of the refugees licked his lips. "They went in," he whispered, "and then they came out. And then...then it was just gone."

"They didn't bring anyone out with them?"

A collective shaking of heads.

Briony took a deep breath and left them. The cottage remains looked even less recognizable up close. What would do this to a building? Too destructive, too fast to be a fire. Briony gingerly picked her way across the grass—all laid perfectly flat, as if whatever had destroyed the building had killed it so fast that it didn't even know it was dead—to where the door had been.

"Briony!"

She turned to find Kishan hurrying up from town, waving one hand. He had her supplies in the other. He froze in place when he saw the remains of the building, then scanned his eyes across the gathered people, with more townspeople showing up every minute. Apparently not seeing anything worth his interest, he joined her at the threshold.

"Old Ones," he breathed, passing her her supplies, "what did this?"

"The Scarred," Briony replied. She ignored his sharp intake of breath and set the supplies down on the grass. Hopefully there wasn't anything caustic left that would melt them, or her boots, for that matter. On second thought, she retrieved a set of thick gloves from her pack and slid them on.

She waded into the remains. Up close, it smelled terrible, like something that had been dead for far too long. Briony held one gloved hand up to her nose to try and block it.

Kishan stayed outside, of course. "Is…someone in there?"

"They didn't see anyone come out." She stepped onto the black mass at the center of the cottage. It was hard. There'd be no digging through this. And what did she think she'd find anyway? If Carys had been here, she'd have melted together with the rest of it. "I mean, other than the Scarred. If someone had been home…"

"Old Ones," murmured Kishan again.

Briony retreated to the edge of the mass and tried to pry up one edge, or break off a piece, but it was fused to the ground. She gave up and walked the edge of the building, trying to ignore the bile building up in her throat. Poor Carys. Had they killed her first, tortured her? Carved the symbols into her face like the rumors said, relishing in her screams?

They'd do that to her family if she couldn't get to Theo in time.

The smell was making her eyes water. Briony left the charred remains to themselves and pushed past Kishan onto the path beyond. She dropped her hands onto her knees and bent over, trying to keep her breakfast down. Old Ones. Poor Carys.

How had they'd known that Carys knew about the other realm? Did they know she was a spirit talker?

Briony's hand strayed to her amulet. Would they be able to tell she was too?

"Bree?" Kishan's hand on her back, trying to be comforting.

Swallowing, she straightened. What was she going to do? If they could track spirit talking, she'd put her family in danger if she went home. She could see their ancestral home, all blackened and melted, hear the screams of the children. How had the Scarred known? How could Briony protect those she loved from them?

Part of her wanted to believe that Carys was an easy target, outside of town and all alone. But their house was on the edge of town and backed up to the forest. It would be easy enough for the Scarred to melt out of the trees and do what they wanted before anyone else in Westenaedre knew.

"Bree?" She was vaguely aware of Kishan leading her away from the cottage, of him sitting her down on the dirt closer to town. "Bree? Talk to me, dear one."

"They're *here*." Briony looked up, meeting Kishan's eyes. She could feel tears creeping into the corners of her eyes, but couldn't seem to stop them. "I'm not ready for them yet! I don't have any way to protect Jael and the children."

Kishan took her hands in his, kissing her knuckles. "Calm down. Calm down." He pulled her against his chest, running his hand down the back of her head in a comforting manner. But Briony could feel the tension in him, too.

She extricated herself from his embrace, took a few calming breaths, and rubbed her eyes. Her tears had left dark spots on the red of his robe. Right. Panicking wouldn't help anyone. And she suspected the Scarred had been here, patrolling the forest, looking for the remains of the Old Ones' knowledge and power. And if Theo and her people were that knowledge, well, Briony wasn't going to let them have it.

"I need to talk to Jael," she said.

"Sure, sure." Kishan rubbed her shoulders. "Whatever you need. Take the rest of the day off if you want."

"No!" At Kishan's surprised look, Briony tried to give him a smile. "No, I mean, could you have him come to the shop?" The shop was on the other side of town from the house. Surely that was far enough from the forest to keep everyone safe. "That should be fine."

Kishan walked her back to the shop, holding her hand and rubbing the back of her knuckles. That horrible smell of death followed her the whole way, but Kishan thankfully said nothing, though Briony wanted to wretch. As they passed through town, she was aware of whispering surrounding her, but she wasn't sure if it was aimed at her, or if the story of what had happened up north had spread.

After getting her some water and making sure she could properly sit on a stool, Kishan left, in theory to retrieve Jael, and Briony stared at the wall. Old Ones, what was she going to do? What had the Scarred wanted from Carys, and had they gotten it?

Briony closed her eyes. Right. She needed to be calm. It took several deep breaths for the world to come back into focus. She would need to stay somewhere else to make sure the Scarred didn't do to Jael and the children what they'd done to Carys. Maybe with Kishan. He'd wanted her to sleep over forever, so he'd probably agree easily.

The idea wasn't as attractive as it once had been. Briony had a brief flash of Theo's face, her eyes, but shook it away.

That was one problem hopefully solved.

As for the other—how was she supposed to open the way to Theo's realm? She had no idea where to start, but seeing how the

Scarred were *here*, out of everywhere in Aelduende to be, they might have a clue. So she'd have to move fast.

Somehow.

Briony reached up and rubbed both temples. Surely some sort of Old One knowledge survived somewhere. All of it couldn't have vanished with the Old Ones. She knew some of Kishan's books—or at least the information in them—predated the War. Somewhere there had to be something like that, except useful.

Kishan would be the one to know. Maybe now that the Scarred were here, had killed someone, he'd be more willing to help. Maybe he would understand, finally.

But maybe not. And for some reason, Briony didn't want him to know about Theo.

The front door of the shop creaked open. Briony turned her head to find Jael hurrying in, Kishan behind him.

"Old Ones, look at you," said her brother. Before she could say anything, he'd gathered her up, holding her tight in his massive arms. "We've got to get you home. I've heard all about what happened up north. You can't go two feet in this town without someone stopping you to tell about it again. Bad shock, I know, but some food and sleep will clear you right up."

"Jay." Briony pushed lightly at her brother's chest, and he let her go. "I promised you we'd talk. Let's talk."

Jael's brow knit, but he nodded once. "Can we use the back room, Kishan?"

The healer blinked. "You can talk right here. I don't think anyone's going to come in for a while."

"Family stuff." Jael clapped Kishan on the back hard enough that the healer stumbled a little. "You understand."

Kishan mumbled something under his breath that sounded like, "I'm practically family," and then turned and headed for the room they'd put the old man in. Briony pushed herself off the stool and headed for the back room, hearing her brother's heavy footfalls behind her. She waited until her brother had entered before she shut the door firmly and locked it, something which would probably infuriate Kishan shortly if—when—he came over either to eavesdrop or try to barge in.

When she turned back to her brother, he was watching her intently. "What is it, Bree? You're acting strange. Are you sure you don't want to go home and sleep?" He laid a hand on her shoulder. "It won't hurt to take care of yourself, you know."

Briony laid her hand on top of her brother's. "Did you ever see Mother…" How to ask this? *Did you ever see Mother routinely perform an act that would have gotten her shunned and feared by the community?* Briony paused, sighing, and rubbed her temples again. "So, that cottage north of town. Do you know who lived there?"

Jael narrowed his eyes. "Yes. Carys. The spirit talker."

Did you know Mother was a spirit talker? Briony couldn't seem to get the words out. She gazed up at her big brother, remembering being much smaller. She'd done something, something not worth remembering, all these years later, but something idiotic, and something she needed Jael's help with to save her hide. But she couldn't make herself ask—she didn't want to see his disappointment in her.

In this moment, she was reduced to being eight again.

"Have you…" she started, then stopped, still not sure this was the right way to get it out. "Have you ever noticed any strange abilities in our family? On Mother's side?"

"What do you mean?"

Oh, Old Ones. There was no good way to do this. "I went to see Carys," she said, then barrelled on before she had a chance to think better of it. "And she said Mother had been a spirit talker too."

Jael looked down at her, blinking his eyes slowly. Briony braced for whatever was coming, but, instead, her brother nodded once. "Yes."

Briony stared at her brother. "You saw her do it?"

Jael sat down on Kishan's stool and used one hand to smooth his beard. "Mother was not...discreet about it, at least not when I was very young. I mean, around family. It wasn't hard to figure it out, but I never got the courage up to ask her about it." He crossed his arms over his chest, then looked up, gazing at Briony. "You can do it too, can't you."

Not a question. Briony felt her cheeks flush. "Yes." She fished her amulet out of her blouse and wrapped her fingers around it. "Carys said our family has always been spirit talkers."

"Magic does run in families." Jael looked toward the examination room next door. Briony could barely hear Kishan and the old man talking. "Is that what you told the Academy? That you could spirit talk?"

"No, of course not." Briony ran a hand over her hair. "I'm not stupid. I didn't tell them anything specific, but they didn't care. Look, Jay, forget about the Academy. I told them I wasn't going to go. We've got a bigger problem."

Jael's jaw tightened. "The Scarred."

"More than that." Briony took a deep breath. Jael was taking the spirit talking thing far better than she'd ever hoped for, but she'd need to tell him everything. "This realm I can talk to, the people there—they're not the dead. They're alive right now, just...somewhere else.

133

Carys said they're what's left of the Old Ones. And the Scarred are looking for them."

Her brother went perfectly still. Briony felt sick to her stomach. Saying it out loud somehow made it a hundred times more real. Who knew what the Scarred remembered from the War? Maybe they understood how to access Theo's world. Maybe they'd never lost that knowledge. Maybe all they needed was to be in the right place at the right time, and then they'd get everything they needed.

"Bree?" Jael pushed himself off the stool. "You've gone all pale."

"We can't let them get there first," she whispered. "We have to beat them."

Jael pulled at his beard and nodded once. "What do we need to do?"

CHAPTER THIRTEEN
THEOSOPHY

THEOSOPHY LED her trio across the rooftops, shadows thick in the alleys below, though the three-quarters moon meant visibility on the roofs was good. They were patrolling far from the ruins, playing rearguard for the more experienced trios. That didn't mean she could afford to be distracted. She pulled her mind back from wishing it were Astro beside her instead of these tyros. They had to learn sometime, and it was her job to make sure neither she nor they got killed while they were doing it. She was armed with a spear to let both her partners get experience with muskets, but it wasn't her favorite weapon; she hoped the location of their patrol would mean little action tonight.

A shriek echoed across the City, and Lever flinched.

"Don't worry," said Theosophy. "That's monster, not human. It's their hunting cry."

"Right," muttered Synthesis.

She turned on him, quick as a spear-strike. "Where is the monster?"

Synthesis swallowed. "It was...maybe five blocks in from the ruins. Closer now."

Another shriek, this one closer. Theosophy grimaced. "*That* was a human."

Lever raised their musket, the bayonet shining in the moonlight. Their voice trembled, but the blade was steady. "Do we go in?"

"No," Theosophy said sharply. "It's not our territory tonight. We hold the blocks we've been assigned, unless another trio gets in trouble and calls for help. If we leave, this neighborhood will be left undefended, and we can't—"

She stopped abruptly. Something was wrong, a shift in the air, a tickle in her nose...

A monster leapt over the next rooftop, all claws and tentacles and an uncountable number of heads. Her trio-mates yelled in unison and charged.

"Get back here! It's not alone, get—"

A second monster lumbered up the roof-tiles behind its mate, but where was the third? Theosophy ducked as she ran, spear at the ready, casting about with all her senses. Synthesis reached the monster first and swung his lowered bayonet—too slow, for the creature spun aside, tentacles flailing. He dropped to the rooftop and bounced up again, bayonet angled upward this time. Lever held the high ground on the peak of the roof, swinging overhand at the larger and heavier monster. Their bayonet stabbed home and Lever threw all their weight behind it. The monster fell out of sight on the far side of the peak, and Lever, off-balance, fell with it. Theosophy swore and ran up the roof, dodging tentacles. She reached the peak and looked down the other side.

The third monster hunched over Lever's splayed body, its shape almost human but for the glowing eyes. It looked up and hissed.

Theosophy yelled and launched herself off the peak. A rush of air, and then she slammed into the monster, both of them rolling, the edge of the roof coming up fast. Theosophy grabbed with her free hand and hung on as her spear and the monster fell past her. A burning pain shot up her leg and she kicked out, felt her foot connect. The monster shrieked, thudded against the opposite wall, and fell out of sight. A moment later she heard a sickening *crunch* on the cobblestones five stories below.

Something grabbed her wrist. She nearly lunged with her other hand before realizing it was Lever. They heaved her up and back over the edge, then leaned over her, face splattered with gore and one eye swollen. "You all right?" they asked.

"Fine," Theosophy said, pushing herself up though she had to grit her teeth against the pain in her leg. "Where's Synthesis?"

They found him curled in pain next to the body of the first monster, limp tentacles splayed across the tiles. As Theosophy approached, he looked up and grimaced. The monster had splattered his leather vest with acid, but the thick material had mostly held; in the moonlight Theosophy could see only a few spots where it had been eaten away to the skin beneath. His hands, though, were covered in welts from the suckers on the tentacles. She knew from experience how painful those were, but they would heal well, after she got him back to HQ for some herbal salve. The worst injury she could see was his left wrist, which he cradled to his chest.

"Broken?" she said.

"I don't think so. Just sprained." He pushed himself up, wincing, and even accepted a hand up from Lever.

"Good. You can't afford to let yourselves be injured like this every patrol. You have to be out here night after night. The City is depending on you now."

"What about you?" said Synthesis.

Theosophy looked at him blankly. He nodded toward her legs. She looked down, and saw one leg of her trousers stained dark at the thigh.

She swore and rolled up the trousers to inspect the wound. Blood, but no ichor; the cut had been clean, the monster's claws not poisoned. "It hurts, but so what? It's stopped bleeding. I'll get it cleaned up when our shift is over. So will you."

Her trio-mates stared at her.

"What did I say earlier? *We can't leave our post.* You can still fight, so we're here until dawn. Now march."

The rest of the night was uneventful. They came upon a lone monster, the rest of its triad dead or lost, and dispatched it quickly, with no further injuries. Dawn came and they headed back to HQ unmolested. If Theosophy was relieved, she told herself it was just because she needed her trio ready to take their next shift. The dean, and Theosophy herself, needed to see that they were pulling their weight. That was all.

She certainly wasn't worried about what Briony would think of her leadership methods.

"THEOSOPHY, you have to do better."

Theosophy paced in front of the dean's desk, wishing for a swig of the drink, but Dean Prosody didn't offer this time. "We're a raw trio, sir. I'm good, but I'm not that good. They need time."

"I know that." The dean shook her head. "I'm not saying this to punish you, or to imply that you're not working hard enough. The fact is, we're down too many people. Until we can get the newest recruits up to a bare minimum of fighting skill, we're shorthanded. We need your trio pulling their weight."

"And what then? You send out the tyros, integrate them into trios, whatever you have to do to get them up to speed, but where's the next cohort? I'm not seeing a whole lot of able-bodied young folk who aren't already in the Militia. Are you going to take twelve-year-olds?"

The dean's face closed down. "You worry about your job. I'll worry about mine."

That gave Theosophy pause. She'd expected to be shouted down, to be lectured about how she didn't understand the finer points of long-term Militia strategy. If the dean didn't have a comeback to her question...that was bad.

"What did you learn about your new trio last night?" the dean continued.

Theosophy understood that the dean was changing the subject, and decided she'd better not try to change it back. "They act before they think. They don't work well together. And they both hate me."

The dean snorted. "Those first two sound familiar, don't you think?"

Theosophy stared back blandly. "I don't know what you mean, sir."

"Do try to remember that you're supposed to be a unit of three, not two against one. It's not their fault that neither of them is Astrolabe."

A fist clenched inside of her. Fuck. She'd been with Astro too long, if his death was still bothering her. "That has nothing to do with anything, sir," Theosophy said through gritted teeth.

"Think about it, Theosophy. And don't forget: I need you at full strength."

Theosophy could do nothing but bow her head and murmur, "Yes, sir."

EARLY EVENING found her in the practice room, shadow-boxing. Usually it was a good way to work out her frustrations, to make the world go away for just a little while. But she kept seeing Astro's face before her, the maps, the device, Briony's lithe body. Everything was just too fucking distracting.

She drilled harder, sweat dripping off her body. Turn, kick, turn, kick, turn, kick—

Someone caught her foot. She blinked sweat out of her eyes. At the other end of her leg, Synthesis gave a shove. She dove and rolled, coming up with a shout. He blocked her with a knee, she twisted and he danced back out of range. Then she lost herself in motion again, only this time the shadow fought back. Sparring with a partner was less fluid, more unpredictable. She felt more alive, not like she had since...since Astro.

"Why do you hate us?" Synthesis said, panting.

"I don't. I'm trying to get you to be better. The City needs you to be better."

"There are other ways to do that."

She snorted. "What, like coaxing and babying you along?"

He didn't answer for a moment, dancing back and forth on the balls of his feet, hands up. "The way I see it is, we have two options. We could push each other to the edge, always harder, always rougher, be more brutal so we can survive. That's your way. Or we could support each other. Push each other to be more, yes, but working *together*, not at odds with each other. That way, we stay human."

She lowered her hands and glared at him. "So I'm a monster now?"

"No. But you could be. What separates us from them?"

"We're not shapeshifting beasts that like human flesh, just for starters."

"Community," he said. "Compassion."

"They fight in threes too."

"Sure. But do they come back for their injured fellows?"

Theosophy blinked. Astro's face flashed before her eyes again. She hadn't wanted to go. And look where going had gotten them: Astro useless, Lever's partners dead. Pointless. Except for the device...and that had been worth everything.

Maybe she'd been wrong.

Lever's light voice cut across her thoughts. "Am I late for warm-up?"

She looked from Lever to Synthesis. *Community, huh?* "Yes, but it doesn't matter. Follow me."

She took them to the rooftop, knowing Solvent wouldn't be there after curfew. The twilight air felt cool, hinting at a chilly night ahead. Once they were well away from the attic door and comfortably seated, and she'd checked for both monsters and stray ears, she turned back to the other two.

"I have an offer for you," she began, clumsily. "It's not an order, because I can't order you to do this. But take the time to think about it, if you need to."

They stared back at her, confusion and concern on both faces. She'd been such an asshole to both of them, she didn't deserve concern, but never mind that now.

She went on in a rush. "I'm going into the University ruins. There's something I need to do. It's strictly unofficial business, the dean doesn't know about it, and I'm probably going to be in big trouble when I get back. That's why I'm not ordering you along." She paused to take a deep breath. "But I am asking."

Into the silence, Synthesis said, "Why are you going? And where?"

"For something big that could change everything. I need to get to the laboratories."

Lever said, "Is this about that thing you brought back?"

Theosophy froze, then made herself laugh. "Aren't you the clever one? Yes, as a matter of fact, it is."

"The thing you wouldn't show me and haven't mentioned since?"

Theosophy felt her heart drop. "Well, yes, but..."

Lever shook their head. "With all due respect, you haven't been treating us like a team. You don't trust us. And you don't respect us." They stood up. "The answer is no."

Theosophy turned to Synthesis, but he too was shaking his head. "They're right, sir."

"But you were just talking about community..."

"For community to be there for you, you have to be there for it first."

This was completely wrong. "But I am! Everything I *do* is for this fucking City!"

"Maybe that's the problem. You care about the City, but not the individual people in it, and you sure as shit don't care about yourself." He took a deep breath. "Look. What I will do is cover for you. If you want to go in, that's your business and I can't stop you. But I won't follow you in there. I'm sorry."

Synthesis got up and followed Lever off the roof, leaving her alone.

CHAPTER FOURTEEN
BRIONY

BRIONY FELT STRONG arms embrace her from behind. She turned to find Theo standing there, a real Theo, with real skin and hair and eyes, unlike the blue glow that had always accompanied her before. Briony looked up into Theo's eyes, getting lost in their warmth. She could feel the other woman's breath on her face. Theo leaned in closer and Briony closed her eyes, feeling Theo's lips brush gently against her own. They were chapped, but soft, and Briony pulled her closer, wrapping her hands in the other woman's short, wiry hair.

Briony lost herself in that kiss. But it ended, eventually. Theo smiled down at her and said, "Good morning, beautiful," in Kishan's voice.

She blinked the sleep out of her eyes. Kishan's face hovered about a foot over hers, smiling. Briony fought down a sudden wave of disappointment and returned his smile as best she could after being awakened from what was a lovely dream.

Kishan rolled away, leaving Briony staring at a blank, wooden ceiling and trying to hold onto the dream. But it was too late—it slipped away, like fog in a brightening morning. She raised herself up on her elbows. It had been days since the Scarred attack north of town, and she hadn't gone home since.

The healer hummed as he dressed for the day. Briony lowered herself back down and folded her hands over her stomach.

What was she doing? Both Jael and Kishan had been enthusiastic when Briony had suggested she move in with the healer, but it was merely for her family's safety, not because she was ready to make things more permanent with Kishan. She felt bad for preying on their hopes.

She missed Jael and the children. She could picture them at home. Auberon would be up and working on breakfast, and Marcea and Brin would be gathering eggs from the chickens. Leo would be flitting about behind Jael as he fed the goats, begging to help. She should be there, with them. This was for them, though. And hopefully Kishan would understand when this was all over and things could go back to normal.

She had to believe they would, that this state of fear wouldn't be the norm.

Briony swung her feet out of the bed and set about retrieving her clothes for the day. Her stuff was a mess—Jael was bringing her things from home as he could, but it was mostly haphazard. She only had the single shirt she'd been wearing still, and had taken to borrowing from Kishan, though that made her look ridiculous and had nearly given Yara apoplexy.

How could Kishan be so nonchalant about this whole thing? It was like, since the Scarred hadn't shown up again—hadn't even really been seen the first time—the whole thing hadn't happened.

But Briony couldn't push things out of her head. Poor Carys. She had to do something, if only so her own fear didn't immobilize her.

"I'm meeting Jael for breakfast," she said as she pulled her boots on.

Kishan's humming trailed off. "What, again?" He came around and sat next to her on the bed. "Why don't you ever eat with me?"

"It's hard, being away from home. Please, bear with me a little longer."

He gave her a sad smile. "Of course, Bree, whatever you need."

Briony could feel his eyes on her back as she left the room, and she couldn't help but suspect that his patience was wearing thinner than he pretended.

She met her brother at the inn near the western edge of town, looking out over the prairie. It was mostly deserted each morning, the late-night revelers still sleeping off their ale, and Westenaedre rarely got travelers, as they were not on the way to Cynestel and were situated dangerously close to the forest. Fractures did exist outside of the forest, of course, but they were more obvious and easier to avoid. Or easier to see coming, at least.

They took over a table in a back corner. Briony sat immediately next to her brother. There was something comforting about his bulk, and it reminded her of when they'd been children. The thought of simpler times was appreciated.

"How's it going?" she asked quietly. In the silence of the inn, it always seemed like her voice echoed too far.

Jael shook his head, pulling at his white-blond beard. "Poorly. There's some talk of appealing to the government in Cynestel for protection, but if they haven't defended the border, I can't see that they'll bother with us either."

"We're closer to Cynestel."

"Maybe, but not close enough." Jael glowered down at his mug as if it had personally offended him.

Briony let him sulk for a minute. "But what about information about this other realm?"

Jael's grimace grew. "Not a thing. I've tried everything short of actually suggesting spirit talking to get information out of people, and no one's said a thing." He sighed. "I can't believe I let you talk me into this."

They'd agreed to have Jael look for information, since it would be less suspicious coming from him—a man looking to protect his family, rather than a strange and perhaps questionable woman, like much of the town seemed to consider Briony, peering around into forbidden and sinister knowledge.

So far her brother had been sidling up to neighbors and colleagues, bemoaning the threat of the Scarred, suggesting that maybe there was something in the past that their ancestors had done to protect the town from them the first time around. It was dangerous ground. He couldn't hint too heavily because it came too close to the idea of trying to access the Old Ones' knowledge.

Briony wrapped her fingers around her own mug. If—when—she managed to open the way to Theo's realm, would the town even accept them and their help? Or would they scream and demand they be hunted down, exiled and reviled like the spirit talkers?

What was wrong with people?

It didn't matter. She needed to protect her family, and this was the only way left to her. Westenaedre could deal as it saw fit, as long as Jael and the children were safe.

Jael laid a hand on her shoulder. "We may need to go about this another way, Bree."

"Like what?"

There were very few repositories of books in town, and most of those only had newer books, many people having decided throughout the years that it was best to burn the Old Ones' teachings, what were left of them, and let that information die. Briony had stopped by the shops and centers that she knew had books and invented excuses to look through them, but there was nothing old enough, and nothing that even mentioned Theo's city or where it used to be. It was hard enough to find mentions of the Scarred and the War.

In theory, Jael's manipulation would have ferreted out any hidden stashes, but maybe there were none.

The serving boy scurried back with plates of eggs and bacon, then scurried off again.

Jael watched him go. "Maybe you need to go back to this Theo and ask her how this whole thing works."

Briony stabbed absently at her eggs. "I don't think she has any idea. She didn't even know there was anything outside her city before. Whatever the Old Ones were before, they're not that anymore. They may not know any better than we do."

"Forsaken spirits." Jael pulled at his beard. "So...we capture a Scarred and force them to tell us what they know."

Briony almost knocked her plate off the table. "You can't be serious."

"We may be running out of time. You said that yourself." Jael stopped, looking around the inn. Briony followed his glance. It seemed so peaceful right now—just people going about their lives, doing the best they could for themselves. No signs that anyone was worried aside from them. "If the Scarred are looking for something specific and manage to find it before we can even figure out how this whole thing works..."

He had a point. Briony blew out her breath slowly. "I don't know how we would do that. They travel in packs. And even if we managed to grab one without bringing the wrath of the others down on us, how would we make them talk? They torture themselves for fun."

"They've got to have some weakness." Jael balled his hands into fists. "Forsake it all, Bree, I almost wish you'd kept all this to yourself. No wonder you've been so wound up lately."

Briony took her brother's hand under the table and gave it a squeeze. "How is everyone?"

"They miss you." Jael sighed. "I understand why you've gone, and I do think it's good for you and Kishan, but...I miss my little sister. The house doesn't feel right without you."

The sentiment was unexpected. Briony wiped at one eye with her other hand. "Yeah."

"But, anyway," said Jael. "How are you and Kishan doing?"

They talked aimlessly of other things while they ate, and then Jael went off to see if he could make any better headway, but Briony suspected they both knew nothing was going to come of it.

Kishan was sulking at the main counter in the shop when Briony arrived. "What are you and Jael up to?"

"Up to?" Briony hung up her cloak, then started putting her hair up. She'd need to do some grinding today, and it was always best to have her hair as out of the way as possible. Plus she tended to get hot, and letting her neck be exposed helped. "It's just breakfast, Kishan. You have to remember this is the first time we've lived apart since we were little."

That was not technically true—while their mother and Nerys had been alive, Jael and his family had lived in a different building on their land. But they had still been close enough.

"I don't mean breakfast." Kishan waved one hand dismissively. "Breakfast, great. But you two are working on something, and you won't tell me what it is. Bree, if we're going to be partners, you need to trust me. If you need help, let me help you too. You don't need to always rely on your brother. He has his own family to take care of."

"I am his family," Briony snapped.

"No, *we're* supposed to be a family." He pushed himself up off the stool, causing it to slide loudly across the floor. "You and me, Bree. We're supposed to be partners, have children of our own, love and cherish each other for the rest of our days." His voice rose in volume as he went on, and he swallowed when he was done, panting a little.

Oh, Old Ones. He meant it. Briony hadn't realized how serious he was—or maybe she had, and had ignored it, too wrapped up in her own goals to think about how she was leading Kishan on.

Or maybe she hadn't realized she was. Not until Theo had come along.

She held out her arms to him, and he came around the corner and buried his head into her shoulder. As she pulled him closer, she wondered what to do. She'd come to rely on him so much, but surely it wasn't right to continue to do so if she didn't know if she could give him her heart or her commitment.

"It's really nothing," she murmured. "We've just been trying to think of a way to protect the rest of the town from the Scarred."

Kishan's chuckle was muffled by her shoulder. "Old Ones, you've managed to recruit Jael into that particular brand of madness?"

Briony stiffened. "How can you say that? They *destroyed* that cottage!"

"Yes, but they haven't touched the town, and no one's seen them anywhere nearby, if anyone actually saw them at all. It was a fluke, that's all. Maybe they're worried about spirit talking as much as the rest of us are."

"The only thing they're worried about is someone *else* spirit talking, and getting the information they need, if anything." Briony dropped her arms and stepped back from Kishan. The healer looked up, surprise written on his face. "I can't believe you're being so callous about this. Someone died in there, Kishan. Doesn't that go against everything you believe in?"

Kishan frowned. "Look, Bree, you *know* what the Old Ones did. Think about how nice it would be to enjoy the forest without having to worry about a choke vine grabbing you, or to be able to safely walk to the next town over without an armed convoy."

"They did good things too! Look at your medicine books—and don't tell me the information in them is from after the War. Yes, they made mistakes—horrible mistakes—but they knew good things, too. How to help people and keep them safe. You still use what you can of that knowledge today. And what about the Senders? That's also old magic." Briony sighed and looked down. "I'm sorry. I just don't think it's fair to hate someone for something like that—to be glad that they're gone."

What else could she have learned from Carys, given the time? Yes, the woman was a mess of half-useful comments and riddles, but Briony would be more lost than she already was without those few conversations.

That last visit had been so rushed. Had Carys known the Scarred were coming?

"And what have you found?" Kishan asked.

Briony looked up sharply, not quite sure what he meant.

Kishan swept one arm in the general direction of the forest. "For protecting us. From the Scarred."

"Nothing." Briony turned away from him, dropping her shoulders. What had happened at the end of the Great War to finally end it? For all she had been taught as a child, she had no idea. It's almost as if those that had lived through the War had tried to forget the whole thing had ever happened. But the scars lingered to this day—the Fractures, the Scarred, even the hole where Theo's city had once been, now filled up with water, all signs that anything had ever been there erased.

"So give it up," Kishan said. He came up behind her, running his hands down her arms. "Forget it. Don't waste your life worrying about something you can't control."

"And when the Scarred come for us?"

"They won't."

It wasn't worth fighting with him over it. They would. They would find whatever they were looking for in the forest. They would access the City, gain whatever knowledge they were looking for there. Then they'd sweep in from the border, a destructive force made more terrible by the Old Ones' information, and all Aelduende's armies and their magic wouldn't stand a chance in the face of it.

"I have work to do," she said, and went into the back room.

CHAPTER FIFTEEN
THEOSOPHY

WHEN NIGHT FELL, Theosophy was inside the barricades. She'd chosen a spot just inside the blockade and well hidden. Still, she felt very vulnerable—alone. She'd never been in here on her own before. No one had, and no one in their right mind would, either. Fucking so-called partners.

This close, she felt it in her bones when the Rift tore open and the monsters came.

They swarmed past her hiding spot, a blur of limbs and tentacles and teeth, half-glimpsed eyes where no eyes should be. Some shambled, others flew, and still others hopped, covering the length of a prone human with each leap. The shadows shifted and she pressed herself even farther into the crack she had found. If they smelled her, she had no chance.

She waited until the swarm had thinned and the last few had gone creeping past, then waited longer still. They would be out hunting in the City for most of the night, but she dared not wait too long.

She checked the musket slung across her back, touched her jacket to check that the device was safe, then crept out of her hiding place into cool night air that made her shiver. Unnatural shadows still moved among the ruins, and she flitted from one piece of cover to the next. Luckily the monsters didn't think like humans: they hadn't cleared the cover. Or maybe they just didn't care. The thought chilled her.

The ruins were eerily quiet. She passed the place where Astrolabe had holed up, but didn't go in—maybe there was more stuff in there, maybe not, but she didn't have time to look. Her boots crunched on debris no matter how lightly she tried to walk. She rounded a corner and saw a dome, and stopped.

The only other time she'd been this far in, she and Solvent had watched their third partner die in front of that dome. He hadn't been the only one—the whole expedition had been a disaster, the muddy streets churned with blood—but they'd been young and his death had hit them the hardest. Solvent, closer than Theosophy, had been splattered with his gore.

After that was when Solvent had started taking the rock salts.

Theosophy shook herself, hard, and moved on, past the dome, farther than any human in living memory.

Moonlight flooded the rubble-filled street and the Rift ahead. The moon made the streetscape stand out in stark relief like paper cut-outs, but the shadows kept shifting. Musket in hand, she crept forward into the growing heat. One last corner, and then the Rift, dead ahead.

She couldn't believe she was this close to the Rift and not dead yet. It steamed and roiled practically below her; she could feel the heat and smell sulphurous gases, and the noise of hissing was immense. A sickly light flickered off the buildings that teetered precariously around it. Shapes moved constantly over the lip, both up and down. She looked away, fighting queasiness. Did they *live* down there? She supposed they must; that was where they had come from, after all. Of course, it wasn't really a rift in the earth, but a tear in the fabric of the world. But the other world it led into was clearly underground. That much had been theorized long ago.

A little ways down the length of the Rift, there leaned a solitary building with letters engraved into its side. She made them out one by one: Academy of Theoretical Dimensionary Science and Philosophy.

Theosophy glanced up at the clock tower. It had taken her longer than she'd hoped to work her way through the ruins. She'd have to hurry.

She worked her way along the Rift carefully, freezing every time she saw something move in its depths, which was often. The queasiness returned and settled at the back of her head. Here, most of the buildings had collapsed into heaps of rubble. When she reached the Academy and came around the other side, she realized her mistake: the wall she'd seen was a facade. Half the building had been torn away, leaving the rooms open to the air. Yet still it stood.

She climbed over heaps of rubble, sweating in the heat, to the massive front doors. But they were jammed shut and she could not budge them from her precarious perch atop sliding detritus. Finally she gave up and slid back down the heap, to circle the building and try from another angle. A second door on the side of the building opened, but the hall beyond was completely blocked with fallen beams from above. At last she came around the back.

Here the rubble stood even higher, but beyond that, three-walled rooms beckoned. She clambered over the piles, slipping and sliding and cursing, and at last stood within what remained of the walls of the Academy.

She moved across the warped floors with excruciating slowness, testing every step before she shifted her weight. One wall was still hung with a row of portraits, some labeled with *Dean* and others with an unfamiliar word, *Professor*. She looked at the *Dean*s searchingly, but saw nothing familiar in either their faces or the names beneath. A wave of unexpected disappointment crashed over her. She hadn't realized how much she had hoped...what? That her people had been somebody?

But the glass she remembered, with the Academy stamp on it...what then?

She went over the lower rows of portraits, the *Professors*. Like the *Deans*, they were labeled with dates, too short to be years of birth and death: the years of their service at the University, then. Way down at the bottom, the last of a few portraits that had only beginning dates and not end dates, she found him—Farhan. Her father's face, the skin much darker but the features unmistakeable. He looked shockingly young. What year had the Rift opened? He could only have served a few years before—before what?

"What happened?" she said aloud. "How did your world end and ours begin? *What did you do?*"

The professor stared back at her, silent.

Theosophy took a deep breath and turned to the stairs.

They were rotten, of course, and she had to do some acrobatics and contortions to attain the second floor. Here the doors were labeled with names, none of them his. The third floor was the same, and above that she could not reach; the gaps in the ceiling were too large, the floors above clearly too unstable. What now?

Back on the main floor, she looked around. And saw what she had not before: behind the stairs leading up, a shadowed door and a stairwell leading down into darkness.

She dug in a pocket to find her multi-purpose crystal, brought it to life, and descended.

At the bottom of the stairs was a door labeled *Farhan*. It opened onto a room lit with moonlight, filtering through the pile of rubble balanced precariously above. Plaster and a thick layer of dust covered everything.

Theosophy stepped cautiously into the room. It was littered with long narrow tables, glass, and shattered equipment. One wall was covered in bookshelves. Her gaze swept past them to the center of the room. There sat a metal structure that looked like a giant barrel—as wide as she was tall, and about as high as she could reach. The mesh covering it was studded with empty slots for crystals, all linked together. Her mind was boggled, imagining the amount of power that would result. "You can *do* that?" she whispered.

Finally she saw the label: "Dimensional Modulator."

She'd found it—the thing that had created the City.

It was the largest device she'd ever seen, yet it looked like such a small thing, insignificant, to have done such a momentous task—to cut off a city from the rest of the world, and to change the lives of thousands of people for generations. She still couldn't fathom how it was created, or even more, *why* anyone would do such a thing—trap all these people with monsters, and not leave instructions on how to escape. The original residents—or at least some of them, like the professor himself—must have known how to reverse the Wall. So why hadn't they done it?

Unless there had been something worse outside.

This was raising more questions than it answered. She cast a quick glance through the broken ceiling. The moon was beginning to drop.

"Shit. Briony!" she said aloud. They'd arranged to meet tonight, and she'd been so focused on getting into the ruins that she'd completely forgotten.

Her stomach was tight but not getting any worse; the room was warm, no doubt due to the Rift being so close, but not too uncomfortable. She still had time before the monsters returned, and this place looked undisturbed. Maybe she could risk contacting Briony here, sharing what she had found. She wouldn't get another chance.

She pulled out her device.

CHAPTER SIXTEEN
BRIONY

STUPID KISHAN. Briony brushed the hair out of her face and ducked underneath a low hanging branch, staying well back from the vine dangling off one end. He suspected, but she wasn't sure what. Every time she looked up from her work he was watching her, and she'd woken once in the middle of the night to find him doing the same, a blank, unreadable expression on his face.

Well, too bad. She had to figure out a way to stop the Scarred from reaching the City, and that was the end of it. More and more tales filtered in from the border, but now they involved rumors of marching troops and large, metal vehicles, clearly visible in Scarred territory. They were coming, Briony didn't doubt, and this new war would be bad enough without the Scarred getting access to what the Old Ones had known.

Beside her, Poes stopped and turned his head, looking behind them. Briony did likewise, peering through the dark of the forest, but she couldn't see anything. Poes looked for a moment longer, then resumed padding through the undergrowth.

She hoped she wasn't too late to meet Theo. Briony hadn't been able to think of some way to get out of dinner with Kishan, so she'd just taken off without telling him when he was in the other part of the shop. Hopefully he'd assume she'd gone to see Jael and the children. If not, well—she was going to have to tell him what was going on eventually.

The trees started to thin and the lake loomed before her. It was so large; Briony couldn't see the other side. Was that whole space Theo's city? Briony hurried forward, looking for Theo's glow. Instead, a dark mass sat on the edge of the water. Briony slid to a stop, then slipped behind one of the trees, listening to some instinct deep within her. It was just in time—the mass stood, and Briony could make out the general shape of a person. But what were they doing in the water?

For a wild moment, she thought it might be Carys, that the other woman had escaped the Scarred's destruction of her cottage, but the figure turned its head, and the waning sunlight reflected off of the mask on its face.

Briony's breath caught in her throat. A Scarred? Here? Did that mean that they'd figured out where the City was?

But why only one?

Beside her, Poes growled low in his throat and bared his teeth. Briony laid one hand on him, though she wasn't sure whether it was to stay him or calm her own nerves.

The Scarred looked around for a moment before returning to its work in the water. What if Theo came now? Briony wrapped one hand around her amulet, as if she could will the connection to not work. The Scarred would see her, would know it was in the right area, if it didn't already.

Maybe she could distract it—throw rocks at it or something to get it to go away. Or maybe—Jael's idea echoed back to her—she should try to capture it. Briony listened as hard as she could, but she couldn't hear anyone else, and it seemed like the Scarred generally made a fair amount of noise when moving through the forest.

Poes was fairly large, and while Briony wasn't much of a fighter, she knew enough to protect herself if necessary. Maybe if she got a large branch, and snuck up behind it...

But who knew what it was armed with? Rumors from the borders spoke not only of the knives they used to carve up their victims, but metal rods that could send lightning at will. And then there was whatever they'd used on Carys's house.

But, if Jael was right, and they might be able to get information out of it, wouldn't it be worth it?

Before Briony could decide one way or another, the Scarred stood again, nodded once, and ambled back into the forest. Briony stayed still for several minutes, hardly daring to breathe, but no further Scarred appeared, and all she could hear was the sound of chirping crickets and the distinct hoot of an owl.

Finally, she crept over to the edge of the lake. She knelt down where the Scarred had been and examined the water, but there were no signs of what it had been doing. Maybe she would need to look when it was fully light out. She debated sticking her hand in the water, but there was a distinct possibility that she would regret that.

There was a sudden glow behind her. Briony turned to find Theo there, and she felt a sudden rush of joy that she wasn't quite sure what the source was. "Theo!" She went to—she wasn't sure, hug her, maybe—but remembered that the other woman was insubstantial. "I'm so glad to see you."

Theo seemed surprised. "You...are?"

Briony felt her cheeks flush, and she looked down at the ground, brushing her hair behind one ear. "Yes, I've...I've been thinking about you a lot lately."

That seemed to surprise Theo as well, and Briony silently kicked herself. What was she doing? Theo no doubt had better things to worry about than Briony and her problems.

"I've been thinking about you, as well," Theo said. She reached one ethereal hand out toward Briony's hair, then seemed to recollect where she was and what she was doing. "I've found out how the Wall was created."

"The Wall?" Briony drifted closer to Theo, though logically she knew the other woman wasn't really there.

"The boundary around our world. It's not a physical wall, just an area of darkness and mist that surrounds the City. But it can't be entered, let alone crossed."

Briony frowned. "How do you know?"

"We have stories of people who tried." Theo shuddered. "Trust me. It's where the world ends. I think it was created by my people during the War."

Briony felt a lump settle hard in her stomach. Carys had been right, after all. She hadn't expected Theo to confirm it. "They did abandon us," she murmured.

"You said that before. If that was us..." Theo grimaced. "I hope it wasn't, but I don't know anything about it. Nobody does. That's why this is so hard—my people have forgotten so much of what we must once have known."

"So how do we undo it?"

Theo shook her head. "I don't know yet. But I think I'm getting close. I've found this...device, this dimensional modulator. It's the key to everything. I just don't have a clue how to work it, and I've already

161

scoured all the books and archives I can find with no luck. I'll have to think of something else to try."

Some of Briony's hope dampened, but it was really too much to hope for, that Theo would be able to do all the work for her. "We haven't found anything out here. No one will talk about the City, if they know anything. I'm going to need to search somewhere else and see if I can find something. You had a map, before. You said—you knew where the City was on there? Do you know if there was anywhere on there that would be a good place for me to look?"

Theo looked around at the trees and the lake, frowning. "It's hard, trying to match this place to what I know. But if this was the southern part of the City, and your town is Westenaedre, then the university ruins—the center of the City—would have been..." She looked over her shoulder, then pointed toward the middle of the lake. "...that way, I think. It certainly seems to be the center now."

Briony glowered at the water. She'd need a boat, probably, and no one she knew had one, because Westenaedre was completely unaware of the existence of the lake. Well, maybe Jael would know something she could use.

"Do you think we can do this?" Theo asked, her voice low. She opened her mouth, like she wanted to say more, but closed it again and shook her head.

Briony reached for Theo's hand. Her hand passed through the other woman's, and Briony mentally cursed. She *wanted* Theo to be there, and be real, but all the wishing in the world wouldn't make that true. Only figuring out how to pull the City back into this realm would do it, and she had a fat lot of nothing to show for trying to do that.

"We need to," Briony said. "The Scarred—they're getting bolder. I think they're looking for the City too." She took a deep breath. "I think they're closer than we are to figuring it out."

Theo looked off to one side, cocking her head as if listening to something, something Briony couldn't hear. After a moment she looked back to Briony. "Why would they want the City?"

Briony blinked. "Because...because you're the Old Ones. Because the Fractures and this Wall and the Scarred themselves were all formed by your people, back during the Great War. And if they can get a hold of that knowledge..."

Theo shook her head. "We don't have it anymore. It's lost."

"Maybe. But they don't seem to think so." Briony was tempted to tell her about Carys, about what the Scarred had done to her, but it felt like there was no time. "We'll get there first. We *have* to. Or this is all for nothing."

Theo looked down at a small metal box in her hand. "Listen, Briony—there's dangers from this side too. I just want you to know what you're facing. We have these monsters that come every night. When you bring the City back into your world...you'll get them too."

Monsters? Briony bit her lip. She remembered Carys telling her to beware of Theo, that she was an Old One with her own agenda, and here it was—some new kind of monster that would be unleashed on the world.

But Theo wasn't trying to hide it. She was warning Briony. That was good for something, surely.

Briony ran her hands through her hair and turned toward the lake, staring at the rising moon's reflection on the water. Was the risk of new monsters worth releasing Theo's warriors to help with the Scarred?

Was having Theo by her side worth new dangers?

"I understand," Theo said quietly, "if you don't want to go on with this." There was some odd note to her voice, something that seemed to be a mixture of worry and hope and...something else.

Briony shook her head slightly and turned her head just in time to see Theo drop her shoulders and reach for her metal box.

"No, wait!" Briony held out both hands. "No, don't go, Theo. We'll make this work. What's a few more monsters between the Fractures and the Scarred? Maybe they'll even take each other out, and we won't have to worry about them anymore. We'll think of something."

Theo stared at her. "I don't think you understand—"

"There's got to be a way," Briony said, aware that she was saying it as much for her own benefit as Theo's. After all, what choice did she have? Her family was tied here, and she wouldn't leave them. And if Theo's warriors weren't enough, or if the monsters were too much of a new threat, then maybe they could at least see what knowledge was holed up in the City. Maybe there would be something in there.

She smiled wryly. Which was exactly why people feared spirit talkers.

"We don't even know how to bring the City back anyway," Briony continued. "There's no use in worrying about it before that point. Maybe we'll find something else we can use while we work on that."

"You're taking this very calmly," Theo said.

Briony shrugged. "What choice do I have? Things are what they are." She smiled at the other woman. "A lot of the rest of this," she gestured vaguely, "we can talk about when you're here with me."

Theo went very still. "What?"

Oh, Old Ones, she wasn't being clear. Briony brushed a strand of hair over her ear. "I like you, Theo—I like you a lot." She kicked at the ground, feeling her cheeks heat up. Had she even admitted this to herself yet? "And while I'm mostly doing this for my family, I'm doing it for myself too. So I can hold your hand." She waved at Theo's glowing hand. "So I can touch your hair, and so I can..." She trailed off, afraid to go on, afraid to look up at Theo's face. What in the world was she doing? They had things to do, and here she was, flailing about her feelings like a child. Theo probably didn't feel the same. Briony was probably just a means to an end, the only person who had answered when Theo had reached out.

"...so you can what?" whispered Theo.

Briony forced herself to look up and meet Theo's eyes. She wasn't sure what she read there, but something told her it would be all right to go on. "...so I can touch your lips, with mine."

Theo's gaze went to Briony's lips, and she visibly swallowed.

Her cheeks felt like they might catch fire. "Well!" Briony said. "Anyway. I'll go give the lake a look, I guess. Do you...do you need anything from me?"

"Briony," Theo said. She reached out again, and Briony felt a tingle as Theo's hand passed through her arm. "I will do whatever I can to help. You know that, right? And I'll check back every night, if you need me to."

Briony thought again of the Scarred by the water and a chill went down her spine. "I don't want you here when I'm not—if they see you here..."

"I don't come if you're not here." Theo shook her head. "It doesn't work."

Briony's hand went to her amulet. "Oh. Then thank you. Though I imagine it'll take a few days for me to go out to the lake and take a look, at the least."

Theo nodded, but she didn't seem to really be looking at Briony.

She should get back, before Kishan realized she was gone. "Good luck to you, Theo. Be well until we meet again."

"And to you, Briony." There was a crackle as Theo disappeared. Briony stared at where she'd been for a moment, then heaved a sigh and ran her hand through her hair again. What was she doing?

She turned to head home and caught movement within the trees. A flash of familiar red accompanied the retreating figure.

"Oh, shit," Briony said.

CHAPTER SEVENTEEN
THEOSOPHY

THEOSOPHY'S ARMS ached as she lowered the device, but her heart soared. Briony wanted—she felt—oh, fuck, Theosophy couldn't articulate it even to herself, but there was a lightness all through her that she'd never felt before. Oh, she'd lusted after and lain with plenty of people of all genders, but this was different. A fuckbuddy for a night, even one like Solvent that lasted multiple nights, was one thing—it was easy to seek comfort where it could be found, never getting too close. But with Briony, the openness in her eyes made Theosophy want to unburden herself, to speak of old fear and guilt and grief, things she'd never even told Solvent during the long years they'd spent moving from lovers to friends to casual acquaintances and back again. She had a feeling Briony would not only listen, but *want* to listen, and then know exactly what to say after. And then...would an innocent like Briony have any secrets? Any burdens that might be lightened in the sharing? Theosophy wasn't sure, but suddenly she wanted to know.

But the only way she would ever find out was by getting through the Wall. And with Briony working on it from her side, she had a flash of confidence. Maybe, together, they could really do this.

"That's it," she said aloud. "I'm coming, Briony. I'll do whatever it takes to bring the Wall down. For the City, and for you."

As Theosophy headed for the bookshelves with a bounce in her step, something crossed over the moon, dimming the pale light. She looked up and saw wings.

Shit! How late was it? The hunt was returning. She was out of time.

Theosophy raced up the stairs, took a running leap out of the building, hit the ground and rolled, and came up running again. No time for stealth now, or indulging her queasiness, or second thoughts about how close she'd been to learning everything. She had to get out of here.

It helped, a little, that the monsters were coming in the opposite direction. They were intent on getting back to the Rift before daylight. At first, hiding until each group passed wasn't hard, except when she had to keep reminding herself that she had no backup, could not try to save anyone the monsters had taken. But there came more and more of them until they were a steady stream, and she had to focus. She vaulted piles of rubble and took to the rooftops until she realized more monsters flew than walked and let herself drop back into the streets below and ran. *Concentrate,* she told herself fiercely. Almost there. Just two more corners and she'd be at the barricades. And sunrise was coming, the sky growing light, the rays already cresting the Wall but not yet touching the buildings of the City.

There—the blockade around the University ruins. They wouldn't pass that in daylight. The daytime guard wouldn't be there yet, but if she could somehow get up on her own...

She ran and leapt and something snagged her ankle and she hung from the defensive wall, dangling, trying to kick with her other leg as the monster below her morphed to avoid her attack but did not let go of her foot, and she hung on grimly knowing that the monster would pull her down. Something flashed past her head so close it ruffled her hair, and the monster below wailed and let go but it was too late, she was falling, and then her arms were nearly yanked out of their sockets and she was being pulled up and over to safety.

SOMETIME LATER, Theosophy came back to herself. She lay still, eyes closed, taking stock. Her whole body ached dully, some parts more than others. Wincing, she opened her eyes. She was in her cot, in her quarters, and the door was opening to admit Solvent. She wondered briefly if she could pretend to be asleep, but Solvent had already seen that she was awake.

Solvent closed the door without speaking. Theosophy narrowed her eyes—Solvent was never at a loss for words, so this had to be bad. A flurry of movement—Solvent crossed the room—her hand lashed out at Theosophy's face—Theosophy blocked with her left arm—and Solvent backed away, holding her wrist, tears in her eyes.

"What was that for?" Theosophy demanded.

"For not saying goodbye."

"Oh, for fuck's sake. I couldn't. If I'd told anyone—"

"You told your trio. You wouldn't have gotten over the blockade if they hadn't been keeping a lookout for you."

"That's different. As you of all people should know."

"So you trust them but not me?"

"Solvent—"

"We were partners before we were lovers. I have the right—"

"You forfeited that with your stupid rock salts. If I can't trust you to have my back on the streets, why would you think I'd tell you secrets?"

"Oh, I knew you didn't trust me with your secrets."

"Wait...what?"

Solvent said quickly, "Never mind that. I just...if you were going off to get yourself killed, I'd like to hear about it first."

"I wasn't planning to get myself killed."

"That's a first. You *have* changed."

Theosophy blinked. Solvent wasn't wrong, but she'd have to think about that later. "Go back to the part about my secrets."

"It's nothing. I'm just glad you're back." Solvent leaned over the bed, clearly aiming for a kiss, but Theosophy put a hand out to stop her.

"I *thought* somebody had been following me around lately. It was you, wasn't it?"

"You lied to me about that thing you found in the ruins."

"It was none of your business."

"Why not? I thought we were...friends, Theo. More than friends. I thought we were everything to each other."

Yes. And no. But Theosophy had other worries just now. "How much did you see?"

"See? Nothing. You're hard to follow, you know that? You're way too jumpy."

"Yeah, there's a reason I'm not dead yet."

"But I did hear you talking to someone. I don't understand how."

Theosophy had a flash of insight. "I'm cheating on you," she said. "If you can call it that when we never meant this to be long-term. I've been meeting someone else."

"That's what I thought at first, but it's not true. You're using the device."

"Yes. I'm using the device to talk to someone elsewhere in the City."

"That's all it does?"

"What else would it do? Solvent...what do you know?"

A knock came at the door. Solvent turned away quickly and went to open it.

The dean's voice said, "I'm not intruding, am I?"

"No, sir. It's fine. Go on in, she's awake." Solvent brushed past the dean and out, leaving Theosophy clenching her fists under the blanket.

THE DEAN SAT down beside her. "How do you feel?"

Theosophy groaned. "Like I've been run over by all the monsters in the Rift, that's how."

The dean shook her head. "And you should. Exactly how did you get out of there?"

"Pure luck, I'm afraid. No words of wisdom to impart."

"And exactly what were you doing in there in the first place?"

Theosophy swallowed. "Exploring."

The dean tensed. "Where?

"In the—near the Rift." She wasn't ready to talk about her family yet.

"Fuck, Theosophy. I thought you were past pulling stunts like that. You know exactly how dangerous that was."

Theosophy looked away and shrugged. "They were all out hunting. That was the easy part. The hard part was when they came back."

"What did you find?"

Here was the part she'd been dreading. She also wasn't ready to share her discovery, not until she knew more. Which meant lying to her dean, the woman she respected above anyone else. "Not much. Everything was destroyed long ago."

Theosophy expected more swearing, or maybe yelling, but instead the dean got very quiet and said nothing at all for some time. Theosophy waited, getting increasingly nervous.

Finally the dean said, "You know this requires serious punishment."

"Yes, sir." She'd be relegated to training, she supposed, and—

The dean stood up. "I'm putting you on hard labor. Faculty of Hydroponics. Your trio, too."

Theosophy felt as if she'd been punched in the gut, but what made her claw her way back from shock was the sense of injustice. "Sir, they didn't do anything wrong."

"You should have thought of that before you made them cover for you, Theosophy."

Theosophy swallowed. "How...how long?"

The dean looked at her coolly. "That will depend on you."

And she walked out, leaving Theosophy alone.

CHAPTER EIGHTEEN
BRIONY

BRIONY HADN'T BEEN able to force herself back to the house. That it had been Kishan in the forest, she had no doubt. Why now, of all times, had he decided to brave it? Had he been there the whole time?

She should have told him what she was doing. He wouldn't have understood or approved, but she wouldn't have been lying to him. Now it was too late.

The thought of having a confrontation with him—or worse, having him close the door in her face—was too much. And since she couldn't go home, she meandered into the inn past midnight. News would travel, she was sure, and the whole town would probably know before morning that she and Kishan were fighting. Or that something was up, at least. Knowing some townspeople, the story would probably go, in some quarters, that Kishan had finally come to his senses and gotten rid of her.

The bed at the inn was hard; the room was cold. It didn't really matter. Briony spent the whole night staring at the ceiling anyway.

When morning came, she forced herself out of bed, tried to straighten her clothes to a presentable level, and pondered her next move over some runny eggs. Theo had indicated that she needed to look at the lake. Well, Briony'd exhausted the lake down here, so she'd probably need to head deeper into the forest and follow the shore until something useful showed up. She could just go to Jael and then disappear into the forest without talking to Kishan. But that felt dishonest. Kishan had put up with a lot from her over the years. She owed this to him.

To the shop?

Briony tried to untangle her hair and managed to get it into a halfway decent braid, and then headed out into the streets.

"Good morning, Miss Ealadgast," said a man Briony had never seen before. He was leaning on the fence outside the inn, apparently waiting for her. Slight, probably about Briony's height, and dressed in a thoroughly impractical purple waistcoat. It was tight with no pockets, and didn't seem to be doing anything to keep the man warm. He bowed slightly, then straightened. "A pleasure to make your acquaintance."

It was too early for this. Briony felt messy and unkempt, and immaculate strangers first thing in the morning were probably a bad sign of things to come. "You have me at a disadvantage, I'm afraid."

Who was this man? His clothing was too fancy for Westenaedre, and he certainly wasn't a refugee coming from the border.

The man looked around the town, hooking his thumbs under his waistcoat and smiling. "We've been hoping to hear from you, you know, or another of your family. Been ages since I've been up this way. Hear old Carys is still around somewhere."

Briony was in no mood for this madness. "The Scarred killed her. Now, if you'll excuse me, I have to go have a thoroughly unpleasant conversation with someone else." But when she went to go around him, the man moved to block her.

"The Scarred killed her?" he echoed, the chipper manners of a moment ago forgotten. "There are Scarred here?"

Briony frowned. "Who *are* you?"

"Ah, my apologies." The man bowed again, lower this time. "I am Mardu Bodere, from the Academy. I thought you had been getting my messages."

It was definitely too early for this. Briony closed her eyes and took a deep breath. "You must have set out before receiving my last message, then. I'm sorry you came all this way, but I don't intend to go to the Academy right now."

She tried to go around him again, but Mardu again blocked her path. Briony glowered at him. Carys's words, about the Academy not easily giving up knowledge, floated back to her.

"Oh, no, I got it," he said, still smiling, though Briony was starting to seriously consider knocking his teeth in, "and since you can't come to us, we decided to come to you! We want everyone to get the best possible education."

Briony closed her eyes, wishing she'd gotten some sleep last night. He'd come for her—and he'd said something about hoping to hear from her family, which meant that they *knew*. The Academy knew her family were spirit talkers.

That opened up new questions that she really did not have time for.

"I'm sorry," she said, opening her eyes, "I didn't sleep well last night. Why all this trouble for me? You don't know what magical aptitude I have, nor to what degree. It seems awfully...convenient."

Mardu's smile lessened, and he examined Briony a bit warily. "Why don't you tell me what you can do, and we can start from there."

"Why don't you tell me why you really came," Briony retorted. Maybe she should whistle for Poes. She wasn't really anywhere near the forest, but his hearing was very good, and with luck, Mardu might have never seen a mountain cat before and be distracted long enough for Briony to make a strategic getaway.

"You know why I came." Mardu dropped the cheerful facade completely, which, to be honest, made Briony feel better.

"Do I?" She went around him again, and this time he let her.

"If the Scarred are here," he said, "then your skills are more important than ever."

Briony paused despite herself.

"Do you know where the anchor is?" he asked.

Anchor? She had no idea what he was talking about. Part of her wanted to stop, to ask him what he meant, but she wanted to get this conversation with Kishan over with, and she wasn't sure he knew what he was talking about either. It could be a ploy to get information out of her. And if he realized she had no idea...

Now, more than ever, she wanted her big brother.

"If you'll excuse me," she said, and left him standing in the road by the inn.

IT WASN'T TERRIBLY surprising to find Yara at the shop when she arrived. Briony even managed to not punch the other woman in the face when she smirked at Briony and then returned to simpering at Kishan.

Kishan, for his part, looked about as terrible as she felt. Briony hung her cloak on its peg by the door and turned to face him, trying to ignore the fact that her heart felt like it might hammer its way out of her chest. She was sorely tempted to flee and find Jael, but she knew her brother would hear things and probably seek her out here anyway.

She braced herself, in case Kishan started yelling or told her to get out. "Good morning."

"Briony," Kishan replied, his voice like ice.

Briony winced.

Yara grinned triumphantly. "Well."

What little patience she had left cracked. "Oh, stuff it," Briony snapped at her. "Get out of here. Even if I weren't in the picture, Kishan has no interest in *you*, so why don't you take your services to other pastures and get out of our way?"

Yara's face darkened. She turned to Kishan, perhaps expecting him to put on his cheerful countenance and say something to contradict Briony's words, but the healer merely looked at her and crossed his arms over his chest.

She deflated, and Briony felt a momentary pang of guilt. But, then, the woman had been trying to steal Kishan for as long as Briony could remember, so it's not like a dose of reality was that bad for her.

It also was probably a bad sign that Kishan wasn't even pretending to be nice.

Yara left without another word. Briony had thought it would be better, with her gone, so there was no one to witness this conversation, but now that she *had* gone, it just seemed worse. Briony could practically feel the chill in the air.

"Look, Kishan," she said, "I have some things I need to tell you."

"Do you now," Kishan said. He turned and went into the back room. Briony wasn't sure whether or not she was supposed to follow. Again, the urge to flee reared its head, but she wouldn't give into it. She squared her shoulders and followed after him.

Kishan was standing in front of his workbench, facing away from her. His shoulders were tense, and he was supporting his weight on his hands hard enough that his fingers had turned white. Briony reached out toward him, as she had so many times over the years, then pulled her hand back. Her comfort probably wouldn't be welcome.

"You lied to me," Kishan said, still not looking at her.

She hadn't, not technically. She'd just...been evasive and misleading. But that was no defense, so she didn't say it out loud. "Kishan," she said, but it came out quieter than she'd intended.

"How long have you been spirit talking?"

"It's not—it's not spirit talking." The excuse sounded flat, even to her. It *was*, for all intent and purpose. "Theo's not dead. She's not a spirit."

"Theo." Kishan laughed, low and pained. "I saw how you looked at her."

Briony had never really believed in the concept of heartbreak before, but now she could see it. How could she have been so cruel to Kishan? Yes, he'd always been a bit of a pompous ass, but he'd been kind to her even when few other people were, and he'd truly cared for her. "I'm so sorry," she whispered.

Kishan chuckled before turning to face her. He leaned against the bench like it was the only thing keeping him up. "What, not even any attempts at explaining it away?" He sounded close to tears, and Briony felt her own treacherous prickles of moisture. But what could she say? Theo was, well, she didn't know what Theo was. But she was exciting and special, and as much as Briony cared for Kishan, it had been a while since she had truly planned to spend her life with him.

"There's no way I can make this right," she said. "I *am* sorry, Kishan." She reached out a hand to him, and, after a moment, he took it, squeezing it too tight.

"Please, Bree," he said. "Say something to make it better. Say you'll stop spirit talking. Say you won't see her again."

Briony looked down, shaking her head. "I can't, Kishan, I really *can't*. Theo and her people can help protect us from the Scarred." *And possibly expose us to new dangers.* What sort of monsters were they that could fashion the Old Ones—intellectuals, if the stories could be believed—into fearsome warriors like Theo? For a moment, Briony's resolve wavered. It had been easy to believe that there'd be some easy solution when Theo had been there in front of her, beautiful and strong and honest, but now, in the light of day and distance, it almost seemed like too much to hope for.

But what other choice did she have? The Scarred, and war, were coming. Unless some miracle solution came from the Academy or the government in Cynestel, they'd be overrun. Briony didn't know Theo's monsters, but she knew the Scarred.

And she had to protect her family.

Kishan was silent for a long moment. "There has to be another way."

"Maybe you can ask the Academy man if they have some way to save us," Briony snapped, and then was immediately sorry. It wasn't Kishan's fault that Mardu was there, or that Briony hadn't gotten any sleep. It was just that she'd been trying to think of something else for so long.

Kishan paled. "Academy man?"

"Yes, name of Mardu Bodere." Briony gave Kishan's hand a squeeze. "What's the matter, Kishan? I thought you didn't like the Academy because you thought I was going away."

"Yes, that's the reason." Kishan visibly swallowed, and Briony knew he was lying.

"If that's the reason, then why worry? His business is entirely with me."

Kishan hesitated for a moment. "He doesn't know about me?"

179

The statement was so similar to what Carys had said—*If the Academy comes looking, please don't tell them where I am*—that Briony's instinctual reply died on her lips. She examined Kishan closely, as if that would tell her something new that she hadn't learned over the decades. "You're afraid of them."

Kishan shook his head violently and dropped Briony's hand, turning away from her. "No, of course not. I'm just..." He stared off into space, as if willing a good excuse to come. "I'm just mad to have someone poking around. Now is not a good time for it, what with the Scarred and all. And I'm annoyed that you bothered to talk to the Academy at all."

"Well, don't worry about it." Kishan's head snapped up, but Briony ignored him as she crossed over to her own bench. Her nerves felt oddly jittery. First Carys and now Kishan. What did he fear from the Academy? "I'm leaving soon, and he'll probably clear out."

"Leaving?"

"I can't stay here right now, can I? I can't go home, and I'm sure you'll want me out as well."

Kishan took a few steps in her direction. "If you'd promise not to see her again..." he whispered. "Please, Bree."

She didn't bother to reply. She grabbed her notebook off her bench and slid it into her bag. It would be good to have, especially if she was going to have to traipse about in the forest for who knew how long. She'd never spent the night in the forest before. Hopefully nothing would eat her.

"Bree." Kishan laid a hand on her shoulder. "Please don't. It's not up to you to save us all. Stay here, with me. Don't throw everything we've had away."

The tears threatened again. "It was better when I thought you were mad," she said. Briony brushed his hand off and headed back out to the front room. Kishan trailed a few feet behind, and Briony was acutely aware of his presence, like a cloud of guilt and sadness hovering just off her left shoulder.

She should go, now. Drawing this out wouldn't help anything.

The bell on the front door chimed, and Briony looked up, welcoming the distraction. A customer would sidetrack Kishan long enough for her to escape without a long goodbye. But it was only Jael. Her brother ran his eyes over both of them and apparently didn't like what he saw, because the worried look on his face darkened. "What's happening?"

"Bree's leaving me," Kishan said.

"What?"

Briony resisted the urge to glower at the healer. "I need to talk to you." She crossed the room, trying to ignore Kishan melting like a kicked puppy, and took Jael's arm. "I'll explain everything, I promise."

Jael's frown deepened, but he allowed himself to be led away. As they left the shop, Briony tried to ignore the terrible feeling that settled around her heart by focusing on what the healer could possibly fear from the Academy.

CHAPTER NINETEEN

THEOSOPHY

A FEW DAYS LATER, Theosophy emerged from the cocoon she'd made of her quarters and reported for day-shift duty with the water team. She brought Synthesis and Lever with her; they trailed along behind her, subdued and unspeaking. They must be furious at her, but she didn't care to ask.

The Faculty of Hydroponics was a small, boxy building that didn't look like much. Maybe the work wouldn't be too bad.

She knocked. The door opened and there stood Solvent, jaw dropping, eyes hardening. "What are you doing here?" Solvent demanded.

"Your dean didn't tell you? This is my punishment." Theosophy tried to put a sardonic angle on the word, but it fell flat, and Solvent only grimaced.

"Our dean doesn't show up much. Better get it started then, huh?" Solvent looked past Theosophy to the other two standing behind her, and jerked her head in a come-along gesture. She yelled over her shoulder, "Hey, people, come and see what the Dean of Militia sent us."

182

A group of people converged on the door from various corners of the building. There was a tall, heavyset woman with a wrench in her hand, dreadlocks tied up, and a smear of oil across her face, a handsome young man with a confident swagger and an equally confident grin...and Astrolabe, with his right sleeve pinned up and empty. Theosophy turned away.

"My team," Solvent said to Theosophy with a grandiose wave of her hand. "Team, this is Theosophy."

The handsome one hooted. "Oh, come on. *She's* the reason you won't sleep with me?"

Solvent tossed her head. "There are many reasons, Paradigm. First is that you think you're better than she is."

"Wait," said Theosophy. "Paradigm? The chancellor's son?" His skin was olive, his black hair loosely curled; Chancellor Dialectic was paler, but now she could see the resemblance in their features.

He sketched a bow. "The very same."

So this is what they had him doing. Her eyes swept over the others: the woman, who was clearly too fat to fight, and Solvent, who'd washed out of the Militia years ago on account of her rock salts. Great. Paradigm seemed able-bodied enough, which meant one of two things: either he was feeble-minded, or his father had gotten him this post to keep him out of the Militia. Not many people in the City could get away with that, but Chancellor Dialectic, head of all the faculties, was surely one of them.

"If you're done looking down your nose at us," said the dreadlocked woman sharply, "I imagine your dean didn't send you over here for fun."

Theosophy felt her cheeks heat up. When was the last time she'd felt shame? Stupid punishment. "Where would you like us?"

Paradigm sniggered. Solvent kicked him as she passed. "Cosmogony is not wrong, but that doesn't mean you should laugh at them. They don't know what they're in for. This way, my tyros. But watch your step."

Theosophy followed, biting back the question—*why?*—just because she knew Solvent wanted her to ask it. They descended a flight of steps, then passed behind a bank of machinery and—there was her answer—onto a narrow metal catwalk that stretched over a vast underground pool. A chill rose off the water. It was poorly lit; she couldn't even see how far it stretched. Her mouth hung open; even swears deserted her.

Solvent tossed a grin over her shoulder. "Welcome to Hydroponics."

The pool wasn't just a pool, Theosophy soon realized. It was divided into sections, all of it moving. "Dirty," Solvent explained, pointing to each in turn. "Distilling. Greywater. More distilling. Clean and ready for drinking and cooking. Nutrients added and ready for the hydroponics pipes. If you're going to fall in, fall into the dirty pond."

Theosophy wrinkled her nose; she could smell it from here. "Because it's easier to get out of?"

"Because if you contaminate the clean pond, you won't be the only one dead."

Behind her, Synthesis gagged.

An immense tunnel emptied into the dirty section. Slightly smaller pipes led from the greywater, clean, and hydroponics sections, accompanied by water-wheels.

"Since this is a punishment..." Solvent considered. "Your two trio-mates can help Cosmogony add the nutrients. You, Theo, can clear out the dirty-water filters."

Theosophy followed her pointing finger, saw the junk up against the screen at the end of the tank, and grimaced. "No loyalty, huh?"

Solvent dropped her slightly smug attitude. "Someone has to do it. Might as well be you. Besides, it was Paradigm's turn, and I like it when he owes me."

She was about to go crawling around in muck so the chancellor's son didn't have to? Theosophy swore and grabbed the long-handled net that Solvent pointed to. This couldn't get much worse.

As a matter of fact, it could. Half a shift later, when it was finally time to break for lunch, she had to admit she'd been wrong about that. Solvent had been kind enough to give her a spare coverall, kerchief, boots, and gloves—none of which fit—but even so, she was covered in filth. Her nose had given up smelling it some time ago. Everything she lifted in her net was sodden, so it was heavy, and her shoulders ached. Worst of all, she'd found dead squirrels and rats, pieces of clothing, lengths of rope—all sorts of things that could have been useful, if they had not been literally covered in shit. The shit itself went into a series of giant vats where it would age until it was ready to use for compost.

By the near side of the ponds, she met Synthesis and Lever, who looked equally exhausted and disheartened. Both were soaked through, if not as dirty as she was. Neither would meet her eyes.

They cleaned up as best they could, then followed the other workers to a space behind a large metal drum. Theosophy frowned at it. "What...?"

"That," said Solvent with a grin, "is the great perk of working here. Theo my friend, let me introduce you to unwatered liquor. Only a small one at the moment, since you've still got the afternoon to go."

She passed out tiny glasses full of an amber liquid. Theosophy sniffed at hers, felt her sense of smell wake up again with a start, and swigged it down.

First she choked, then she coughed, and then a warmth spread through her all the way down to her toes. "Fuck," she managed at last, and the water crew laughed—but, she thought, in a friendly way for the first time. "And you prefer numbing your pain with rock salts because why?"

Solvent's smile disappeared. "Theo, you asshole."

Theosophy thought about this through the fuzziness in her head. Did Solvent's crew not know? Yet they didn't look surprised; maybe it was something they'd silently agreed not to talk about? She'd never been good at subtlety.

"And this," Solvent announced to the group at large, "is why you may still have a chance, Paradigm."

He raised an eyebrow, but Theosophy noted that he was smart enough to keep his mouth shut.

"Only a chance?" said Cosmogony. "She must be quite a catch."

"She knows her stuff as a fighter," said Astrolabe unexpectedly; he hadn't opened his mouth once.

"That doesn't mean she's good in bed, Astro," said Cosmogony. "But I guess she must be. Right, Solvent?"

Astrolabe looked away. Theosophy, remembering bedding Astro back when he was whole, had no idea what to say.

"That's enough, all of you," said Solvent, but Theosophy was startled to see that she was smiling. Joking around was one thing—if Theosophy didn't allow that in her trios, they'd all go mad—but teasing their leader? Didn't that undermine Solvent's authority? Maybe it did. She knew a little about Solvent's job, but only from what

Solvent had told her; she'd have to pay attention while she was stuck here.

THAT AFTERNOON, Theosophy was struggling with the long-handled net again when Cosmogony came up behind her. Theosophy heard her approach but did not bother to turn around.

"Need a hand with that?" said Cosmogony.

"No, I'm fine." Theosophy swept the net through the water emphatically and almost overbalanced.

"Mind if I show you something?" Cosmogony laid her hand on the net's handle without waiting for an answer. Theosophy gripped it tighter for a moment, then looked over her shoulder. Cosmogony returned her gaze levelly. Theosophy forced herself to let go. Best not to annoy Solvent's team, especially when Solvent was already out to get her.

Cosmogony angled the net so that it was half out of the water, and skimmed it through with apparent ease. It came out half-full. She flipped it expertly over the pile of junk that Theosophy was making, then when it was empty, swung it back to the foul water again.

"See? Looks slower, but it's more efficient, and easier on the arms, too."

Theosophy grimaced. "Thanks."

Cosmogony studied her. "You're not used to being bad at something, are you?"

I'm not used to being shown up by a civilian, Theosophy wanted to say, but she didn't. "Not exactly."

Cosmogony's mouth quirked; maybe she'd guessed anyway. "You must have really pissed off your dean."

Did she expect Theosophy to tell her why? "Guess so."

"Relax, fighter. Who stuck a rod up your ass? I was just asking." The other woman shrugged at her and wandered off.

Theosophy watched her go, but didn't call her back. Maybe she hadn't been prying. Maybe she was just being friendly. That still didn't mean Theosophy was going to open her mouth—aside from all the other considerations, she was in no way ready to share Briony with anyone—but she'd try to remember to be a little nicer next time.

And, once she got the hang of them, the motions Cosmogony had demonstrated really were easier. Shit.

The rest of the day was just as bad as the first half. Her body ached in ways it hadn't since her earliest days in the Militia, training with Solvent and the rest of the tyros. She hadn't eaten much at the midday meal, as her stomach had been tight all morning, but by midafternoon she was regretting not choking the food down anyway. By the time Solvent released them, she was starving.

After washing up again, she stumbled out into late-afternoon sunshine, completely disoriented. How long had it been since she'd last worked through the day? The streets were bustling with civilians finishing up their business for the day—just like her. It was an odd feeling. She wasn't even armed, except for a knife in her boot, just in case. As far as anyone could tell, she was one of them.

Or maybe not. As she strode through the crowd, it parted for her. She didn't *think* she still stank of shit, so it must be due to the way she moved or looked, somehow. The civilians around her were slow-moving and seemed to be ignoring their surroundings for the most part. They'd be more observant as night drew closer, or at least she hoped so.

"Theo!"

Astro's voice. She froze, then turned.

He stopped several paces back of her, letting civilians stream around them both and occasionally between them. For a long time he didn't speak. Her eyes kept drifting to that pinned-up sleeve, and she kept jerking them away.

Finally he seemed to realize that she wasn't going to start the conversation, and did so himself with an effort. "Look, I know this is awkward. I was a jerk to you, before."

She shook her head. "I deserved it."

Astrolabe made an impatient gesture. "Never mind that. I've had time to think now, and I do get it. I didn't want to see ex-fighters either, when I was—well."

Theosophy made herself shrug. "I'm just as useless as you right now." Then she winced. Briony wouldn't have said that, especially not to a former partner, and someone she'd slept with, too.

But he shook his head, seeming not to care. "It's not like that. When you're in the Militia, you feel like there's nothing outside of it, right? Like any life not spent fighting is a life that's wasted?"

"Or lazy," she muttered. "Not you, but..."

"Paradigm. Sure. But the thing is, everybody in this city is fighting in their own way. You just can't see it until you're forced to look outside your own experience. What Solvent does, what I do, is just as crucial for the City's survival as what you do."

"The hydroponics and the sewers? I guess so." She glanced around, at all the civilians around them, and Astro followed her gaze.

"You think they're weak. They're not. I've only been out of the Militia for a little while, and...Theo, I've learned a lot. I thought I'd

189

feel useless, like you said. But I don't. And not just because Solvent was nice enough to get me into Hydroponics."

Theosophy paused, distracted. "Solvent did that? I thought our dean must have approached theirs—yours."

He grimaced. "The Dean of Hydroponics is dean in name only. He's completely shot on rock salts. Solvent's been running the operation on her own for the last couple of years."

Theosophy felt her mouth sag open. Solvent had occasionally complained about work, about her responsibilities, about the team she supervised, but...to take charge, without letting her addiction interfere with her job? That required more toughness than Theosophy had dreamed she had. "She never told me."

"Maybe because she knew what you thought of her washing out of the Militia."

Theosophy blinked.

His expression softened. "You weren't the only fighter she still counted as a friend, you know."

She'd known that Solvent and Astro had slept together now and then, just as she and Astro did, but somehow she had never thought of them confiding in one another. Not that she'd ever shared her own struggles, or listened to Solvent's; the two of them had been through a lot together in the early years, had shared such comfort as they could, but that didn't mean they were confidantes. Had Solvent needed more support than Theosophy could give? She examined her thoughts and decided she didn't feel betrayed, exactly, just...left out.

"Anyway," Astrolabe went on, "you might try talking to a civilian sometime."

Theosophy raised her eyebrows pointedly.

Astrolabe gave a choked laugh. "No, not me. Someone who's never been in the Militia. You might find they sound like...like people worth listening to. Worth respecting. After all, they're the ones you're fighting for. If you don't think they're worth anything, why protect them? Think about it." He raised his left hand and punched her in the arm, like old times, then faded away into the crowd.

CHAPTER TWENTY
BRIONY

THE DARK LOOK on Jael's face didn't go away as Briony explained what she'd learned from Theo and repeated the events of the morning, leaving nothing out. She had thought maybe that she'd leave her feelings for Theo, whatever exactly they were, out, but it felt good to not keep any secrets. Jael stroked his white-blond beard the whole while, saying nothing.

When Briony finished, he shook his head. "I don't like it, Bree. The forest is no place to be wandering around for days on end. Who knows what's in there?"

"What other choice do we have? If anyone around here knows anything, they're keeping it to themselves. I've got to look elsewhere."

"What about the man from the Academy?" Jael's mouth twisted in distaste. Briony had a thought that he didn't like the Academy, either. Maybe their mother had said something to him, something she hadn't lived long enough to pass on to Briony.

This is what came of keeping secrets.

Well, it was too late now. Briony sighed and leaned back in her chair. They'd sequestered themselves in the corner of the inn again. It was surprisingly busy, despite being mid-morning. There were quite a few newly arrived refugees about. This was the first bunch to arrive that could afford lodging, which probably meant something.

She leaned back in toward her brother. "I don't know, Jay. I don't like how much he knew about me without being told anything."

"That just means he knows more about what's going on than we do. That might be a good thing."

"In theory." Despite the early hour, they'd each ordered an ale, since it seemed like it was going to be that sort of day. Briony swirled hers in its mug, though not too fast as it was still mostly full. "But he does make me nervous. And you should have seen Kishan when he heard about him. He looked like he might pass out. Besides, Carys warned me against the Academy too."

Jael frowned down at his own mostly-full mug. "What could they possibly do that wouldn't be worth the risk?" he asked, though it sounded like he was asking himself as much as her.

Briony didn't know, and that bothered her. "All right, I'll give you that. If I don't find anything in the forest, I'll talk to Mardu."

"I don't want you going into the forest, especially not with the Scarred there. I'll go."

"This is not the time to play big brother, Jay. I know the forest better than you do. Besides, you've got the children to think of. I can't stay with them at the house, not if the Scarred can trace me or the spirit talking or whatever, and there's no one else."

Jael growled. "Well, if you hadn't alienated Kishan, we could have asked him."

Briony felt that horrible, heavy guilt tighten around her heart again, and found she couldn't respond. After a moment, Jael took pity on her, patting her shoulder with one giant hand.

"I'm sorry," he murmured. "I know you didn't do it on purpose." He was silent. "I suppose that reasoning also eliminates both of us going. Forsaken spirits!"

"I'll be fine." She'd have to be; that's all there was to it. "It would be nice to have a boat, though. Then I could stay on the lake, and out of danger."

With a grunt, Jael rolled both hands into fists. "I *don't* like it, Bree."

She didn't either, but there were no boats to be found here. The river that Westenaedre had been named for had long since gone dry, and the lake was deep in the forest. Besides, how would she get a boat to the lake anyway? Dragging it through town would be more than suspicious, and it would slow her down in the forest. And if the Scarred saw her with it, or if they took it from her, she might only be helping them.

"What do you think he meant by 'anchor'?" she asked, since the subject of the boat seemed to be a dead end and it looked like Jael could use a distraction.

"I haven't the faintest idea. Do you?"

"It must be something related to the City." Briony's going theory was that, since Mardu had been waiting to hear from her family and knew about the spirit talking, he probably knew what realm it was that her family could access. Which meant he knew the City was there. But beyond that... "But I haven't gotten any further."

Jael stared down at his ale. "Maybe Kishan would go with you."

Yesterday, Briony would have bet that he wouldn't step foot in the forest. "I really don't think that's a good idea."

"Hey, if he's as worried about this Academy man as you say, he probably wouldn't mind disappearing for a day or two."

"Or a week. Be realistic, Jay. We can't leave Westenaedre without a healer." Why had they bothered with the ale? It had sounded good, but Briony had no urge to actually drink it. "Besides, Kishan is Kishan. If I took him with me, I'd just have to worry about protecting him from choke vines and Fractures the whole time."

"Sometimes I think you sell him too short, Bree."

She shrugged unapologetically. "Can we please just accept that I need to go, and I need to go alone?"

"Auberon could go with you."

Briony jerked upward hard enough that some of her ale spilled on the table. "Auberon? Jay, he's not even fifteen!"

"And how old were *you* when you started going into the forest by yourself?"

Barely older. "That was different."

"He knows his way around the forest. All my children do."

"I can't believe you'd even suggest that."

Jael sighed. "I know, but I really hate the idea of you going alone."

Briony brushed a stray lock of hair out of her eyes. "If I had said yes, would you really have sent Auberon with me?"

"I don't know. Probably not." Jael glowered down at the table. "I give in. You go by yourself, but if you get eaten by something, I will never forgive you."

"Fair enough." Briony pushed her chair back and stood. "Come on. We've got to gather supplies so I can go."

Jael muttered something under his breath that Briony couldn't hear, but suspected was uncomplimentary. He stood as well. Briony slipped her cloak back on and started for the door, listening to Jael grumble the entire length of the room.

As she went to pull the door open, it swung inward, almost hitting her in the face. Jael caught her as she stumbled back. A ragged man, blood streaming down his face from a forehead wound, crashed into both of them, tumbling onto the floor. Jael caught Briony and himself against one of the tables and heaved them back upright.

"Are you all right?" Briony asked the man. She didn't recognize him, but there seemed to be new refugees every day, so that wasn't necessarily strange. "Let me look at your head." She knelt beside him, but he batted her hand away.

"There's no time for that," he snapped. "They're at the border. They're coming!" He looked wildly around. It was completely silent in the inn, everyone's conversations having died away. "We're too close here. If you value your lives, you must go!"

"I wouldn't worry," drawled a voice from behind her. Briony turned to find Mardu there, weaving his way through the tables. Had he been there the whole time? Briony would have sworn not, but there was only one way in, unless one came through the kitchen. "The government in Cynestel is well aware of the situation at the border, and they've dispatched the army to deal with any and all unauthorized troops in the area."

He spoke loud enough for everyone to hear him, but he watched Briony. She felt her skin crawl, though she wasn't sure why.

Jael examined Mardu. "How do you know?"

"My good fellow, I just came from the capital. The border is *days* away. Nothing to worry about."

"Hmm," said Jael. He set his hand on Briony's shoulder and led her out the door. Once outside, he murmured, "Was that your Academy man?" At Briony's nod, he ran one hand down his beard. "Right, not the Academy then. I'll go get your supplies so you can go."

"Thank you, Jay."

Her brother grunted, patted her shoulder, and headed off. Briony watched him go, then wondered what to do with herself now. She couldn't go home, and she didn't want to go to the shop.

She found her gaze drifting toward the north and the border, as if she would be able to see what was happening there if she looked hard enough.

THE NEXT MORNING, she and Jael stood at the edge of the forest. Briony straightened the pack on her back. It was heavy and felt too large, and she wasn't entirely sure she'd be able to maneuver with it. Poes wove his way around her legs. Beside her, Jael crossed his arms and frowned at the forest. "I still don't like it."

Briony wasn't going to dignify that with an answer. The stream of refugees from the border had intensified, and it seemed like the war that Briony had been dreading had arrived. Even if she found the City, if she could bring it back, would it be enough?

There was only one way to know. She straightened her pack again. "Let's go, Poes."

"Wait!"

For a horrible second, Briony thought the voice belonged to Mardu. She—and after the Academy man had made the connection between her and her brother—and Jael had been ducking him as best they could. On some level, Jael's plan of talking to Mardu and asking him what he knew made sense, but Briony couldn't shake the idea that the man was trouble. For both Kishan and Carys to be so afraid...

But it wasn't Mardu—it was Kishan. Briony hadn't seen him since the previous morning, and it looked like he hadn't been sleeping.

He'd been running, and, as he reached Jael and Briony, he leaned over, panting from exertion.

"Is something the matter?" Jael asked.

Kishan took a few more deep breaths, then let the air out in one long stream. "I brought you something."

He fumbled in his bag for a moment, then held out some brilliant red fabric to Briony. It took her a long moment to realize it was his healer's robe.

"I don't understand," she said.

"Please, take it." Kishan pushed it at her more insistently. "You don't have to wear it. Just keep it in your bag."

Briony held both hands up. "What do you think I'm going to do with that? I know it's important to you, but I've barely got room for what I've already got packed."

Kishan bit his lip. He looked down at the robe in his hands, then back up at Briony. Then, apparently coming to some sort of decision, he huffed, blowing his hair out of his eyes. "You can't just do magic, Bree. You have to have the right kind of focus."

Blinking, she remembered that day with the boy when the magic didn't come. And how her amulet grew warm and glowed when Theo was near. "You need this to cast your spells."

Kishan pushed it at her again. "Please take it."

Briony was torn between the selflessness of his gesture and wanting to punch him. "I can't take this, Kishan! The town needs its healer, especially with those refugees streaming in. And I've got my own healing skills, you know."

"It's not just—" Kishan bit off whatever he was going to say. "I *know* you do, but I would feel better if you took this with you. I'm sure Jael would too."

"Don't bring Jael into this," Briony replied before her brother could say anything, because he probably would feel better, and she didn't need them ganging up on her. "I'm not taking your robe, and that's final."

"I have another that I used while I was training. It's not as strong, but it's not like I won't have anything."

"Old Ones, Kishan!" She thought she might cry, and that was unacceptable. "Why are you being so nice after—after everything?" Poes butted his head against her hand, and Briony absently patted it. "I don't deserve this."

"Bree, look at me, please." Briony forced herself to look up, to meet Kishan's eyes. "We've been friends forever. Things aren't going how I hoped, but—I would hate for something to happen to you all the same. Please take it." He held the robe out again. "To be honest, I wouldn't mind it being conveniently missing while that Academy man is around."

Briony reached out for the robe and took it in her hands. She'd never handled it before, and now, it felt *wrong*. A laugh escaped her. All that hoping for healing magic to find her, now to have it in her hands, only to find, decisively, that it wasn't for her.

She handed it back, silently, and Kishan took it without protest, perhaps reading what had happened in her face.

"It was worth a try," he said, and tucked it back in his bag.

Jael looked between the two of them. "I'm not even going to pretend I have any idea what's going on." He glanced up at the sky. "It's almost midday. You'd best be going, Bree. The less time you spend deep in the forest, the better."

Nodding, she scratched Poes behind the ears. "Yes, I'd better." She wrapped her arms around her brother's midsection and squeezed him tight like she had as a little girl. "Keep everyone safe while I'm gone. And tell Auberon to stop stealing my supplies when he thinks I won't notice."

"The only person I'm going to worry about is you." Jael returned her hug and kissed her on the top of her head. "Don't be a hero, Bree." He frowned down at Poes. "And you'd better earn your keep."

Poes twitched his tail and otherwise ignored Jael.

She had to extract herself from her brother's hold. Patting him reassuringly on the arm, she turned to Kishan. For a moment, both stood, awkwardly. It was ridiculous. Briony shook her head and forced herself forward to embrace Kishan as well. His arms fell around her, familiar and automatic.

"Be safe," he murmured.

Briony pulled back. "Well, I'll be back before you know it," she said. "Let's go, Poes."

It was surprisingly hard to leave Jael and Kishan behind her and head under the trees. Briony mentally chided herself. How many times had she ventured into the forest? She knew its tricks and habits. She would be fine, and Westenaedre would be fine while she was gone, and she would find what she needed, and everything would fall together in a way that would protect them from the brewing war.

But, as she detoured around a choke vine, she couldn't help but think that she'd never been so deep in the forest. The lake had seemed endless. There might be Fractures there that she'd never seen before, perhaps had never even heard of. And who knew where the Scarred were.

Were they tracking her, or maybe her amulet, even now?

Taking a deep breath, she wrapped her fingers in Poe's fur and ventured deeper inside.

CHAPTER TWENTY-ONE
THEOSOPHY

OVER THE NEXT few days, Theosophy watched Solvent and the water team do their jobs together. They had an easy camaraderie that Theosophy recognized from her time in training, and from seeing some of the other fighter trios work; she'd never managed it herself. She'd always had more important things to think about, like staying alive and keeping other people alive and making sure all the monsters she met ended up dead. But this teasing and joking and friendliness made the team seem close, not in a comrades-in-arms kind of way, but like...friends maybe?

Yet when Solvent spoke, they listened and did what she said, even the unpleasant tasks. Somehow, she had made them respect her. It was a side of Solvent that Theosophy hadn't seen before. Or maybe Astrolabe was right and it had been there all along—she just hadn't acknowledged it. Maybe she'd been an asshole to Solvent all this time. Fuck.

She finally decided to approach Cosmogony again. The woman had been friendly before, maybe she'd be receptive now to...what? Theosophy couldn't decide what to do: offer her an apology? Ask to hear her life story? Demand to know why she hadn't joined the Militia? Shit, this was why she didn't bother with niceties, for all Granddad's attempts while she was growing up. This stuff was too hard, and she'd always thought it was unimportant—why bother, when monsters could take away your family on any given night?

But for Astrolabe's sake, and maybe Briony's too, she had to do it.

She found Cosmogony alone at a long, scarred table near the hydroponics tank, measuring something that looked like coarse salt into glass bottles. Cosmogony looked up as Theosophy approached, her expression guarded but not openly unfriendly, as best Theosophy could tell. "Need something?" the other woman asked.

"Listen, I know I wasn't too friendly before." Theosophy had spent a lot of time thinking about how to start the conversation. Now that she said it out loud, it sounded stupid. Shit.

But Cosmogony smiled, her eyebrows going up. "Is that an apology?"

"Guess so. I just..."

"I know. You fighters think you're better than us." Cosmogony was still smiling.

"It's not that." Well, it kind of was, but... "When you spend your time fighting for your life, for everyone's life, it's hard to relate to people who don't."

"Why did you join the Militia?" Cosmogony asked abruptly, setting the bottle down on the table.

Theosophy shrugged. "Same reason anyone does. I lost someone."

"And you joined the next day?"

"No. I was a kid. I joined as soon as Dean Prosody would take me." Which was earlier than most. She figured the dean had gotten tired of the fourteen-year-old girl hanging around outside HQ, watching the fighters and pestering them to teach her. The dean had insisted on getting permission from Granddad, which he'd given despite his misgivings, but after that, she'd treated Theosophy like an adult—but gently. She'd brought Theosophy to the trainees' dorm and assigned her the bed next to the other newest recruit. Solvent had been there for a season or two already, but she still had nightmares, like Theosophy. They'd taken to comforting each other, falling in and out of being lovers but always fast friends. When Solvent washed out of the Militia after the failed expedition a few years later, the dean had taken one look at Theosophy's face and agreed to let Solvent stay at HQ—even if she was a failure now. Theosophy had never forgotten the new divide between them, and if Astro was right, neither had Solvent.

"Huh," said Cosmogony, drawing Theosophy back to the present with a jolt. "See, I lost someone when I was a kid, too. My brother." Her face shifted into grim lines. "They came right into our rooms and yanked him out through the broken shutters."

"And you didn't want to fight after that?"

"My father did. He joined up, and I barely saw him after that. It was like losing both of them. So I decided to join the Faculty of Engineering instead and learn all I could about reinforcing our defenses, so our homes would be safe."

Theosophy snorted. "It didn't work."

"No. There's simply not enough strong material around. But Hydroponics—there's something I can still tinker with and improve." She gestured at the table, and Theosophy saw tools, funny-shaped bottles, bits and pieces of things whose purpose she could not guess. "More nutrients, better filters. That saves lives, too. And it means I still get to see my kids."

"You have a family?"

"Sure. One mate, three kids."

Theosophy thought about this. It had always seemed pointless to her, having children, getting attached to a single lover. "Why?"

"Coming home to my mate and the kids...it makes everything worthwhile. You know—human connection. Kindness. Love. Hope. It's a way of fighting back, too. Just not as obvious as yours."

Theosophy thought of Solvent, how they'd always stayed close. Of Briony, and how she'd given Theosophy a new kind of strength. She nodded slowly. "Thank you."

"Anytime, fighter."

"Call me Theo."

BRIONY HAD BEEN preying on her mind ever since their meeting in the ruins. But what she had told Briony was the truth: she hadn't seen any papers, either in the archives or in Granddad's library, that had anything to do with the dimensional modulator...but then, she hadn't known what to look for. After her return, she'd gone back into the archives and looked through them again, with no luck. She had tried once to contact Briony just to check in, but no luck there either. She could only hope Briony was all right.

The next step was to try Granddad's library again. But if she did find something, what then? She couldn't go back into the ruins alone—Dean Prosody had confiscated her musket. Lever and Synthesis still had their weapons, but they wouldn't follow her. Unless...

She was going to have to be Solvent and Briony both.

She found Lever and Synthesis the next morning in the HQ dining hall. They were lingering glumly in a corner over their mugs of chicory, watching the fighter trios come in exhausted after their shifts. How long had they been avoiding the others? She suspected she knew the answer.

"Listen," she said, "I need to talk to you."

They both glanced up at her, then away. Synthesis said, "We report to Solvent now, not you."

"I know. And it's my fault." Astrolabe had told her that his injury and Rhetoric's death were not her fault, and she could see his point now, but this... "I pleaded with the dean not to punish you because of my actions. I never thought she would."

Lever said, "It doesn't matter now. What's done is done. The past is over."

Theosophy grimaced. They weren't making this easy, but then she didn't deserve it to be easy. "Yes. But the *meaning* of the past can be changed. And so can the future." They looked up at her blankly, but she pressed on. "I wanted to say thank you. For helping me get into the ruins, and watching for me to come back. I wouldn't be here without you."

Synthesis said, "If we hadn't helped you, *we* wouldn't be here, working at Hydroponics."

Lever put a quelling hand on his arm. "What did you find?"

She took a deep breath, glancing around, but the dining hall had emptied out and they were nearly alone. She had to give them her trust now, and hope it would be enough. "A device that could change everything for the City." She explained, as best and as honestly as she could. Everything except her feelings for Briony—those were too private to share.

"So you've come to make nice to us because you need our help," said Synthesis after a moment.

"That doesn't make her thanks any less genuine," said Lever.

Synthesis shook his head. "Words are easy."

Theosophy wanted to argue. Those words had been anything but easy. Instead she said, "So what can I do to make it up to you?"

SHE VOLUNTEERED for sewer duty that day. Even Synthesis looked a little sorry as Theosophy stepped into the hip-waders and strapped a mask across her face. Theosophy didn't need anyone's pity and would have rejected any spoken overtures, but she found herself grateful that they were feeling kindly enough for sympathy.

"Here goes nothing," said Theosophy aloud, and jumped off the ledge.

She landed in knee-deep muck. It splashed up around her, sending up an awful smell that threatened to make her retch despite the mask. She wouldn't give Solvent the satisfaction, though. If she was going to retch, she would do it out of sight.

Better get moving, then. Holding up her multi-purpose crystal, she waded into the tunnel.

"Check for blockages," Solvent had said, "and keep your bearings." Theosophy had thought her sense of direction was pretty good, but that was aboveground, where the Wall was always on one side of you and the Rift on the other; even if you couldn't see them, you could sort of feel them both. Here, under the ground, she could feel nothing but the weight of the City pressing down on her. Fuck, she hated the dark. Solvent knew it, too, had held her when she'd woken from nightmares. But Theosophy had never chosen to tell her why.

The tunnels forked and re-converged and twisted back and forth at angles that had nothing to do with the streets above. It unsettled her, right down to her bones. She knew the City so well she could walk it in her sleep, every rooftop and lane and shortcut and ladder. To be somewhere *else*, somewhere unfamiliar...was this how Bree felt, in her world, with so much *space* around her? Theosophy shuddered and almost couldn't stop.

But she pressed on, checking each grate she passed. Some were clogged with bundles of cloth or tangles of leaves. She freed them, sent them spinning back into the main flow and away, though she didn't see what good it would do when she'd just have to fish them out of the dirty tank later.

And then she hauled on a bundle of cloth and it came apart in her hands and she was holding an arm bone. Human, not monster. And gnawed.

She dropped it and swore, holding her crystal high and shining it into every corner, until she realized she was being silly and there could be no monsters here. She wasn't sure how far she'd come, but it wasn't that far—she was definitely not under the University ruins yet. Besides, there must be underground barricades around the ruins to match the ones at street level. Right? She would have to ask the dean.

So where had the bone come from? If the monsters had gotten in here, under the City...either the City was in big trouble, or she'd come much farther than she'd thought.

She tried to retrace her steps, following the tangled map in her head. All the tunnels looked the same. A draft blew through and she traced it to its source, only to find a dead end. She backtracked and found herself in a small cave with five exits, all identical, and as soon as she turned around, she couldn't even tell which one she'd just come out of.

"Deep breath, Theo," she said aloud. "Bree wouldn't give up."

The effluent around her legs was eddying back and forth, fetching up against walls and corners, but sluggish and circuitous as it was, it mostly oozed in one direction. She followed it carefully, stopping at intersections to watch before moving forward again. Sometimes it seemed to stop and go around and around and around before suddenly uncoiling and oozing onward. Then it started to flow backward.

"You've got to be kidding me," Theosophy said. The wall tilted and the ooze rose up to meet her and she went down on her knees in the muck. Her crystal went dark.

CHAPTER TWENTY-TWO
BRIONY

IT MIGHT HAVE BEEN her imagination, but it seemed to get darker the farther she wandered into the forest. She and Poes reached the lake easily enough. Briony paused, looking into the water where she'd thought the Scarred had been, that night, but nothing was obvious.

Her general plan was to stay close to the lakeshore. It would keep her out of range of dangerous plants like choke vines and hopefully help her find whatever there was to be found relating to the City.

It also made her more visible to things inside the trees—Fractures and Scarred—but she tried not to think about that.

That first afternoon was a useless, horrible affair. Briony startled at every sound, but saw nothing. The lake seemed impossibly large. If what she needed was in the middle of the lake, how would she find it?

How would she even know where to look?

By nightfall, she and Poes had found nothing and camped on the edge of the forest, curled around each other under the cover of a rotting tree that'd fallen against its companions. The gentle rhythm of Poes purring was the only thing that drew Briony to sleep.

TIME SEEMED TO blend together. At first, Briony had tried to differentiate her path, but she didn't dare leave any physical markers and everything looked the same. It had been a long time since she'd visited a new part of the forest, the discovery of the lake not withstanding. Even with Poes at her side, she felt unnerved. Were those flowers the same ones she used for her sleeping draughts? Or were they a Fractured variety, designed to poison their pickers? Had the Old Ones made Fractured trees, and Briony's mother hadn't warned her because she'd never thought Briony would leave the relative safety of the forest by their house?

The lake continued to stretch out, descending into fog part of the way across. Sometimes, Briony thought she might have seen something on the other side, looming through the mist, but nothing ever came of it.

ON WHAT MIGHT HAVE been the third day, Briony found the Scarred again. She had been along the edge of the lake, refilling a water skin, when she'd heard them, their heavy march through the forest silencing the surrounding wildlife.

The dark of the forest made it hard to see where they were, and she didn't dare stay by the lake, outlined against the shining water, so she and Poes managed to scale a tree on the edge, hopefully out of view. The Scarred's marching grew louder, and Briony closed her eyes. *They've found me*, she thought. *They're tracking me or the amulet or whatever they used to find Carys, and there's nowhere for me to run.*

They emerged out of the forest underneath her, like maggots from a corpse, dispersing from their marching formation to blanket the edges of the lake. They didn't look up toward Briony, and she didn't dare move lest she draw their attention, even though there was a branch poking her in the leg. Just above her, Poes watched them intently, though he thankfully stayed silent.

They had devices in their hands that Briony was unfamiliar with—small and metallic—that occasionally beeped. Briony's blood froze in her veins. They were searching for her, they'd tracked her this far, and it was only a matter of time before they found her.

It seemed like she should go out fighting. That's what Theo would do, right? Jump down in the middle of them, directing Poes to use his claws and teeth, take out as many as she could. But she couldn't force herself to move. Instead she watched, waiting for the one who would point his device in the right direction.

A few inserted their devices into the water, like the Scarred Briony had seen the other night must have done. Their devices beeped, slow and steady, loud enough to echo across the lake. After several minutes they reconvened, and Briony could hear the murmur of voices, low and scratchy and unnatural in their rhythm.

Her hands were going numb. Why didn't they find her?

One of them pointed down the shoreline, south, toward Westenaedre, and the entire pack of them disappeared back underneath Briony into the forest.

She waited until Poes relaxed before she began her descent.

They weren't looking for her—they were looking for something else. Going along the lakeshore, just like Briony was. It was the City, of course. Should she follow them? Try to get ahead of them?

But she'd come from that direction, and she hadn't seen anything that seemed helpful in the least. And when she stood still and closed her eyes, breathing deeply, it still seemed like she should continue north.

Maybe the Scarred didn't know what they were looking for. Or maybe what they and Briony sought were not the same things.

THE LAKESHORE WAS ENDLESS. Briony had a terrible vision of her following it forever, what she needed always staying out of her reach. She was beginning to think that she'd been wrong to come. Or that what she needed was unreachable, buried deep underneath the waters of the lake. The weather was temperate, but the water was frigid.

Briony sat down on a large rock. Old Ones, what should she do? If she gave up and went home, she'd still have no idea how to help Theo—and the City—get back, and she had no idea where else to look. She'd have to talk to Mardu, probably, though the idea made her skin crawl. Somehow, she suspected she didn't want the Academy in the mix, and that would give him power over her.

But she couldn't wander the forest forever. She'd been lucky so far, but eventually her luck would run out. Something would catch her scent, or she'd run out of food and accidentally eat something from the forest that was unsafe, or the Scarred would eventually come for her.

Briony scrubbed at her face. What was the right thing to do here? She'd give anything for some sort of a sign.

She shifted her weight; the rock she sat on was sharp and uncomfortable. But there were few rocks on the lakeshore aside from pebbles, so she didn't have much of a choice. This was one of the first she'd seen the entire time she'd been out here.

Well, she'd at least give it to the end of the day. She pushed herself off the rock and continued down the shore. There were a few more rocks, all white and sharp, right here. Beyond, there was just lake.

Poes padded along beside her, occasionally wading into the water to cool off. Briony wished there was something useful up ahead, like a dock with a boat, or even some sort of sign. Something obvious, something like...

Something like rocks when there hadn't been any elsewhere.

Briony retreated back to the rocks. Upon closer examination, they weren't just rocks—they were stone that had been deliberately shaped. This had once been part of a building or a wall. Running her fingers over where she'd been sitting, she found a number, mostly covered with moss and worn with time. It could have been a fifteen, but that didn't mean anything to Briony.

She stood and huffed. Did this help her at all?

If these were part of Theo's city, they still didn't seem to be useful. A handful of ruins, caught behind when the City went away, left to decay.

Briony picked up one of the stones, just a fragment really, and turned it over in her hand. Was this all there was to find? She wanted to scream, but that would be a bad idea, so instead she just threw it as hard as she could. The stone skipped across the water and eventually settled with a dull thud.

Thud?

She crept to the edge of the water and peered in. The lake was a little cloudy here, small clumps of algae covering the surface, but she could just make out a few more stones under the water. Some even ghosted the surface.

Well, it wasn't a boat, but it was all she had.

Briony tugged off her boots and, after some consideration, left them at the edge of the forest rather than on the beach. She left her cloak as well, and her pack. Then she coiled her hair on top of her head as best she could and rolled up the bottoms of her trousers.

"Stay here," she said to Poes. "Keep an eye out."

The mountain cat tilted his head up to look at her. He flattened his ears back.

"I'll be fine," Briony said.

Poes didn't look convinced, but he yawned, then stretched out across her cloak and promptly went to sleep.

Briony hesitated on the edge of the lake. Had the Scarred done something to the water? She slowly stuck one foot in, ready to abandon the effort at the first sign of danger, but nothing happened other than the fact that the water was almost numbingly cold.

Her first plan had been to use the stones as a kind of pathway, scrambling over them and mostly staying dry. That had lasted for about twenty feet before one had proved too algae-covered and Briony had tumbled into the water. She was not the best swimmer, but she could use the stones to pull herself along.

It was probably for the best, anyway. It was terribly cold, but at least now she wasn't standing on the water, visible if the Scarred were along the edge of the lake somewhere.

The trail of stones—a wall, Briony decided—led her far out into the center of the lake. The shore, and the forest beyond it, became just lines in the distance, all detail lost. Briony's hands went numb, but she kept going. She pictured Jael and the children, imagining what they'd be doing right now. It had been mid-morning when she started swimming. Now, maybe, it was mid-day, and Jael had come in from his work, and Auberon would have laid out food on the table. Leo would climb all over his sisters, and there they'd all be, laughing and fighting, secure in the knowledge that they'd be fed and that they were loved.

The wall disappeared beneath Briony's fingers and she plunged into deeper water. Spluttering, she pulled herself back to the surface. The water here was deep blue, like a starless night, and she couldn't make out anything through it. A chill made its way down Briony's spine. Who knew what lurked out here, under all the water? Who knew what monsters had made their home in this lake?

She fought down her rising panic. She refused to believe that she'd come all this way just to be lost to the cold and the depths. Clinging to the edge of the wall, she took a few deep breaths, then forced her head under the water, searching. There was just dark and water, not even any fish.

Briony dragged herself back up. The cold seemed more biting here, her limbs heavier. She took another breath, submerged again. Nothing. Nothing.

Then, off to her left, she noted a blackness that seemed slightly darker than the surrounding water. It was so far off, though, if it was anything other than her imagination. And if she left her wall, would she ever be able to find it again? It was so very cold.

She thought again of Jael and the children, of Kishan. Of Theo. Beautiful, fierce Theo. Briony would never see her again if she didn't try. She took a deep breath, tried not to think of giants lurking below, and pushed off toward the blackness.

It was so hard to move her arms and legs. The water seemed to want to drag her down. The blackness wasn't getting closer fast enough. Briony closed her eyes, forcing her arms to keep moving. One stroke. Then another. And another. As long as she kept going, she'd be okay, she wouldn't give into despair and let herself sink.

A million years later, one hand hit something solid. Briony clung to it, so cold even shivering seemed impossible. It was so much work to pull her eyes open again. It was another wall, more complete than the first. Briony stared at it, tired, cold, unsure whether or not it was actually useful toward her quest.

Then, finally, she realized that there was no water on the other side.

CHAPTER TWENTY-THREE
THEOSOPHY

THEOSOPHY GROPED IN the muck for her crystal, her head spinning to match the sludge that she could somehow still see even though the crystal had gone dark. "Round and round and round..." she muttered.

Then someone was beside her, arm under hers, pulling.

"Bree?" she mumbled.

"Stupid, stubborn asshole...never thought you'd be out here this long...why you didn't...long ago...here, eat this."

Something crunched between her teeth. Rock salts. She tried to spit them out, but someone held her mouth closed until she chewed and swallowed.

Her head cleared almost at once. Solvent was holding her up, still swearing inventively.

"What the ever-living fuck?" said Theosophy.

"Oh, good, you're back. Come on, let's get you out of here."

The walls were back where they belonged. The muck around her legs flowed steadily in one direction. Solvent followed it, still half-supporting Theosophy until Theosophy noticed and shook herself free.

Her body felt light and tingly—that was the rock salts working—but at least her thoughts were still clear.

"What the fuck was that?"

Solvent snorted laughter as she walked. "Do you hear yourself? You sound amazed. Did you really think we sat around all day dabbling our fingers in water and cooing to plants? Did you think your job was the only dangerous one? I've got news for you, Theo. Everyone lives and breathes danger. It's just how life is."

"Not everyone," Theosophy mumbled, thinking of Bree. "It doesn't have to be like that."

"Excuse me?" said Solvent.

Theosophy realized what she'd said out loud. Shit. Her head must still be muddled after all. "Never mind that. I meant...well, let's start with the rock salts."

"Oh, those. Listen...they're kind of a secret. I mean, everyone knows they give you a buzz. But not everyone realizes that we on the water team take them for *work*. There are bad vapors down here, and the rock salts are protection against them."

"And you didn't think to give them to me *before* I almost passed out in the whole City's shit?"

"I didn't think you'd last down here half this long! Silly girl. The dean wants to punish you, yes, but she didn't intend you to work yourself to the bone while you're doing it."

"Why not? I overstepped and almost got myself killed. I wouldn't be any use to the City dead, would I?"

"*Use*? Theo, you've given every fucking bit of yourself to the City. There's barely anything left for yourself or...or anyone else."

Theosophy looked away as Bree's face flashed before her eyes. She and Solvent had never made each other any promises—most folks didn't, and why would they? Even so, she felt a stab of guilt. "I've never touched anyone else," she said, choosing her words carefully.

Solvent shook her head. "You've never touched me either, not really. There's a wall of ice around you every bit as impenetrable as the Wall itself. The only thing that gets through is your desire to get yourself killed."

"I don't *want* to get myself killed."

"You expect it. Isn't that the same thing?"

Before Theosophy could figure out what to say to that, they were emerging from the tunnel, stumbling back into the light and the dirty tank and—she was surprised to hear—glad shouts from above, where Lever and Synthesis hung over the edge of the railing with hands outstretched. She let them heave her up and onto dry land.

Then she just lay there for a while until Solvent brought her another glass of what she'd called unwatered liquor. It went down just as nasty as the first, but after Theosophy had finished choking, she did feel better.

Her head cleared further, and she remembered something.

"Solvent," she called. "I saw some odd things while I was down there."

"It's the hallucinations," Solvent said.

"No." Theosophy was very sure of that. "This was before that started. I found a human arm bone that had been gnawed on...Solvent, are there monsters down here?"

Instead of answering, Solvent looked at the oldest member of her team, Cosmogony.

"I've never seen one," she said. "But we stay away from those areas where we know our tunnels intersect with theirs. And we don't work at night. People on the team have disappeared before."

Theosophy couldn't believe what she was hearing. "Does the dean know about this?"

Cosmogony looked at Solvent, who said, "You'd have to ask her."

"I will. This could be a huge security problem."

"Theo...don't go to her right away." Solvent swallowed. "She's not exactly happy with you right now. Give her some time to cool off."

Theosophy considered it. Briony's problem was urgent, and waiting didn't suit Theosophy at all. She wanted to be taking action, preferably something involving a blade. Then again, research was action of a sort, wasn't it? And she knew exactly where to start.

AFTER HER SHIFT was over, Theosophy parted ways with her trio, saying she had an errand to run. She stopped long enough to barter for onion-stuffed dumplings and a skewer of fried rats from a street vendor, then wandered alone through the City. Knowing what lay beneath the streets made her feel more vulnerable, as if they might crumble and fall into a lair of monsters at any time. Children ran and laughed among the garbage, and overhead an old woman tended her hydroponic tomatoes.

Theosophy let her thoughts turn to Briony, but the image of Bree's face, her expression last time Theosophy had seen her, only made her heart ache. She'd had such hopes that maybe Bree's world was safer, that if only they could find a way through, everyone could stop living in fear all the time. But that wasn't true at all. From what Bree had said in the ruins, the other world was almost as dangerous. It wasn't going to be that easy.

Still, Bree's people had knowledge that the City didn't, and the same held true in reverse. If they could pool their knowledge, they'd be better equipped to fight all the threats, inside and out. And with Bree by her side...no, that was a childish thought...but then again, if they *could* find a way through, surely they could do anything. Together.

She turned the familiar corner and climbed the ladder.

Granddad was sitting in the main room, a closed book on his lap, though he was looking off into space. When he saw her, he smiled. "You came back."

"Of course I did," Theosophy said curtly.

"You weren't done asking questions. But indulge an old man. How are you?"

Theosophy paused as embarrassment rushed over her, first with the realization that he knew she hadn't come just to visit, then as she considered how to answer the question. "I'm...on sewer duty right now, Granddad."

His head came up. "Be careful."

She laughed. "You know about the danger of the sewers, too? Does everyone know except me?"

"No. There's a map of them in one of these..." he waved his hand vaguely in the direction of the bedroom. "But tell me, did you visit the ruins?"

Theosophy nodded and sat down on the floor in front of his chair. A flash of memory came to her, looking up at him from this same vantage point, but his hair was darker and his skin smoother... She shook the memory away before it could go any further, and told him about her solo excursion into the ruins. "I found the Academy," she said. "And our ancestor, and the device they used to wall off the

City—all of it. But I don't understand why, and I don't know how to reverse it."

"*Reverse* it? Theosophy, you must stop this line of thinking at once. Our ancestors—not just yours and mine, but everyone's—died to create the Wall."

"And all of their descendants are going to die if we can't bring it down," Theosophy said.

"My grandmother used to tell me stories that her grandmother told her. There was a cataclysmic war, she said. The Wall was put up for protection."

Theosophy had never heard this. "Ours or theirs?"

He shook his head. "I don't just remember now. Only that there was great danger, and the scientists at the Academy did what they had to. They had some warning, otherwise the City would have been even worse off than we are."

"And on the other side? Granddad, I didn't even know there *was* another side."

"It's not surprising. Folks don't talk of it now. Even when I was a child, only the old people did, muttering of old-people things. Stories, legends. Most didn't believe them."

"But you did," she said.

"It's our family history. There's truth in it somewhere, even if I'm not certain where."

"There's a whole world out there, Granddad. And I'm about to find out. I *have* to get through."

"No. Absolutely not. You don't know what could be on the other side now."

She swallowed. "Actually, I do. I can't tell you how, but I've seen it. On the other side is...people, just like us. And so much more—

room, and enormous plants as tall as buildings, and water just lying out in the open...we could be *safe*. We could all be safe."

He was silent for a long time. Then he murmured,

" 'The trees they grew high,

the waters blue as sky...,

there once lay you and I. "

Theosophy froze, the lyrics running through her mind again and again. "What did you say?"

"I never thought it was real. We used to chant it, and the old people would tell us how they learned it from *their* grandparents. But we thought it was a nonsense song."

"It's not. And you'll be able to see all of it. If you help me."

He only smiled and closed his eyes. She took that for permission.

There were fewer books in the bedroom than the last time she had come. He hadn't mentioned trading them away, and she didn't want to bring it up now. So she held her tongue as she flipped through them, looking for maps. She found several: parts of the City that were barely recognizable, a roughly hand-drawn map of what had to be Briony's forest, and finally, a diagram centered around what she recognized as Hydroponics, though it was labelled "Sewage treatment". The diagram showed a snarled network of what must be tunnels. They extended straight into the center of the City—into the ruins.

"Granddad," she said, hurrying back into the main room, "I've got to go."

He lifted his face to her, though she wasn't sure he could see her. "Are you going to find the trees?"

"I hope so."

He took her hand in his frail one. She leaned down and hugged him, hard.

THAT WAS IT. The dean might still be irritated with her, as Solvent had said, but this was too important—it couldn't wait. She had to bring the sewer map and warn the dean about the security risk, *now.* Theosophy hurried through the narrow streets. Around her, women gossiped about nothing while men sat in silence together—all civilians, all with their lives and their friends, their children and their petty concerns that persisted despite the nightly danger. *This* was what she was protecting. This was what she had to save.

Theosophy dashed into HQ and hurried to the dean's office, avoiding the startled looks of the other fighters. But outside the office stood a young man, burly enough, but the light dusting of fuzz on his cheeks and the anxiety in his eyes betrayed his age. When she would have barreled past, he moved to stop her. She dredged her memory for his name and couldn't find it.

"Is the dean in?" she asked instead.

"No, sir."

"Do you know when she'll be back?"

"No, sir."

Theosophy gritted her teeth. This wasn't getting her anywhere. "Did she leave any instructions?"

"Not for you, sir." He said it in a slightly embarrassed tone, and that gave Theosophy an inkling of an idea. Something a more socially astute person might do, like Briony.

She jerked her thoughts away from Briony when they threatened to linger. "I need to speak to her second-in-command, then," she told the boy. "It's urgent."

He swallowed. "Sorry, sir, he's busy drawing up plans for tonight's shift."

The sun was setting fast, Theosophy knew without having to look. Maybe the dean had left some note, or *something* that could tell Theosophy where she had gone.

"I left my musket in her office earlier," Theosophy said. "Do...do you mind if I go in and grab it?"

The boy looked at her skeptically. "Aren't you on duty...elsewhere? Sir?"

"Yes." Theosophy grimaced for his benefit, though it wasn't all feigned. "But she asked me to go on patrol tonight."

"Because we're shorthanded?" The boy nodded without waiting for her to answer. "Fine. But be quick, and please don't tell her I let you in." And he stepped aside.

Theosophy stared at him for a moment, surprised, before she managed to collect herself and walk past him into the office.

Her musket was propped in one corner, but the blade was gone. She swore. But she couldn't worry about it now. She moved to the desk and glanced out the door. The boy had left the door ajar, but resumed his position facing outward. Clearly he trusted her. *And why not?* she reminded herself. She hadn't done anything except talk her way inside. Though that was amazing enough.

Theosophy turned back and looked over the desk. Various tools and parts were scattered across its surface, but no papers—no hints there. She pulled open the drawers, one after the other. One of them seemed a little too heavy when she pushed it back in. She pulled it out again, lifted out the contents—the dean's bayonet-sharpening kit—and poked at the flat bottom inside. It seemed too thick, almost as if...she got her fingernails under the edge and pulled. It lifted off, revealing a folded sheet of paper.

She took out the paper, unfolded it, and froze. It was a carefully drawn schematic of the device she had found in the basement of the Academy, the one called "Dimensional Modulator."

The dean knew. Knew what, Theosophy wasn't certain, but definitely more than she had told Theosophy—about that device, about the Wall, maybe even about how to get through it.

Well. The dean wasn't obligated to tell Theosophy everything. She probably knew all sorts of things that others didn't—she was the dean, after all.

But if she knew how to open the Wall and free everyone from the monsters...why hadn't she done it?

Theosophy didn't understand any of this. It frustrated her, and beneath the frustration was a rumbling of uneasiness. Suddenly she wanted very much to talk to Briony—she was the only one Theosophy trusted to help her make sense of this.

She folded the schematic up again and stuck it back in the drawer, replaced the drawer bottom and the drawer as she had found them, then remembered to grab her musket. She took a deep breath and went to the door, forcing herself to stay calm. "I found my musket, but the blade is missing," she told the boy, trying to sound irritated. "Do you know if she gave it to anyone else?"

"No sir," he said, sounding nervous.

"Fuck." She swept past him with an air of impatience, which lasted just long enough to get out of sight.

Then she hurried to her quarters, pushed aside her cot, and stared at the hiding place.

Empty.

Theosophy forced herself to think past the inexplicable panic that gripped her at the thought of never seeing or speaking to Briony again.

There was only one possible explanation: the dean had taken her device. And Theosophy knew where.

CHAPTER TWENTY-FOUR
BRIONY

IT HAD TAKEN ALL of Briony's remaining strength to haul herself over
the wall, and then she had let herself drop down on the other side
without bothering to check if it was safe to do so. Then she laid there,
numb to all pain, and let the sun shine down on her face.

The sun had disappeared from overhead when she finally forced
herself to move. Her muscles ached, but she didn't seem to be
seriously injured. Slowly, she sat up. What had she been thinking? She
should have taken off her wet clothes as soon as she'd gotten out of the
water. That was how the cold got you in the end. Luckily, however, it
was still hot and she was now mostly warm and dry.

Briony pushed herself to her feet and surveyed her surroundings.
She was in a small stone chamber, just slightly taller than her height,
and it was completely empty except for a metal door in the wall
opposite the one Briony had come over. She ran one hand down it—
she'd never seen metal used for a door before. There was a lock above
the door handle—also metal—that had rusted out, but when Briony
tried the handle, the door popped open, scraping loudly on the stone.

Beyond was darkness, and Briony had nothing with her.

She forced the door open as far as it could go. It screeched the whole way, and Briony could picture the sound echoing across the lake, startling birds and alerting Fractures and Scarred. But that all seemed so far away right now.

There were stairs immediately inside the door, heading straight down for ten or twelve steps, then turning at a landing and heading farther into darkness. And, worse, Briony could feel cold air flowing up.

Still, she had survived the cold thus far. And she had come all this way.

At the second landing, there was a door, but this one was locked and would not budge. The stairs continued down, and Briony followed them. There was a railing that ran down the middle of the staircase. She clung to it as the light from above filtered out.

The next door was slightly ajar. Briony pulled it open and stepped inside, running her hands along the walls of the corridor beyond. There probably wasn't anything to fear in here. It was too remote for the dangers of the forest, and if anything *had* been in here when the City disappeared, it was probably dead by now.

Hopefully.

As Briony inched her way down the corridor, she could feel her amulet warm up. It began to glow, softly, its light not penetrating the darkness, and an answering hum reverberated through the walls beneath her fingertips.

Briony froze. A light bloomed up ahead, so white it was almost blue, revealing that the corridor widened into a room. As she inched forward, Briony wondered if this was under the bottom of the lake, or just deep in the waters. Maybe all that separated her from the icy kiss of the water was the centuries-old stone walls around her.

It was not a nice thought. Briony swallowed and stepped into the room.

She found complete disarray. Large metal cabinets had been tipped onto their sides and their contents were scattered across the room. A large, jagged crack split the floor and continued part of the way up one wall. Shelves full of books had been slashed, either by a large knife, or possibly something with large, and very sharp, claws.

It was oppressively stuffy and smelled like dust and mildew. Briony forced herself farther inside. There was so much here, but was any of it still readable? She reached down and picked up a sheet of paper, which crinkled and cracked upon contact, its ink faded and smudged from time.

Briony set the paper down and edged nervously toward the center of the room. It felt like she was invading someplace sacred, someplace that had been locked away all those years ago. It felt like she was trespassing.

She tried to right one of the metal cabinets, but it was much too heavy. So she turned to the papers instead. Some were within folders. Briony selected one of these folders at random and flipped it open. *Academy of Theoretical Dimensionary Science and Philosophy*, read the top, *Status Report,* followed by some numbers that were probably a date, but which meant nothing to Briony.

Minutes approved. New business. Old business.

Under new business, someone had expressed concerns about one of the graduate students, whatever that was. Worried that they were gathering information for the valdnordri, another term Briony had never heard before. There was some discussion about how one could tell, and whether it was right to deny someone knowledge, no matter what they intended to do with it.

Briony flipped the paper over. On the back they'd gotten to old business. Something about money, something about new students seeking admittance to the program. A sentence note: *The barrier seems weaker at twilight.* But there was no additional information on the topic, as if whoever had written the document had assumed that all other necessary data was known to all.

Briony set the folder down, disappointed, and looked at the sheer amount of paper around her. Her stomach grumbled, but there was nothing to be done for it.

She rolled up her sleeves and went to work.

SHE HAD THREE PILES; the first was for mentions of the valdnordri. It had taken her a while, but now she was pretty sure that this was the Scarred back before and during the Great War, before the Old Ones had warped them into what they were today. The papers treated them as the enemy, after all, and the Scarred had been who the Old Ones were fighting against in the Great War.

The second was full of gibberish about barriers and dimensions, which made very little sense but seemed important.

The third was for anything that sounded like it had to do with locking the City away wherever it had gone. It was mostly fragmented, a sentence here or there, but it sounded like it had been meant purely theoretically, a last ditch step that they never thought they'd have to take. What had happened, what had been so terrible that they'd taken that final action?

There was a name tied to this last pile: *Farhan.* Someone specific who was working on the problem. And there were notes about his—or her—research, but not the research itself. If Briony could just find that research...

But who knew if it was even here? Maybe this was just for odd notes. Maybe research was stored somewhere else. Maybe it was trapped in the City with everything else. How odd that this one building, and not even a building, but what seemed liked the bowels of one, had been left behind.

Briony worked with her back against the wall, keeping the crack in the floor in front of her. Whenever she turned her back on it, it made her nervous. That was ridiculous, of course, but there was something about it that seemed *wrong*, and, as the night went on, she imagined she could hear noises coming from it, guttural, inhuman.

The stairs had continued farther down. There could be more rooms, filled with paper. Briony leaned her head against the wall. The task was insurmountable. There was too much information here. So much of it could be useful, but she couldn't get it out. The swim back to shore would ruin it.

But she couldn't sift through the mess forever. She needed food, sleep, some place warm and dry. And she couldn't shake the feeling that she shouldn't be here, that this place was never meant for the likes of her.

Without realizing it, she had come to the bottom of her current stack of papers. This set was different—the handwriting was hurried, and it wasn't divided into the careful sections the others had been.

Barrier can be breached, read one side. *Formal test to be attempted tonight under controlled circumstances.*

Dimensional pocket to be readied, read the other. *At this time, we do not believe we shall need it, but the argument has been raised that the procedure requires a decent amount of preparation, and that we should do as much as possible now so we do not find ourselves without time later.*

Please see Emergency Procedure 43-CD32X. Preparations will begin immediately.

Where was Emergency Procedure 43-CD32X? What was Emergency Procedure 43-CD32X? Briony tried to throw the paper away, but it just wafted slowly toward the floor. As it neared the crack, it fluttered backward, as if blown by a breeze.

Briony pushed herself to her feet. She wanted out of here. She needed out of here. But she was so close to the information she needed. Licking her lips, she slid around the edge of the crack. Part of her wanted to look inside.

But she didn't. *The engineering department reports that they've developed a portable defensive technique*, said part of a piece of paper at her feet. The rest of the page was missing.

Reports from the border are not optimistic, read part of another.

The released creatures cannot be controlled as hoped.

The surrounding populace has been warned about which paths are safe to take, but there have been increasing incidents.

The dimensional barrier seems to be weakening even without experiments running.

People have been asked to gather within the university for safety.

The biochemistry department has created a new form of chemical gas.

The forest is burning.

Briony looked at the papers spread out at her feet. It was like a slow, scattered decline into chaos, a look at everything going more and more wrong. Soon, surely, soon they would have locked the City away wherever they put it. But there were no details and, Old Ones, Briony needed details.

She picked up a strip of paper from the corner. *Activating Emergency Procedure 43-CD32X. Ealadgast has volunteered to*—and then it cut off. Briony stared at the paper, at her own family name staring back at her. One of her ancestors had been part of this, had helped to lock the City away. It was hard to focus on the words, but then she realized her hands were shaking.

Her ancestor had been an Old One, had sat in on these meetings, had commented on the release of the Fractures like it had been the weather.

Forcing herself to breathe, Briony let the piece of paper drop to the floor. Did that change anything? No. No. She needed this procedure. She needed to know what had been done to seal the City away. Without that, she'd never be able to get it back. Theo would be trapped, locked away from Briony, forever.

The paper she'd gone through had been spread across the room, and it had all been status updates, so it was reasonable to conclude that none of the rest of it would be of any use either. Briony edged her way back over to the metal cabinets. There were five of them. Two were empty, their contents no doubt the papers spread across the floor. One lay face down, its drawers trapped underneath. The other two were on their sides. Briony yanked on a drawer on the one closest to her, but it didn't budge. Locked, or rusted shut. She couldn't tell.

The other one squealed as she pulled the drawers open, the noise echoing throughout the room and down the staircase outside. Briony really hoped that there wasn't anyone, or anything, else in here.

The first drawer was full of identical copies of the same piece of paper. There were large blank spots. Further back, different hands had filled in numbers and equations in those spots. It all meant nothing to Briony, and she moved on. The next drawer was full of papers packed with long words and unfamiliar terms. But nothing said "procedure."

The last drawer had folders with names, but there was nothing inside each folder except notes and records about each person.

Briony tried the locked cabinet again, but the drawers still would not move. The need to get out of this place was getting stronger. She would have sworn that something was watching her, and the whispers from the crack seemed louder.

She shook the cabinet as hard as she could, pulling and rattling until her arms hurt. It stayed horribly, annoyingly locked. Briony kicked it, which helped not at all, and turned her attention to the last cabinet. Managing to squeeze between it and the wall, Briony shoved her back up against it and pushed off the wall with her feet. All that accomplished was to slide it across the floor. Next she braced her shoulder against the top of one side and leaned her whole weight into it.

It took a moment, but the cabinet creaked and, finally, rolled.

One drawer popped open immediately, and its contents slid out onto the floor. Briony pounced on it, keeping half an eye on the crack. It was probably her imagination, but now it almost seemed like there was movement within it.

Just a trick of the light, surely, reflecting off the metal cabinets.

This looked more promising. There seemed to be actual technical details here, though Briony had no idea what any of it meant. She flipped through it as quickly as she could, looking for the correct emergency procedure or anything that mentioned it.

The first drawer exhausted, she moved on to the next, but there was nothing there, either. As she opened the bottom drawer, her heart sank. This one was mostly empty, and the few folders inside were worthless.

She needed to get into that locked cabinet, but there was nothing in the room to use to break it open. Her eyes darted toward the crack, but she wouldn't actually swear that it went to the room underneath.

But there were the stairs…

The locked cabinet wasn't as heavy as the other two, but it still took Briony longer than she would have liked to muscle it to the top of the stairs, and several minutes more to get it back upright. Then, taking a deep breath, she threw her full weight into it. The cabinet tumbled down the stairs, making enough racket that the Scarred could probably hear it in the forest, and crashed open at the bottom.

In the dim light, she could see that at least one drawer was now open. Briony hurried down the stairs.

She could barely read the writing from the glow of her amulet. *Emergency Procedures*, was written on the front of the folder. Briony flipped it open and rustled through the contents. Actual procedures, finally! Each procedure was accompanied by a symbol, which was printed on every page.

But the one she wanted wasn't there. Briony threw the folder down, fighting back tears. From the landing below her came a whispering, like a gentle wind. She froze, listening, but the sound did not repeat.

The other drawers were still locked. Briony pried out the open one, intent on getting into the one below through brute force if nothing else, when something fluttered off the side of the drawer onto the ground. Briony set the drawer down as quietly as she could manage and bent down. Someone hadn't wanted this found, or it'd been tossed in without a thought of where it went.

Her fingers brushed the front of it. It was a large stack of paper bound together. *Emergency Procedure 43-CD32X. Use only as a last resort.*

For a second, the words didn't register. The paper didn't even crinkle ominously, like the stuff out in the room had done. Maybe being locked away for centuries had better preserved it.

Below her, the whisper sounded again, followed by a low noise, like something being dragged.

Briony clutched the papers to her chest and fled.

CHAPTER TWENTY-FIVE
THEOSOPHY

WITH THE PANIC about being out of touch with Briony stuffed safely in the back of her mind, Theosophy moved about her quarters, making preparations. She took a spare blade and fastened it on her musket, picked up Astro's double crystal and made sure it was still tuned to hers, and went to find the only person she knew who could help her.

Solvent was sitting on the rooftop, watching the sun set. Pushing it, as always. Normally Theosophy would have hassled her about being outside so late, for no other reason than the difficulty of protecting civilians who insisted on being stubborn. Then Solvent would have snapped back about Theosophy's tone of voice when talking about civilians, and they would have ended up having a quick tumble before Theosophy started her shift.

Tonight, Theosophy sat down beside Solvent without speaking, trying to find the words for what she had to ask. Talking had never used to be this hard. What was wrong with her?

Solvent must have been thinking the same thing, for she eyed Theosophy and said, "What's up?" in a cautious tone.

Theosophy took a breath and forced the words out. "I need your help."

Solvent's eyebrows went up. "Did the world just get broken open?"

Theosophy laughed, startled by the old saying. "Something like that."

"What is it?"

"I need you to get me into the ruins through the sewers."

Solvent hugged her knees, her body closed off, face in profile so it was even harder to read. "Can't be done."

"I've seen the maps, and those tunnels. They go right through, underneath."

"They're blocked off," Solvent said. "Otherwise, what would be stopping the monsters from leaving the ruins?"

"Nothing, apparently. Or was it a rat that gnawed the arm-bone I found?"

"If they could have overrun the City that way, they would have done it by now. I'm telling you, the tunnels are blocked."

Theosophy studied Solvent. They'd known each other for a very long time, and something told her that Solvent was lying. "Remember the device I found?"

Solvent went still. "What about it?"

"I have reason to believe the dean has taken it and gone into the ruins. I need to get to her—*now*—and I can't do it aboveground." Theosophy waved a hand at the sky, where the last light was draining away. "I almost died last time, and that was in daylight."

Solvent didn't answer immediately. "Can't this wait until morning?"

Theosophy thought of Briony in danger, right now. "No. I promise you it cannot."

Solvent closed her eyes. "Be careful, all right?"

Solvent hadn't said that to her in a while. Theosophy responded the way she always did. "I'm always careful. If I weren't, I'd be dead by now."

"I guess that's true." Solvent turned to face her for the first time. "But you won't be going alone. You need me to guide you, and I'm bringing backup."

Theosophy wanted to argue, but more than that, she didn't want to delay any longer. "Fine. But if you're bringing backup, so am I. I can't be the only fighter down there."

"Deal."

Theosophy stood, and reached down a hand to help Solvent up, before she remembered that they weren't lovers anymore. But Solvent accepted the help. Her eyes met Theosophy's, almost as if she wanted to say something else, but she didn't.

Theosophy gave her a quick hug, shoving Astro's double crystal into Solvent's pocket as she did so. Solvent would never agree to take a fighter's crystal.

"What was that for?" Solvent said.

Theosophy turned away. "Just in case. Let's go, and quickly, before the monsters come."

BY THE TIME the monsters began to stream across the City, Theosophy was safely inside the Hydroponics building, crowded in on the main floor with most of Solvent's squad and Lever and Synthesis as they all suited up. Solvent was having a quiet word with her squad, so Theosophy, feeling fidgety, decided to pull her trio aside as well.

"Thank you for agreeing to come," she told them bluntly.

They both stared back at her with identical expressions of shock. She would have laughed if the situation hadn't been so serious, but she managed to hold back the impulse.

Lever recovered first. "We trust you, sir," they said.

"Why now, and not before?" Theosophy couldn't help but ask.

They looked at each other. At last Synthesis said, "You're nicer now. You're thinking past the end of your blade. Sir." Lever nodded in agreement.

Theosophy's thoughts flashed to Bree, making her chest ache. "Glad you're here," she said gruffly.

Lever shrugged. "You needed us, sir."

It was true. She couldn't go into the ruins at night on her own, even through the sewers. Even with a full trio, the mission was tremendously dangerous. Just like last time, she hadn't ordered them to join her; she had asked, and this time they'd said yes. She didn't like asking the water team to come along, but the sewers were as dangerous to her and her trio as the monsters were to civilians. Solvent had given her team the choice, too. Theosophy was startled, and humbled, that they had all agreed.

She said, "You're right. I do need you."

Saying it out loud, like that, felt good. From the looks on their faces, hearing it felt good, too.

"Are we ready?" said Solvent, coming up to the huddle.

Theosophy checked that her musket was securely slung across her back, turned to see Lever hefting their spear and Synthesis checking his own musket, and nodded. "Whenever you are."

Solvent turned to her squad. "Paradigm, you sure about this?"

He raised his chin. "Yes, sir. I'm not staying aboveground just because of my father."

"Very well." Solvent turned to Astrolabe. "If we don't come back, you know what to do. The leaders of the other shifts know how to keep this place running, and they won't fuck around when you tell them it's time for emergency protocols."

"Yes, sir. And...good luck." His eyes flicked to Theosophy. "Fight well."

She nodded again, and saluted him. He did not speak, but he stood a little straighter.

Solvent said, "I'll go first. Then Paradigm, then you three, and you last." She gestured to Cosmogony. "When we get closer to the ruins, you'll take the lead, Theo. Agreed?"

It felt strange to be giving the command to someone else, even temporarily. Theosophy reminded herself that this was why she had approached Solvent in the first place. "Lead on."

THE SEWERS WERE just as nasty and claustrophobic as the first time she'd been down here, and they still gave her the creeps. Strange eddies ran through the muck, and terrible-smelling breezes from the opposite direction, and drips and splashes that echoed through the tunnels until she had no idea which direction the noises had originally come from. The shifting shadows from everyone's multi-purpose crystals didn't help.

Solvent had set a quick pace, then slowed down once it became clear that the trio of fighters was having trouble keeping up, slipping and sliding on the surface they could not see. Theosophy's two partners slogged through the muck, wide-eyed behind their masks. She didn't blame them. It was one thing to grow up, and to fight in narrow alleys and tiny rooms, but another to be under the streets and know there was no escape except a maze, walls everywhere and no way out except through the monsters that loomed over her and her parents...

"Stop it," she said softly. "This isn't like that."

"Sir?" said Synthesis behind her.

"Never mind. Now shut up, we need to listen."

That was obviously not true—nobody could hear anything, what with the echoes off the arched roofs as the six of them sloshed onward—but Synthesis, wisely, did not argue.

Despite her struggle to remain calm, Theosophy had to admit that trekking through the sewers in a large group was a completely different experience than going alone or with just Solvent, like before. She had people on point, people at her back, people with all the skills necessary for surviving this journey...or at least for having the best shot at surviving. She was determined to get them all out alive, not least herself. The City needed her, and besides, she wasn't about to die without at least touching Briony once.

While keeping her senses alert, Theosophy allowed her thoughts to drift back to the missing device. How the fuck had the dean known it was there? And why would she have taken it, knowing Theosophy had hidden it for a reason? She felt uneasy. The dean was on the list of people she trusted with her life—a very short list, now that Astro was unable to fight. Surely the dean had a good reason, as was true for everything she did. But Theosophy was very much looking forward to asking her what it was.

She knew she was focusing on the dean because she didn't want to focus on the other part. The part where the Wall between the City and Briony had suddenly snapped back into unarguable, impenetrable existence. She'd gotten used to thinking of it as...porous, maybe. If one could talk through it, even sort of move through it—or whatever—as she did to reach Briony, then surely it could be breached, torn down, vanished, or whatever one did to the edge of the world to make it not be the edge of the world anymore. But now that Briony was out of reach—

No, fuck it, she *was* going to see Briony again. This could not be the end. Dean Prosody would help her get through the Wall. For the City, and for Briony.

THEY HAD RESTED and eaten and rested again and gone on still farther when, ahead, the sloshing footsteps halted. Theosophy peered through the gloom. Solvent and Paradigm had come to a stop before a heavy iron gate, the grille so tightly woven that it was almost solid.

"Dead end?" said Theosophy.

Solvent shook her head, looking grim. "Listen."

They all stopped moving. Theosophy held her breath. Faintly, through the iron grille, she could hear movement and eerie calls. Not close, but close enough.

Monsters.

"This is the boundary of the ruins," said Cosmogony quietly, from behind. "They can't come through that gate. To my knowledge, the water squad has never gone farther than this. Even being as close as we are..." She shivered.

Theosophy stepped up to the gate. "This is where my trio and I take over. How do we get through?"

There was a silence. Theosophy turned to look at Cosmogony, who said, "We know how. We've just never done it before." She swallowed.

Solvent said, "I'll do it."

Both trios watched, wide-eyed, as Solvent walked up to the gate. "Sorry, faculty secret," she said to Theosophy, turning her body so that Theosophy couldn't see what she was doing. The lock seemed to resist at first, but then turned with a loud *click*. Theosophy tensed at the sound, unslinging her musket. The gate itself opened quietly and easily, despite its bulk. Every other sewer tunnel she'd seen had been evenly rounded, built of brick or stone carefully laid. But this one was irregular, not quite a circle and not quite an oval but something in between that her mind couldn't grasp. *Wrong.* Her stomach roiled—a clear signal that they were under the ruins now, as if the tunnel hadn't been enough. All was quiet, but Theosophy knew better than to hope it would last.

"Thank you for coming with us," she said. "If you wish, you may turn back now."

Solvent shook her head. "We may be under the ruins, but we're also still in the sewers, and I don't think you want to go aboveground until you absolutely have to. You still need us."

Theosophy looked at Paradigm and Cosmogony, who exchanged a glance and nodded. Paradigm said, "We follow Solvent, sir."

"Very well." Theosophy took a deep breath. "But stay in the center of the group, and if we meet any monsters, get out of the way, and don't let them get near you, understand?" She gave each member of the water trio a ferocious glare until they nodded. Good at navigating sewers they might be, but they were still civilians and non-fighters, even Solvent. She was used to fighting in cramped quarters—some of the alleys weren't much bigger than this—but not with civilians around, and certainly not so many. They'd just have to watch themselves. "Synthesis, with me. Lever, take the rear guard. Let's go."

Solvent locked the door again. They moved forward more slowly this time, with Solvent murmuring directions as quietly as she could, just at the edge of Theosophy's hearing. Each time they met a cross-tunnel, they stopped and crept forward until Synthesis on one side and Theosophy on the other could spin around the corner—as much as the *wrong* tunnels had corners—with musket blades at the ready. Each time, they were met with silence.

Until they weren't.

At the third tunnel, Synthesis yelled. Theosophy spun to throw a knife over his head. It glanced off the tunnel roof and fell, narrowly missing Synthesis's shoulder and dropping harmlessly into the muck. Then the triad of monsters was on them.

The fighting was nasty work, the footing slippery. She'd never liked fighting on roof tiles in the rain, and this was worse. The dim lighting from their crystals made it hard to see clearly, especially when it reflected off the muck. Worse, the monsters seemed bolder here in their own tunnels. Maybe they were expecting backup and her only chance was to dispatch them quickly. Easier said than done, though. One got past her and among the water squad, leaving Lever alone to fend it off while she and Synthesis dealt with the other two. Then the one she'd chosen got her backed up against the wall. She fought hard, and finally slid the musket home, past the shifting tentacles, to its heart.

The monster collapsed into the muck. Theosophy pushed herself away from the wall—there was slime all down the back of her jacket, fuck it—and looked around. Synthesis had killed another, and the third...

The third was gone. Lever, clutching a bleeding arm and staring at her helplessly, mouthed, "I'm sorry."

She counted. One, two—

"Where's Solvent?"

Paradigm answered, his voice stiff with shock. "I think the monster took her."

CHAPTER TWENTY-SIX
BRIONY

IF THERE WAS something in the depths, it didn't get Briony before she reached the outside and closed the door, though, with the squeaking, it certainly knew where she was. It was dark, though lightening; dawn would be soon. Briony wished she had something to bar the door with. As it was, she huddled in the corner farthest from the door, watching it, papers clutched against her chest.

With the growing light, she was finally able to look at her find. She should have looked inside. If she was missing something essential, she wasn't sure she'd be able to go back in. Each page was labeled with the same symbol, perhaps to make sure other procedures didn't accidentally get mixed in. Something about the symbol was familiar, but she couldn't put her finger on it. There were a lot of words that Briony didn't understand, and she couldn't help but feel she was out of her depth. What had she been thinking? She wasn't an Old One. If she could get it to Theo—but she couldn't, and Theo probably wouldn't understand it either.

But there was a word she recognized that ran throughout: anchor. Mardu had mentioned an anchor too. And eventually there was a picture of the City, within a bubble, with ties coming off of it to a single point outside the bubble. The point was labeled "anchor" as well.

Okay, so the anchor was important somehow. Tied directly to the City. Briony rubbed one temple, then flipped back through the papers. If she understood the concept—which she probably didn't—then the anchor tied the City to the rest of the world. It needed to be activated to bring the City back.

That was good. That was something useful. There were instructions on how to pull the City back. Those weren't immediately important—she needed to figure out where this anchor was first. Near the end of the stack of papers were a series of pictures, each showing different parts of the process. Apparently there'd been someone stationed at the anchor, to talk to the City and start pulling the City back when the danger had passed.

Briony turned the page to the picture of the communication device and almost dropped the whole stack. Staring back at her was a picture of her own amulet. Not on a chain, but unmistakable nevertheless.

A horrible, sickening feeling wormed its way through Briony's core. The amulet had been in her family for generations. Her family had been spirit talkers for generations. Hardly daring to breathe, suspecting what she might find, she flipped through the pictures until she found one of the anchor.

It was a square fence-post looking thing with that same symbol on top, surrounded by other things Briony had long believed were the remains of many different fences. And she'd passed through it nearly every day of her life back home.

BRIONY AND POES hurried through the forest undergrowth as quietly as possible. Briony had composed her nerves enough to pry the door back open and replace the procedure in the stairway so that it wasn't lying out in the elements. It had been perfectly quiet inside, no hints of whispers or anything else. Briony still didn't know if she'd imagined them.

As they went, she ran over what she'd learned from the procedure. The anchor would need to be activated in order to pull the City back, but Briony couldn't do it on her own. Someone on the inside would need to activate the other end, and so Briony would need to talk to Theo about it, coordinate something.

To think—the anchor and the key to everything had been under her nose this whole time. Her heart leaped a little. She'd get to relay the good news to Theo—to see her and talk with her again—and then, maybe in as little as a few days, they could be together. She'd be able to see Theo with her own eyes, to touch her, to…Briony shook her head, cutting the thought short. Priorities. They'd have all the time in the world later.

She and Poes had been lucky on their trip back. They'd not run into any signs of the Scarred, and the lone Fracture they'd encountered—a large, black bird that Briony's mother had definitely never told her about—had fallen under Poes's claws without too much damage to either her or the mountain cat.

Briony slowed as they reached familiar edges of the lake. It was near dark, the sunlight rapidly fading. The forest was silent, as if it were waiting, but Poes seemed calm and Briony couldn't hear anything alarming. She wrapped one hand around her amulet and looked around for Theo.

The other woman didn't appear.

Briony watched the sky. Was it too early? Theo had said she'd be there every night, hadn't she? Had something happened to her? Briony wasn't actually sure how long she'd been gone. Maybe Theo thought something had happened to her, and that she wouldn't come back.

Brushing her hair out of her eyes, Briony huffed. Well, what had she expected? Theo had her own things to do, and she couldn't be expected to hang her attention on Briony's return. It didn't matter. Briony would go home, tell Jael what she'd found, and she could come back tomorrow night and wait for Theo. She'd just have to assume that Theo would still check in periodically, even if she wasn't every night. Surely she wouldn't have given up on Briony completely, no matter what.

Jael was going to be so pleased to see her. Briony picked up her pace, relying on Poes to warn her if something unfamiliar got too close. Her brother would frown and tell her how stupid she'd been, but then he'd gather her up in his massive arms and everything would be okay.

Briony slid to a stop and Poes twisted his head to look up at her. Could she risk going home? Surely it wouldn't hurt to visit for a moment or two before heading farther into town. They were *so* close to a solution now, and Jael would want—

There was a loud bang in the distance ahead of her. Briony could feel the force of it. She threw a hand up to block her eyes, and, beside her, Poes hissed and raised his hackles. What, by the Old Ones, had that been?

A thin scream followed. Briony's heart dropped into her stomach.

She broke into a run. She'd heard that scream before, but never like that—before, it'd always come as a result of laughter, from a sibling jumping out from behind a corner, or from being tossed up into the air. But now—

The forest flew past. If there were choke vines or Fractures, Briony never saw them. As she neared home, other noises, all foreign, joined in. Other screams, crashes, a weird mechanical noise Briony could not place.

The forest disappeared around her and home came into view. But it was not recognizable. Several outbuildings were on fire, the smoke and heat wafting into the now-dark sky. One, the one Jael spent so much of his time in, had been leveled just like Carys's cottage. Dark shapes were everywhere. A horrible smell, charred and burning, assailed her.

Briony swallowed around a lump in her throat. She wiped at her face, which was unexpectedly wet, and dropped her bag on the ground. "Poes," she said, "come."

Slowly at first, then faster, she stepped into her home. The first Scarred loomed out of the darkness in front of her. Briony raised one arm and pointed, and before that horrible insectoid mask had fully turned to her, the mountain cat pounced, snapping hoses and bone in one leap. There were more ahead. They saw her coming. Three more went down under Poes's bulk, still chattering to each other in their strange, almost comprehensible, language.

The rest fled.

Around her, the fire crackled. Where was her family? Briony wiped at her face again. *Please, please, Old Ones or whoever is out there, don't let them have been surprised. Please let them have gotten out beforehand.*

Briony rounded a corner, flinching away from the heat. The flicker of the flames illuminated a small figure on the ground, flailing beneath a larger figure. The fire reflected off the Scarred's mask, and its knife.

Letting out a yell, Briony charged. She drove her shoulder into the Scarred's side, knocking him off the smaller figure. The Scarred tumbled satisfyingly before stumbling to his feet, but by then Poes was already on him.

Briony bundled the smaller figure into her arms. It was Brin, shivering and crying, but seemingly otherwise intact. Briony murmured something—she wasn't even sure what—and stumbled to her feet. She'd need to get the girl out of here, but where could she take her? And what about everyone else? Brin never went anywhere without Marcea.

That weird, mechanical noise that Briony had noticed earlier clanked closer. Briony looked up and her breath caught in her throat. Illuminated by the burning building behind it was a large, metal carriage. Several long tubes decorated its sides. Clutching her niece closer, Briony darted for the nearest building.

The carriage groaned ominously, and the building exploded around Briony. She ducked her head and wrapped her body around Brin's. Beside her, Poes yelped. As soon as bits of wood stopped flying, she ran again, unsure what had happened to the mountain cat— he no longer seemed to be beside her. Maybe she could duck back into the forest, backtrack into town, get some help, if there was any to be had.

Briony rounded the corner into several Scarred. These were armed with smaller versions of the metal tubes from the carriage. Briony slid to a stop. In her arms, her niece whimpered and dug her face into Briony's blouse. There was nowhere to go. Behind her was fire and destruction. Ahead of her, the Scarred raised their tubes. Briony hugged Brin closer and closed her eyes, waiting for the pain.

The sound from the tubes was deafening. But when nothing more happened, Briony risked a glance.

In front of her, the red of his robe flashing in the flicker of the flames, was Kishan.

She must have whispered his name, because he turned to look at her. Beyond him, between them and the Scarred, there was a thin, almost translucent wall. He gave her a wry smile. "I told you it was more than just healing."

He offered her a hand. Briony allowed him to pull her up, a million questions dancing on the tip of her tongue. But she fought them down. She needed to focus. "Jay?"

Kishan opened his mouth, but the Scarred's tubes flashed again. Briony flinched and the wall cracked. The healer grabbed Briony's arm and abandoned the wall, pulling her and Brin back the way they'd come. The noises around them were louder and more confusing now, and Kishan occasionally threw up more of his barriers—and he could move them quickly if necessary—against assailants Briony hadn't even noticed. It was a side of Kishan she'd never seen before.

Around the chaos, it was hard to tell where they were on the property, but eventually she realized they were heading back toward the cottage. They found Auberon cradling Leo and cowering behind a bush near the house, but there was no sign of Jael or Marcea.

What were the Scarred doing? They seemed to be everywhere. Briony handed Brin off to Auberon too and peeked around the side of the house. For a terrible moment she thought the anchor was gone, but then its outline, as well as the outline of several Scarred, was illuminated by the fire.

Were they trying to access the City? Briony stood. She couldn't let them! Unsure exactly what she was going to do, she darted out from behind the building, shouting something. Kishan grabbed for her, but she eluded his grip. None of the Scarred even looked in her direction. Panic made her throat dry. They needed to stop, they needed to leave it alone, that was all that could connect her to Theo—

Something bowled her over and dragged her behind the remains of a wall. Briony shrieked and dug her nails into an exposed bit of flesh before realizing it was her brother. It was hard to see his features in the flickering light, but his size, and his beard, made him unmistakable.

"We need to get out of here," he said.

"Jay," she said, more breath than an actual word, "we need that anchor. We can't—the City…"

"Come on." He dragged her to her feet and back across the clearing, heading for town.

No! There had to be something they could do. Briony pulled against her brother's grasp, but he was, as always, annoyingly larger than her. She caught a glimpse of true red—Kishan—and some shivering figures following him, heading the same way. Someone else ran past—Mardu; she'd recognize that ridiculous waistcoat anywhere—pulling out purple ribbons. He wrapped them around one of the few remaining upright portions of wall, then pulled. They exploded, bringing what was left of the roof down on some Scarred.

"Jay!" She tried to wrench her arm free. "You said we needed to stay here, you said—"

"I know what I said!" Jael snapped. "And, look, you were right, we should have gone. We're going now. Stop fighting!"

Briony twisted her head to look back at the blaze engulfing their home. The Scarred were paying them no mind now, busy spreading mayhem and gathering at the anchor. Briony pulled once more at Jael's grip, but her heart was no longer in it. What could she do? She wasn't a fighter—that was why she needed Theo. And now…now Theo was beyond her grasp forever.

Westenaedre was calm beyond the edge of their land. Mardu was waiting there now, Marcea huddled next to him, bruised and bleeding and crying, but there, thank the Old Ones. Briony's hopes rose a little. Maybe he'd prove that he was actually helpful, show off the reason everyone seemed to fear the Academy, maybe help her get back in. But instead he handed Marcea off to Jael, patted him on the shoulder, and led the way back into town. Briony caught his eye, but he just turned away from her.

Stepping into town was almost unreal. All was quiet, peaceful. Very few people had noticed what was happening. Briony paused. She turned back to what had been her home, letting Kishan and the other children pass her. The fires were calming down, but the Scarred were still everywhere.

Theo seemed farther away than ever.

CHAPTER TWENTY-SEVEN
THEOSOPHY

THEOSOPHY LOOKED around at the aftermath of the fight. Her double crystal was silent; its companion in Solvent's pocket was either damaged or out of range, maybe already in the Rift. The two remaining monsters were good and dead, and backup didn't seem to be coming. Perhaps all the monsters were in the City, so none were left to be drawn by the sound of combat. The group had moved down the tunnel while fighting, so they were no longer in the four-way intersection—only two sides to defend. Here was as good a place as any, she supposed.

"We'll take a few hours to rest," she announced. "My trio and I will keep watch. Do what you need to."

Paradigm stared back at her blankly until Cosmogony nudged him and said, "Thank you." He echoed her; then they moved off together, both blinking back tears.

She had never understood how tears helped. But maybe if she had let Astrolabe have this moment, he'd still be whole.

She turned away and went to lean against the tunnel wall. Only it wasn't quite where she'd thought. She slipped, tried to catch herself, missed, and felt a strong hand grab her arm. Synthesis. "You all right, sir?" he said. "I know you and Solvent were..."

"I'm fine," she said. "Take the first watch. Lever, rest. It only gets harder from here."

He waited a moment, then nodded and turned away to take up a guard stance. Across the tunnel, Lever was squatting down and watching her, but they did not speak.

"Get a grip," Theosophy growled to herself, under her breath. She had never let death get to her—that was one of the reasons she'd managed to live so long—and she wasn't about to start now. Why was she getting soft? It couldn't be because of Solvent; they'd always agreed not to put too much stock in each other.

Never mind that Solvent was the last person alive who'd been a tyro with her. Or that they'd survived the disastrous expedition into the ruins only by watching each other's backs and trusting each other as Theosophy had never thought she could trust anyone. Or that after the expedition, when Solvent had turned to the rock salts, Theosophy had lost that trust and it had taken her years to forgive Solvent enough to become lovers in the first place...or maybe it had taken Solvent years to forgive Theosophy her resentment of anyone who couldn't or wouldn't fight. She would never know, now.

She slept, and woke with dampness on her face. "Weakling," Theosophy whispered. Louder, she said, "Time's up. Come here, all of you."

The two water-squad members drew near, looking grim and determined, and her two partners shifted closer, though Lever did not relax their watch.

"It's time to send you two back," she said to Solvent's squad. "I know she told you to see us through, but..."

Paradigm cleared his throat. "Actually, she told us to obey your orders."

Theosophy stopped, feeling an ache in her chest. "She did?"

Cosmogony nodded. "She said, if anything happened to her, we were to do as you said, because you knew your stuff."

The ache got sharper. Theosophy had confidence in her own abilities, and she knew the others in the Militia did too, but Solvent had never said anything of the sort to her. She said briskly, "Yes. Well. We've already lost one and I'd like to get the two of you back alive. The hydroponics system is too important to lose two experienced workers. Thank you for getting us this far." She glanced at her own team. "Lever, you will escort them back to the gate. Don't come back here—you won't make it alone."

Synthesis and Lever exchanged glances. Lever said, "Sir, if I may..."

Theosophy nodded.

"I'd like to volunteer to come with you instead."

"Explain."

"I'm quicker and quieter. And I've been in the ruins with you before, when...anyway, we have experience together, and you'll need that."

"Fine," she said. "Synthesis, all right with you?"

"Yes, sir."

She nodded and raised her voice. "Let's move out. Good luck to all of you. I hope you all return safely to the sunshine and the City."

"And you, sir," said Paradigm.

Theosophy gave him a shrug and a half-smile. He looked at her for a moment longer before turning away. She didn't want to get into it, but really...depending on what the dean was up to, she wasn't expecting to come back alive.

THE TUNNELS UNDER the ruins were, thankfully, much cleaner. Either the monsters didn't use plumbing, or their numbers were just much smaller. The tunnel bottoms were nearly dry, and the stink lessened enough that Theosophy was able to pull down her mask and breathe properly again. The *wrongness* persisted, but she was almost used to that.

With the drier footing and the smaller group, they were able to make much better time. She and Lever ran lightly through the tunnels, taking turns on point, pausing before each intersection, resting more often now but for shorter periods to keep their strength up. But the tunnels were quieter now—all the monsters must be out hunting. Theosophy wished she were up there, helping to defend the City—but of course she was off the front-line duty, and besides, what she was doing would be the best defense of all. If it worked.

Without Solvent there, she had to keep pausing to consult the sewer map that she'd torn from Granddad's book. It was hard to connect the lines on the paper with her mental picture of the wrecked streets above. But the *wrongness* kept growing, telling her that she was on the right track—the Rift was drawing closer.

The tunnels intersected with various half-collapsed basements. She began to hesitate at each one, trying to see if anything looked familiar.

Then the tunnel ended in a pile of rubble.

"Fuck," said Theosophy.

"Sir?"

"We'll have to backtrack a little and go aboveground. I don't like it, but it's all we've got."

Lever gripped their spear more tightly. "Lead on, sir."

Theosophy stopped and turned to face them. "What did I do to earn your loyalty, Lever?"

Lever paused. "You believe in what you're doing, sir."

She took a deep breath. "It's not just that. I believe that what I'm doing might be enough to save us all from the monsters, once and for all."

She'd never said it out loud to anyone inside the Wall, even when she'd opened up to Lever and Synthesis. Just as she was wishing she could take it back, Lever blinked hard and said, "In that case, sir, I will follow you to the death. Just tell me what to do."

Theosophy shook her head. First Astro, then Solvent—both her fault. "But *why*?"

"Hope," said Lever simply.

She didn't believe in hope, but if others did, if it galvanized them, well...who was she to argue? "Let's do this."

They came up the stairs together, weapons out. The main floor was deserted, but she heard monsters outside, and crouched low as she crossed to the window with Lever shadowing her.

She didn't immediately recognize where they were, but then she sensed the Rift close by. They had overshot—the Academy building was to her right, only a block, but so close to the Rift that the whole street was overrun. She didn't bother to swear; the situation was too serious for that. Outside, monsters passed to and fro. They hadn't seen or smelled the humans yet, but it wouldn't be long. Just for this moment, she and Lever had the advantage of surprise.

Her double crystal pinged, loud in the quiet room.

Theosophy swore. "Stick with me if you want to get out of here alive," she said, and Lever nodded.

She leapt up and over the windowsill, knocking a monster to the ground as she landed and stabbing it through the chest. Other monsters swirled around her, but by then Lever was there, doing sweeps with their spear, keeping the monsters back. She sprang up and charged into the nearest ones, slashing as she ran through. Footsteps pounded right behind her—human, she knew without looking, too light to be monster. The rubble on the street made for uneven footing. She could only hope not to turn an ankle. The monsters sometimes flowed over the rubble more easily, depending on their form; she targeted the ones that were currently in more awkward forms, bipeds or thick-legged quadrupeds. Thick blood flowed among the cobblestones. None of it hers—yet.

Lever fought by her side as they made their way slowly up the block. At last they reached the familiar Academy edifice, leaning empty behind its windows. Theosophy hesitated. She didn't dare lead them inside, into tight quarters, into whatever the dean was doing...

Lever glanced over at her as though reading her thoughts. "I'll hold them off. It only takes one fighter on the stairs."

She took a deep, steadying breath, and nodded. Lever had said, after all, that they were willing to die for her mission. "I'll come back for you if I can."

They nodded. "Go!"

Theosophy leapt up the stairs with Lever right behind. She reached the doorframe, darted inside, and looked over her shoulder. Lever stood at the top of the stairs, spear lifted high, monsters growling and thronging below.

She squeezed her eyes shut for just a moment—*weakling*, something inside her whispered—and turned away.

The Academy lay unmolested, just as she remembered it. She went straight to the staircase, and descended.

The door to the laboratory was closed again. She marched up and opened it.

Two people stood before the dimensional modulator, turning toward the door in alarm. It took Theosophy that long to process what her mind was seeing. The first person was the dean. The second was Solvent.

CHAPTER TWENTY-EIGHT
BRIONY

"HOLD STILL." Jael dabbed at Briony's face with a damp cloth, which stung, but the pain was disconnected, distant. The Scarred had the anchor, and without the anchor, Briony couldn't help pull the City back in. And Theo hadn't come earlier. All that work, all those days in the forest, all that searching through that horrible underwater paper crypt, and now she was cut off from the one thing she needed.

All that work to protect her family, and she hadn't done a damn thing.

"Bree." Jael's hand on her shoulder, shaking her. Had he been talking? It was hard to focus on him. Everything was lost. The City had been her last hope to help with the war against the Scarred, and now they had it.

"Bree!"

It was so much work to look up at her brother, to meet his eyes. He looked tired, so lost. Briony swallowed, tears welling at the corners of her eyes. Her brother had been so determined to stay on their family's land, and now...

"Jay," she murmured. "What are we going to do?"

He shook his head. There was a streak of red through his white-blond beard, and one eye was swollen shut. She'd failed him, somehow. If she'd made it home earlier, if she hadn't wasted time on all that paper, she…

…she would have what? Her presence, her news, wouldn't have changed anything.

Kishan emerged from the back room of the shop. It was weirdly quiet here, in the middle of town. There was no sign here of the destruction that had raged through her home. Briony felt like she was trapped in a dream, nothing quite real.

The healer wiped his hands on his robe. It was stained with soot and smoke, and there was a long rip down one sleeve. "They're all sleeping now," he said to Jael. "They'll be fine. Nothing more than a few cuts and bruises, though I'm afraid some of those will scar."

"Thank you, Kishan."

Kishan nodded at Jael, at Briony, then turned to go. Briony found herself reaching out, snagging the sleeve of his robe. "Thank you, Kishan. If you hadn't been there…" Briony couldn't finish the thought. Would any of them have made it out?

"You don't need to thank me." He managed a smile. "Good to stay in practice, after all."

"Yes, indeed." Mardu lurked by the front door. He still looked immaculate, which Briony felt should have annoyed her. But annoyance was a luxury, and one she didn't deserve. "Very interesting."

Kishan's shoulders tensed, but he didn't look at the Academy man or acknowledge his comments. "How's your head?" he asked Briony.

Her head? The cloth in Jael's hand was stained with blood. She reached one hand up and tentatively felt her forehead. Laceration. Only skin deep, no damage to the bone beneath. "Fine," she said.

"Good." Jael hauled himself to his feet. "Then let's go."

"Go?" Briony echoed.

Her brother looked down at her, his green eyes reflecting a strange fire that didn't come from the light of the shop. "Let's go show those bastards that we won't go down so easy."

BRIONY AND JAEL peered out of the forest. The sun was starting to rise over the horizon, and its faint, weak light illuminated what was left of the only home they'd ever had. Something cold and heavy had settled deep inside Briony, but now, something else flared as well. After this, she would make sure they paid for what they'd done to her and her family.

The fires had gone out, perhaps because there was nothing left to burn. Charred remains dotted the landscape, and the smell of burning still floated in the air. The anchor sat alone, unaffected.

There were small groups of Scarred scattered about. Had there really been so few last night? They had been everywhere, then. Most were quiet, now, as if they were asleep, if they slept. There was a perimeter guard spread out around the anchor.

"That one," Jael said. He indicated a lone Scarred standing near the edge of the forest. It had one of the tubes from the night before in its arms, but it didn't seem alert, and the weapon was pointed at the ground.

Briony nodded, then followed her brother back into the undergrowth. It seemed unnaturally still, and it took Briony a moment to realize that there were no choke vines here, though they normally had an issue with the Fractured plants in this particular part. Had the Scarred killed them as well? Briony found herself actually upset at their loss. How dare the Scarred come in and change the landscape to fit their needs?

The Scarred was looking back toward the anchor, and so never saw Jael dart out of the forest before her brother hooked an arm around its neck and dragged it back in. Briony joined them at the edge, taking one arm and helping heave it deeper inside. The Scarred made a grating, metallic noise, and Jael cuffed it in the head.

Despite being slight in body, the Scarred was heavier than Briony would have expected. By the time they'd judged themselves far enough away, her arms ached. She thankfully dropped her half of the Scarred. It'd lost its tube back a few paces, but it still struggled violently and tried to claw at them. It had metal gloves on its hands, each finger ending in a vicious-looking edge. As Jael tried to pin its arms down, Briony ducked underneath and jabbed her fingers into the Scarred's collar bone. The Scarred choked on its breath, and Jael heaved his bulk on top of it.

"Now," he said, his breathing a little labored, "we're going to have a chat."

The Scarred said something almost understandable in that horrible dialect and hissed. Jael twisted one of the hoses that connected to its mask and the Scarred instantly went quiet.

"Do you understand me?" Jael said quietly.

It took a moment, but the Scarred nodded.

Jael looked up at Briony. She took a deep breath and crossed to behind her brother's shoulder, where she could see herself mirrored in the Scarred's mask. "What do you want with the anchor?"

The Scarred twisted to look at her, then back at Jael. It started chattering in its own language again, despite Jael's hold. Briony's patience snapped. She reached over Jael's shoulder and tore the Scarred's mask off, ripping the hoses that connected it to the canister on its back. A foul, noxious gas, visibly yellow, oozed out of the broken ends. Beneath the mask was what had once been a human face, but it was now crisscrossed with scars, many old and healed, though some were newer and still red. There was no hair, and the scars continued over the top and sides of the head. There was a strange pattern to them, though Briony could not place it.

The Scarred took a deep breath, closing its eyes, as if in pleasure. After a moment, it opened them again, locking eyes with Briony. It grinned at her, showing pointed teeth. "You know what we seek, Devilspeaker." There was an accent to its voice, and there was still an odd, metallic edge to it. Its eyes traveled down to where Briony's amulet hung beneath her blouse, and she fought down the urge to reach for it, as if that would protect it from the Scarred.

Briony forced her voice to be as level as possible. "You cannot do what you want with the anchor."

The Scarred made a raspy sound, and it took Briony a moment to realize it was laughing. "Do you not think we came prepared, Devilspeaker? Now we have what we need in this world, and everything is complete."

"It won't work. It can't be opened from this side alone."

The Scarred's smile grew wider.

Briony's blood ran cold. "But you already knew that."

The Scarred's eyes darted between her and her brother again. "We are prepared," it said simply, shrugging its shoulders.

"What does that mean?" Jael snapped.

Briony stood, taking a step back. "They have someone in the City already." She ran both hands down the sides of her neck. Oh no—how had this happened? She'd missed something, she had to have. Her goal couldn't be the same as the Scarred's. She needed to talk to Theo, desperately.

"Let's go," she whispered to her brother.

Jael pulled his arm back, then smacked the side of the Scarred's head. It went still, those horrible eyes closing again.

As Jael heaved his bulk off the Scarred, Briony tried to clamp down on the panic in her stomach. Someone inside, and the anchor too. Nothing would stop them. They'd access the City first, get what they wanted, and then it wouldn't be so much a war as a slaughter.

The Scarred heaved itself off the ground, moving faster than Briony would have expected, based on its size and amount of modifications. It bent and picked up its mask, tsking to itself and fingering the broken hoses.

"It is too late," it said. "But let it not be said that we are not merciful." It lunged for Briony, claws up and ready. Briony took a step back, grabbing behind her for a branch or something else she could wield. There was a loud bang from next to her, and the Scarred toppled, blood blooming from a large hole in its side. Briony looked up to find Jael holding a smoking tube, a deep frown on his face.

"Well, at least they bleed like the rest of us," he said.

Briony took a deep breath, trying to calm the shaking of her hands. "I have to warn Theo," she said. "I have to warn her about this person inside."

And fast—before the Scarred got there first.

WESTENAEDRE WAS a mass of chaotic movement when they returned. People were everywhere in the streets, carts loaded up with belongings, families huddled together with bundles at their feet. They stared at Briony and Jael like they were spirits—perhaps not that surprising of an idea, since news would have traveled about the destruction of their home. Yara passed them, her belongings packed into a small wheeled cart. She kept her eyes on the road, as if acknowledging Briony in any way would invoke some evil.

It was no wonder people were on the move. Having the Scarred so close would make even the bravest person antsy. Briony saw several refugees already on their way. They'd seen the Scarred up close before.

The shop was busy too; people ordering draughts to take with them. Kishan was up front, fielding questions as well as collecting orders. He nodded to them as they came in. He looked worse in the daylight.

Some of the people took one look at them, especially Jael, still wielding the Scarred's tube, and decided to be elsewhere.

"The children?" Briony asked.

"I gave them a sleeping draught." Kishan's voice echoed his appearance. "Figured it'd be good to let them rest as long as possible. Keep the memories away as long as we can." He shook his head. "I wish there was more I could do about those."

Briony laid a hand on his arm. "We appreciate everything you've done."

Jael tucked the tube into his belt and ran a hand through his beard. "What now, Bree?"

"I meet Theo by the lake." Kishan flinched. Briony patted him on the shoulder, then dropped her arm. "Twilight, usually." She tried not to think about Theo not being there the night before. It seemed like ages ago, before everything had gone all wrong. One of the documents she'd read in that lake complex had said something about the dimensional fabric being easier to breach at twilight.

It was maybe midday now. Briony looked at the other people in the shop, their faces reflecting their fear and worry, and could hear the people rushing about outside. The thought of sitting here, of watching everyone else react to something that didn't yet affect them, and of doing nothing, sounded terrible.

"I need to warn her." Briony turned to her brother. "And I can't wait around here." Though Kishan did look like he could use her help. But she felt like if she stayed still for too long, the reality of the situation would sink in too far, and then who knew what might happen.

Jael nodded. "Let's go."

"You won't make it." Mardu again. Calm and put together in the face of madness. Briony was tempted to shove her fist into his smug face. Why hadn't he helped more? If the Academy was so great, then why couldn't he have protected them—or the anchor? Or at least warned them, so the children wouldn't have had to face the Scarred when they should have been safe in their own beds.

"We'll be fine," she said. Her anger showed in her voice, but Mardu didn't seem to notice. "Come on, Jay."

"I mean it," Mardu said. He actually reached out and grabbed her by the arm. She stiffened and he immediately let go, perhaps aided by Jael's hand going to the tube. "That area will be swarming with Scarred. You'll need help to get there."

"The Scarred are at the anchor," Briony replied, voice dripping with scorn. "Don't worry, I think we can manage not to get to close to that."

Mardu frowned. "Will you think for a moment?"

271

"Come on, Jael." Briony led the way out of the shop, and Mardu, thankfully, didn't follow. Poor Kishan, though. Busy shop, and the Academy man hanging around. He'd seen what Kishan had done back at home—at the anchor, Briony mentally corrected, since home was gone—and whatever the healer was fearing was probably on Mardu's mind now.

The man was daft, though. The lake was nowhere near the anchor. And there had been no Scarred there when Briony came through the day before.

She and Jael ignored the frantic preparations of their fellow townspeople and entered the forest as close to the shop as possible. They moved quietly and quickly, all the skills their mother had taught them working, for once, in perfect harmony. Perhaps, Briony thought, it was because they'd never had a reason to be more focused than they were now.

But, as they approached the lake, the forest quieted. Briony slowed her pace. Something seemed off.

She could hear the marching of Scarred off in the distance. It did sound like they were between her and the lake, though the forest could warp sound, so maybe not. There was movement ahead in the undergrowth, but it was too far away to make out what it was. It could be anything. Scarred, sure, or Fractures, but maybe something more natural.

Briony slowed more, trying to figure out what it was that didn't seem right. Jael moved along beside her, peering through the undergrowth. The skin beneath his eyes was dark. She shouldn't have brought him. What was she thinking? What was he thinking? Those children were going to need their father when they woke up.

Jael stepped in front of her, and without even knowing why, Briony pulled him back. Jael knew better than to make unnecessary noise this deep in, though he looked confused. Briony was as well, but something told her to proceed with caution. There were no Fractures, no choke vines, but still…she inched forward slowly. There was a new plant here, one she'd never seen before. Briony retrieved a stick, not as long or thick as she would have liked, and prodded one.

The plant moved instantly, wrapping itself around the stick. It wrenched it from Briony's hands, spiraling tendrils up the shaft. There was a sickening crunch, and the stick exploded, fragments ricocheting everywhere.

Jael let out an aborted yell and stumbled backward.

Briony retreated a step, surveying the undergrowth. These new plants were everywhere, crawling up the trees and even down some choke vines. There was no clear way through.

"Oh, Old Ones," she whispered.

The Scarred had brought new Fractures, and they had barred the way. She and Jael retreated, trying to find another way around, but it was no use—the way was closed.

"I TOLD YOU," Mardu said.

Briony punched him as hard as she could. She was aiming for his nose but missed, getting his cheek instead, but he still let out a satisfying yell and fell onto the floor.

"Will you shut up?" she said. "We don't need your attitude here. If you're here because of why I think you're here, then the Scarred just came and scooped it out from underneath you, and you don't even seem to care!"

Mardu looked up at her, rubbing his cheek. It was bright red, and if Briony was lucky, maybe it would bruise, too. "What do you want me to do? I didn't come prepared for this! If you had been clear when you contacted the Academy, then I would have known the danger."

"I want you to get me close enough to the lake that I can contact the City."

Beside her, Jael grumbled. "Get *us*."

"No, Jay." Briony took her brother's hand. "You need to stay here and be here for your family." The children were still sleeping, or else faking it, but Briony knew the potency of her own draughts, and it wouldn't be long. "I go alone."

Jael opened his mouth, then apparently thought better of it. Her brother's gaze went to Kishan, across the shop. The healer was watching them, frowning, but probably wasn't close enough to hear what they were saying. Just as well. Kishan would probably want to come, too.

Mardu narrowed his eyes. "You hit me, and then you want my help?"

"Do you have a choice?" Briony put one hand on her hip. "If you want to do something now, then you've only got me. Otherwise you'll have to go back to the Academy and let them know that the Scarred have possession of the anchor. By the time you get back with help, the Scarred will have already pulled the City back into this realm and taken what they wanted."

He'd been in the process of pulling himself off the floor, but now Mardu paused. "What?"

"Apparently they came prepared," Briony said.

Mardu swore under his breath. He stood fully and straightened his vest. "Fine," he said. "Let's go."

BRIONY PULLED the hood of her cloak up over her hair. The day had drained away. It would be twilight soon, and she needed to get to Theo before it was too late. She had a feeling that she was out of time, and even if she could survive until tomorrow night, it might be too late.

Mardu crashed along behind her, muttering to himself. Luckily the Scarred's cleansing of the forest seemed to be fairly complete and she didn't need to worry too much about him stumbling into a choke vine or something worse. She'd briefed him on the new Fractured plants. Briony had whistled for Poes a few times, but he hadn't come.

She could remember his cry from the night before. She shouldn't have dragged the mountain cat into that. He'd been too dear and steadfast a companion to have sacrificed him on an impossible task. Hopefully he was somewhere licking his wounds, and nothing worse. She'd just have to hold onto that thought.

She almost walked into the new Fractured plants in the fading light, but managed to stop in time. Mardu came up beside her, peering down at them, still frowning. It seemed to be his permanent expression when he wasn't in smarm mode. "This them?"

Briony nodded.

"Right." Mardu pushed his sleeves up. He murmured beneath his breath and a ball of glowing light formed between his hands. Mardu twirled his hands around the ball once before sliding them behind it, like he meant to give it a push. He shouted some word that sounded like gibberish. A beam of light shot out from the ball, incinerating the Fractured plants as well as the surrounding ones.

Briony may have made a startled noise.

"I expected their barrier to be a little more resilient," he murmured, quiet enough that he might have been talking to himself. Briony stared at him. Louder, he added, "Best not to hang around here."

"Why?" Briony asked, but she followed Mardu over the charred remains.

The Academy man didn't answer. "Which way now?"

Briony checked their position against the sky and led the way. But before they made it a hundred feet, a squad of Scarred appeared out of the mist, those horrible tubes clutched in their hands.

"Ah," murmured Mardu, "there we go."

Briony slid to a stop, burning images of her home flashing. Mardu grabbed her roughly by the arm and gave her a push, then murmured under his breath, pulling up his ball again. The Scarred raised their tubes as Mardu let out his beam, felling three of the Scarred in one go.

The others fired, and the forest went up around Briony.

"Go!" Mardu said. "I'll catch up to you. Go, while you can!" He fired his light again, but the ball seemed to be getting smaller. Briony paused for a moment, wanting to say something. But nothing came to mind, and so she turned and ran.

As she went, she could hear another set of explosions behind her. Briony set her jaw and kept going.

She had to duck two more squads of Scarred, and the light was growing dangerously faint. But finally, thankfully, the lake came into view ahead of her. Briony let out a sigh of relief and hurried forward.

Straight into a lone Scarred.

He'd been bent over, blending into the undergrowth, but now he hissed and lunged, the claws on his hands flashing in the fading light.

Something in Briony snapped. She was too close now to fail. She ducked underneath the Scarred's reach and slammed her palm into his sternum. He stumbled back, but quickly recovered, throwing himself in her direction again.

Briony let out a yell and knocked his arms to one side. The Scarred recovered slightly, dragging his claws along the side of her leg, but Briony bit her lip and concentrated on putting her full force onto his pressure points: collarbone, jaw, temples.

The Scarred fell and did not get up.

Briony sucked in a few breaths. Her leg burned, but she couldn't see the damage in the fading light. It held her weight, though, so it would have to do for now.

She raised her eyes to the sky and prayed for Theo to come.

CHAPTER TWENTY-NINE
THEOSOPHY

THEOSOPHY CAME slowly into the room, her eyes fixed on Solvent. But it was the dean who spoke first. "I should have known you would find us."

"'Us'?" Theosophy flicked a glance at the dean, but her gaze was drawn back to Solvent, who looked away. "Solvent, you...you knew she was here this whole time?"

"I helped Dean Prosody get into the ruins," Solvent said, still not meeting her eyes.

"And then you let me—us—think you were dead?" Theosophy's voice broke on the last word.

The dean cleared her throat. "Solvent knew that secrecy was imperative for the safety of the City."

"Solvent, how long have you been working for my dean?" Even the question sounded strange. Theosophy herself was working for Dean Prosody. Wasn't she?

Solvent pressed her lips together and looked at the dean.

Theosophy barged ahead anyway. "And my device...you took it. Which means you've been spying on me."

"On the dean's orders," said Solvent quickly.

"But why?"

"I needed to keep an eye on what you were doing with the comm device," Dean Prosody put in.

"But for *what*?"

"Haven't you figured it out yet? We're on the same side, Theosophy. You want to get through the Wall. So do I."

Wait. She and Briony had been trying so hard to find a way through, and the dean had been doing the same thing the whole time? "If you knew what I was doing, why not recruit me?"

"I didn't know if you could be trusted for this. Don't misunderstand me. You're an excellent fighter and not half bad as a trainer. But Solvent had qualities you didn't."

"Like what?" said Theosophy, and winced at the scorn in her own voice. A part of her, even now, hoped Solvent hadn't noticed. A bigger part felt like puking. After all these years, the dean still didn't trust her. She took a deep breath and reminded herself that she didn't have all the information and responsibilities that the dean had—she couldn't expect to be told everything. But it still hurt.

"They're not important right now. What is important are the qualities you *do* have. I'm sorry I had to keep you in the dark as long as I did, but now I need you." The dean's voice grew steely. "The City needs you."

Theosophy swallowed, feeling her back straighten automatically. "Tell me what to do."

"Everything is in place. Our next step is to bring the Wall down by activating the dimensional modulator. Are you with me so far?"

Theosophy nodded. For the first time, she noticed that the fine tracery of metal that covered the dimensional modulator was now sparkling with crystals—not particularly big ones, but more than

Theosophy had ever seen in one place. She'd known that the dean collected crystals, all the fighters did when they had the opportunity—but everyone else traded them for other necessities. The dean must have been collecting them, and keeping them, for years.

"Good. The dimensional modulator created the Wall by drawing on the energy from the monsters' dimension. Once the Wall was set up, it attained a state of equilibrium—it doesn't take a lot of energy to maintain, but there is a constant trickle. So the Wall and the Rift are linked. If the Wall falls, the Rift closes, and vice versa. Bring down one, and the City is saved from the other."

Theosophy stared at the dean. Here were all the answers she had been unable to find. Dismay warred with a strange sense of maybe-this-was-going-to-work-out. Maybe that was what Cosmogony called hope.

She still couldn't quite grasp the enormity of the dean's secret, or the fact that she herself had never guessed—she felt as if her world had shifted. "How long have you known all this?"

"Long enough to figure out how to make it happen. It took until now; there would have been no point getting everyone's hopes up before then, don't you agree?"

"Yes, but—"

"Theosophy," the dean snapped. "We've been over this. You're very good at what you do, but that does not give you leave to question me. Particularly when you're already on sewage duty. Understood?"

The dean clearly had reasons for the secrecy. And really, did it matter when the result would be the same? The City would be saved and she would meet Briony in the flesh. She was only disappointed because she hadn't gotten to do it herself.

"Understood," Theosophy said.

"Good. Then watch." The dean reached into her pocket and pulled out Theosophy's device, the one she had called the comm.

Theosophy glared at Solvent again. "What—"

The dean held up a hand. Theosophy fell silent out of habit.

The dean lifted the comm device, her eyes on Theosophy. "I'm going to get us out of here," she said.

A beam of blue light sprang up around her. Theosophy watched open-mouthed—was this what she looked like when she was talking to Briony?

The dean looked around herself with a kind of wonder, as if taking in surroundings that Theosophy couldn't see. Was Briony there? Was the dean looking at the forest and the lake? At Briony?

"That's mine," Theosophy said. It came out louder than she'd meant.

The dean glanced at her and away, as if barely able to hear her, and spoke. Or at least her mouth moved, but it was as if she stood behind glass, for Theosophy could hear nothing, though she strained. From the shapes of the dean's mouth, she guessed at a few words: "...ready to come through."

BRIONY

A GLOW ANNOUNCED the arrival of Theo, but when Briony turned, it was someone else, an older woman she'd never seen before. The woman straightened, looked at Briony, and said, "The device is ready and waiting. Are your people ready to come through?"

Briony stared at this strange woman. She could see the resemblance to Theo in her bearing—another warrior. But what did it mean that she was here and not Theo? Fear bloomed in Briony's stomach.

"I need to speak with Theo," she said. "I will only discuss things with her."

The strange woman seemed surprised. "I don't understand. Haven't I been speaking with you?"

Been speaking with her? Briony had only ever spoken with Theo. Had this other woman been talking to Carys, before? But, no, she would have been easily able to tell that Briony was not Carys. So...she'd never seen who she was talking to?

And what did she mean about coming—oh. Briony drew a deep breath. Oh, Old Ones. This is what that Scarred meant. Someone on the inside. And she was here instead of Theo. Briony swallowed. She refused to believe she was too late.

This woman thought she was the Scarred. Briony was obviously not Scarred, not if this woman had any familiarity with them. So maybe she didn't. Maybe she—or her ancestors—had been inside the City since before the War. Maybe she didn't know what the Scarred had become. Briony squared her shoulders, trying to remember the terminology those papers back in the lake had used. "You must have been speaking to"—what would they call it?—"my contacts back home. I am the field agent. And I speak to Theo."

"Aren't you in Askavollr?"

The name was unfamiliar to Briony, but it was probably within the Scarred country. Old Ones, they could talk to the City from there? And she had to be on the edge of the lake to get anything. "No, I am in position at the anchor. I will need to coordinate with Theo."

What would she do if something had happened to Theo? Or if this woman called her bluff? Briony hopefully schooled her face into careful neutrality, trying to make it seem like she was supposed to be there and not panicking on the inside.

THEOSOPHY

THE DEAN TURNED TO Theosophy and beckoned. Theosophy stepped hastily into the area of bright light with the dean. Immediately the basement room disappeared. She was standing by the lake with the dean, holding onto the device and looking at her sweet Briony. "I'm here, Bree, what's going on?"

The dean took a firm grip on Theosophy's arm, squeezing hard enough to hurt. "You know this person?"

Briony scowled at the dean's hand. Was she being *protective*? Theosophy felt herself blushing. Fuck. "We've spoken," she said cautiously, hoping the dean didn't notice her blush.

"I will speak to Theo alone, please," Bree said pointedly. She looked as if she'd been in a skirmish, Theosophy thought—there were nasty-looking cuts on her forehead and one leg, but more than that, she had a look in her eyes that Theosophy recognized, with a twist in her gut, as the angry-and-stupid phase that had gotten Astrolabe. What the fuck had been happening over there? Bree was no fighter, she wasn't made for it. She looked determined, true, but also tired and worried. Theosophy felt a pang in her chest.

The dean squeezed Theosophy's arm once more—a clear warning that confused Theosophy even more—and then let go of the device, took two steps to the side, and vanished. Theosophy waited a moment to be sure that the dean was gone and that she couldn't hear anything from the room outside. "Bree, are you all right? You look kind of terrible."

"It was...I had a hard time getting here." Briony waved one hand unhelpfully. "It's not important right now. I'll tell you later. Who was that?"

"Dean Prosody, my commander. It's all right, she's in on it. She knows how the Wall was created, so she knows how to take it down."

BRIONY

THEO LOOKED TERRIBLE TOO. What was happening? But at least she was there, which was more of a relief than Briony wanted to admit. She'd been so scared that she'd lost Theo before she'd ever really had her, and she didn't want to think about how much Theo was like a light in the darkness, a sole point of hope even as everything else fell apart.

Briony fought to keep a relieved smile off her face. Theo needed information, and Briony needed to give it to her, before her dean figured out that Briony wasn't on her side.

"There was a war, many years ago, do you remember? And the City—the citizens locked themselves away because of something that happened right before, or during, it. Do you remember?"

"My ancestor, Farhan," said Theo. "He was involved, he did something with the..." She waved her hand toward something that Briony couldn't see.

Briony nodded encouragingly. "Mine...mine was, too. The City is tied to an anchor out here. In order to bring the City back, it needs to be activated, and so does something in the City. But, Theo, we can't do it now."

Theo looked over her shoulder. "Why not? We're ready. I think." Theo gave her a bright smile. "And Bree, the Rift will close when we do it. It's only open because we were sealed away. You won't have to worry about my monsters."

Briony took a deep breath. Old Ones, if that was true… She shook her head. The Scarred were worse; Briony had to make Theo see the danger. "Do you remember when I told you about the Scarred?"

"They're your enemies," said Theo. "The way the monsters are ours. They're not people either, are they?"

Briony remembered the way that Scarred had looked underneath its mask, the unnatural way they moved. "They were, once. The valdnordri. But Theo, they have the anchor, and they've cut the City off. If we pull it back now, it'll fall right into their hands. They'll take whatever the City tried to keep safe." She took a deep breath. "And I think your dean intends them to. They said they had a person in the City."

Theo leaned forward, as if she wanted to touch Briony. "What?"

Briony really wished she could physically get to Theo, that there was some way to make her understand how important this was. "You can't let them have the City, Theo. They've got machines designed for killing, ones that can melt entire buildings. They'll slaughter everyone inside, and those are just the lucky ones. The unlucky ones they'll carve up first. I hate to ask this of you, to stay with your monsters,"—was she crying?—"But this would be worse. Please believe me. They have—"

And Theo disappeared.

Briony let out a sob, then covered her mouth.

Theo was out of her reach again. Briony couldn't help her in the City, and without being able to pull the City back safely, Theo would continue to just be an image in the dark.

Wiping her eyes, Briony glanced around. The rising moon reflected off the still waters of the lake, and, closer than she would have liked, she could hear the marching of a Scarred squad. Mardu had never caught up with her, she realized. With one final glance at the lake, she scurried back into the relative safety of the forest, heading back the way she'd come. Had he been killed? Taken? Carved up, the Scarred's weird symbols adorning his skin?

Hopefully not; she might not like him, but it would still be better to have him around.

Briony found a stick and prodded the ground ahead of her, worried that she'd walk right into a set of Fractured plants or some other sort of trap. She wouldn't put holes lined with sharp sticks past the Scarred.

Off to her left, a series of metallic calls went up and were answered from somewhere behind her. Briony glanced over her shoulder. Was it just her imagination, or had she seen the echo of a city over the water?

There were more calls. Briony needed to get out of here; she wouldn't be able to do anything to help her family or Theo from here. Keeping her head down and her hood up, she tried to wrap the darkness and silence of the forest around herself.

CHAPTER THIRTY
THEOSOPHY

THEOSOPHY STAGGERED as the forest and Briony disappeared. The basement room blinked back into existence around her. Dean Prosody was holding the comm device. Theosophy reached for it without thinking.

The dean let her take it, focusing her attention instead on Theosophy's face. "Fighter, what was she telling you?"

"She...you..." Theosophy couldn't find the words. Had Briony been lying to her all this time? Stringing her along for a greater plan? The thought hurt more than she would have imagined possible. She cleared her throat. "She said you were speaking to...to monsters."

Pain crossed the dean's face. "No. To our people."

So at least part of it was true. Theosophy felt her knees weaken. "The Citizens *are* our people."

"Not yours," said Solvent quietly behind her. "Ours." She paused, and the dean nodded. "Dean Prosody and I...we're not really Citizens. I mean, the stories we tell each other say that Citizens came from all over the world, back when the world was bigger, to study at the University. But that's not why we're here."

It took Theosophy a moment to realize what she meant. Briony had said the Scarred weren't always monsters. Once, they had been people too—the enemies of Briony's people. And therefore also the enemies of the people who had shut themselves away and become the City. "Fuck. You're..." What was the word Briony had used? "Valdnordri."

"It was wartime," said Dean Prosody sadly. "A few of us were living in the City when the war began. Others entered during the war, as spies. The war grew more ferocious, and we knew the University was planning something big, but we never dreamed they would split the world in two. When the Wall went up, we—my forebears—were trapped. We've kept our culture hidden, knowing that discovery meant death. But we've been trying to find a way to re-establish contact. Some time ago, I was able to muster the resources to explore the ruins and find what I needed, but at the cost of many lives."

"The failed expedition." Theosophy shook her head, searching for words to tell how she and Solvent had clung together, expecting first rescue and then death, and had finally rallied to fight their way back past the bodies of all their friends and lovers. It had broken Solvent, and Solvent had almost pulled her down too. But of course there were no words for that. She settled on, "You almost destroyed the Militia."

"I am sorry for that. I had hoped I could do it with fewer deaths."

"Was that when you recruited Solvent?" Theosophy let the bitterness enter her voice. That much, at least, she knew: Solvent had been spying on her, and even if it was for a good cause, it made Theosophy hurt right down to her bones.

"No," Solvent answered. Her voice was weary. "I always knew who my people were, but I had no idea about...this plan...until much more recently. Theo, forgive me?"

Theosophy shook her head. "That's just a word. Only actions matter."

Solvent flinched.

"Indeed," said the dean, and stepped away to fiddle with something on the dimensional modulator.

Theosophy felt a momentary pang, but focused on the dean. "Sir, my...my contact called your people the Scarred. From what she's said, they don't seem to act human. Do you know what you're getting yourself into?"

The dean made a dismissive gesture. "I've been speaking with them, planning, for years now. I assure you, they're human. A different people than that that formed the University, with their own language, their own culture, but human all the same."

"Their own language...do you speak it, too?"

Again came that flicker of pain. "Only a few phrases—they have to use your language to speak to me. Our culture is fractured...we need them, and they need us. Their world is full of resources, but we have knowledge and technology that they do not, and they are eager to access it."

"What about the rest of us?"

Solvent put in, "There will be no more monsters, Theo. Isn't that enough?"

"Theosophy," the dean said, "do you trust me?"

Theosophy took a deep breath. This was a lot to take in, a lot of lying and pain. But the dean still had the best interests of the City at heart...didn't she? The Scarred weren't monsters, just people. Facing them, even as enemies, was still better than staying here.

Besides, if she didn't trust the dean, who could she trust? She really wanted to trust Briony, but maybe Briony was wrong, blinded by the notion of enemies. After all, she hadn't grown up fighting. And besides Bree, who else was left—Lever, who was probably dead by now? Synthesis, who'd been loyal but was still too new for her to be sure of him? Astrolabe, who couldn't fight with her anymore? Solvent, who had betrayed her and who still wouldn't meet her eyes?

No, she had to trust somebody, and it had to be her commander, otherwise...what was the point?

"With my life," Theosophy said.

"Then give me the comm device."

Theosophy took another breath and handed it over.

The dean passed it off to Solvent, who glanced at Theosophy, set the device on a nearby table, and began to take it apart.

Theosophy reached toward it involuntarily, but let her hand fall. It was too late to stop Solvent now, and besides, she'd promised her trust. She watched uneasily as the dean handed Solvent a similar-looking device. Solvent fiddled with the two of them, connecting them together and swapping out parts. Finally she looked up and nodded to the dean.

Dean Prosody shouldered a musket that Theosophy hadn't noticed before. She stepped forward with barely contained excitement and took the joined devices. Then she turned away from Theosophy and Solvent, and activated the devices together.

A blue light appeared in the room, and beyond it the shadowy forms of trees. Theosophy watched, fascinated—it appeared that Briony's dimension was coming into the City, this time.

"Hello?" said the dean.

A figure stepped into the light.

Its face was hidden under a mask; it reached up and pulled the mask off, revealing facial features covered in scars. Theosophy jumped, and heard Solvent gasp beside her. The dean made a quick motion, so that the light wavered, but she made no sound.

"Prosody?" the Scarred said.

There was a short silence. Theosophy wished she could see the dean's face. "I am here," Dean Prosody answered in a steady tone.

"Are you ready?" the Scarred said. The voice was obscured by a thick accent, but Theosophy guessed it was male.

Dean Prosody raised her chin. "All is in position."

The figure lifted an arm and beckoned, in what Theosophy recognized as a Militia-like gesture. Other figures crowded in behind it. Each one held what she guessed must be a weapon.

"Proceed," the Scarred said.

"I will activate the dimensional modulator," the dean said. "See you all very soon."

The Scarred nodded, and the image disappeared.

Theosophy couldn't find her voice for a moment. It was Solvent who said, in a voice that trembled, "Sir?"

The dean stood with her back to them. Her shoulders rose and fell once, but when she spoke, her voice was firm. "Continue with the plan, Solvent."

Theosophy stepped forward. "But, sir—"

"This changes nothing, do you understand? We had an agreement. The Wall will open, they will come in with weapons, and the Rift will close. We knew this. Proceed. That's an order!"

So everything Briony had said was true. Theosophy felt her hands curl into fists. She glanced at Solvent, who shook her head just a fraction and stepped between Theosophy and the dean. Well, Solvent might be a coward, but someone had to stop this.

"Sir," Theosophy said, "I wanted the same thing you did. I wanted to open the way to the outside—once I knew there *was* an outside. I thought we might have room to flee the monsters, and more people and resources to help us fight them. I wanted the Citizens to live without fear, and thrive. But what you're doing—it's going to be a slaughter, and I can't let that happen."

And she lunged at the dean.

Solvent blocked her and tried to fight back, but she'd been out of the Militia too long. Theosophy decked her without even trying.

Solvent fell, but the dean stood behind her, holding the musket horizontally on her shoulder. Theosophy looked into the open end, confused. "What—"

There was a flash and a terrific noise that almost deafened her. A moment later, pain flared from her left shoulder, and her whole left arm went numb. She glanced down to see blood. Quite a lot of blood.

She stared dumbly at the dean, remembering Solvent talking about muskets. So that was what they were meant to do. "Fuck," she managed.

Then she lunged again.

Even injured as she was, it took the dean and a wobbly Solvent together to subdue Theosophy. She fought back, no longer worried about hurting either of them, but eventually they got her tied to a chair and Solvent bound up her shoulder. Even then she struggled, until the chair tipped and she fell heavily to the ground. Solvent cast her a worried glance, but the dean ignored her, moving out of Theosophy's line of sight. A moment later, Solvent went, too. She could hear them both moving around, the dean giving a steady flow of instructions— what she guessed were the final preparations for opening the way to the Scarred.

At some point, Solvent came to her side, holding a medical syringe. "I've got to draw your blood," she said quietly. "Dean's orders."

Theosophy lay still and let her insert the needle. While she was drawing Theosophy's blood, Theosophy met and held her gaze. Barely moving her lips, she whispered, "Solvent, let me stop her."

Solvent mouthed back, "I can't."

"But...the City!"

Theosophy could see anguish in Solvent's eyes. "She's my kin. I'm sorry. Truly."

Theosophy pulled frantically against the ropes, but Solvent only turned away.

Left alone, Theosophy lay still again, waiting for the pain of her injured shoulder to ease. Gathering her strength, testing the ropes around her wrists and ankles. Her thoughts raced.

If she let the dean finish her plans and phase the City back into Briony's dimension, she would finally meet Briony. But the Scarred would invade—exactly what her own ancestor and the other original Citizens were running from. And, reading between the lines, the Scarred were going to steal the City's dimensional technology and use it as a weapon. She couldn't let that happen.

If she stopped the dean—if she even *could* stop the dean with Solvent there—then where would that leave the City? Safe from the Scarred, but still vulnerable to the monsters...in exactly the same position as before she had learned that another way of life existed. And before she had seen Briony. She would never get to touch Briony, to find out how those lips felt or how her body looked. She wouldn't even be able to see Briony again, now that her device went to the Scarred instead. The prospect made her chest ache; it bothered her more than she would have thought possible.

But it was the only way. The monsters, she knew now, were bad enough, but the Scarred, with their superior weaponry and battle tactics, were far worse. The Citizens could barely defend themselves from the monsters. Against the Scarred, they would be doomed.

So she lay in her bonds, and tried not to think of Briony, and waited.

BRIONY

DAWN CAME MUCH too early. The stars and moon still hung overhead as Briony emerged from the forest at the edge of Westenaedre to a golden glow to the north. And the noise—it was almost deafening. Loud and metallic and strange.

Briony didn't need to be told what the glow was. She'd seen something much the same the night before, when her home had burned.

Town was almost unnaturally quiet. More people must have left earlier than she had thought.

She hurried through town to the shop. The door was locked, which Briony couldn't remember ever having done before. She banged on the door a few times.

"Who is it?" Kishan's voice, muffled by the wood.

"Briony."

An audible click as Kishan drew the latch and let her in. He immediately locked it again behind her, as if the Scarred would care about a door.

There were several packs sitting in the middle of the floor, and her nieces and nephews sat huddled together next to them. Auberon had Leo on his lap, and Brin and Marcea were so close to his sides that all four of them seemed to be one solid mass, inseparable. They stared at Briony but made no move to greet her. Her heart caught. How had they come to this? She choked on her breath. How many times had she endured one of those effusive greetings with a grimace? She would give almost anything to go back to those days, to do a better job of protecting them, of convincing Jael to go.

"We were just about to leave," Kishan said. "I packed your bag too."

Briony stared at the bag. Just…go?

"Where's Jael?" she asked.

Kishan bit his lip. "He went after you."

Briony whipped her head around. "What? Why didn't you stop him?"

"I'm sorry, Bree."

Of all the stupid—Briony snatched the bag off the floor and slung it over one shoulder. "Go," she said. "Get out of here. Go south."

"But—"

Briony picked Leo up, set him on his feet. The older children rose too, as if even that slight distance was too much. She fought down tears as she gave each a hug and a kiss, and helped them put their bags on. "Don't fight me on this, Kishan. I'm counting on you to keep them safe. Go to Cynestel. If nothing else, the Academy owes us."

"But where are you going?"

"To get my stupid brother." Briony took Leo's and Brin's hands and led them outside. The others followed, including Kishan. "We'll catch up." She stood on her toes, giving him a kiss on the cheek. "Please do this for me."

Kishan stared at her with large, sad eyes. "Of course, Bree."

"Thank you," she said quietly. "Please go. They're too close."

The noise had grown in volume. What, exactly, was coming? Troops, machines? A whole army? It didn't really matter, as long as those she loved were safe.

Was Theo safe?

"Go," she said.

Kishan took Leo's and Brin's hands from her and led the way. She watched her family go until they were just indistinct shapes in the dark. Then she returned to the forest.

THEOSOPHY

THEOSOPHY STRUGGLED with the ropes again, growing frantic now. The dean raised the syringe of her blood, and smashed it over the nearest crystals. The crystals absorbed it and began to pulse with light. Then the rhythm of pulses spread across the dimensional modulator until the whole thing was lit. The crystals pulsed faster and faster, and the dimensional modulator began to thrum.

The floor shook, and the dean staggered. Theosophy turned her head and watched as the pulsing merged into a single bright light. The room suddenly looked a little less sharp. At the same moment, her gut wrenched, and the feeling of *wrongness* suddenly grew less.

"The Rift is closing," she whispered. Her whole body felt lighter, and she felt pinpricks behind her eyes. No more monsters...

Solvent glanced quickly toward her, and away. "Sir," she said. "I think the City is drawing less power while it's half-phased. The Rift is going to close before we finish phasing back in to the other dimension."

The dean gazed at the dimensional modulator, her expression rapt. "We're going home," she whispered.

The walls of the room were beginning to fade. Beyond them, Theosophy could see the faint outline of trees.

Theosophy jerked against the ropes. If the Rift closed while the City was only half phased...maybe she could save them from the Scarred and the monsters at the same time. Briony had said something about activating an anchor—maybe she could get through while it was half phased and break the anchor and everything would stay right where it was. If she failed, she probably wouldn't die; she'd be stuck on the other side, leaving the City to fend for itself. Maybe they'd still have monsters here, and she'd be safe with Briony.

She decided the risk was worth it. She'd always thought she would die saving the City. If she could save the City and be with Briony...if failure meant still being with Briony...fuck it all, she deserved this chance.

But she had to move *now.*

CHAPTER THIRTY-ONE
BRIONY

THE FOREST WAS DARK, blocking the glow from the northern horizon, and the noise from the oncoming Scarred faded as she went. Briony leaned against a tree and stared up at the stars through the canopy. She had no idea where Jael had gone, and no way to track him without light, without knowing where he'd entered the forest.

What had he been thinking? If—when—she found him, she was going to give him a talking-to that Mother would have been proud of. Leaving his children with Kishan to go after her!

She was never going to find him.

Surely he would give up, right? And go back to the shop, see they had gone, and go after them. Surely he wouldn't spend the entire night tramping about the forest. Surely he would have given up on Briony at some point, especially if he couldn't find a way through the Fractured plants.

Bile rose up Briony's throat. He hadn't seen the plants before. Or what if he had made it past, only to walk into a Scarred patrol like she and Mardu had?

No, no, She had to be positive. He was probably already on his way back. She just needed to wait, and listen…

Listen.

Theo's dean had thought she was talking to the Scarred. She had been in contact with the Scarred back in their own country, and had expected to be talking to Scarred now. So the Scarred back wherever had probably told the dean that she would need whatever method Theo used to talk to Briony, no doubt to coordinate with the Scarred stationed at the anchor.

But the dean hadn't gotten the Scarred stationed at the anchor. She'd gotten Briony.

Why?

Briony's hand went to her amulet. This tied her to the anchor, to the City. It had been designed to give the City a way to communicate outside, to learn when it was safe to come back and to help coordinate the process. The Scarred must have told Theo's dean to use that line of communication because they had an amulet of their own.

Maybe that was what Carys had died for.

But maybe whatever Scarred had Carys's amulet hadn't been in position, or Briony had been closer, so it had defaulted to her.

Or maybe they hadn't been able to get Carys's amulet. In which case, they would need Briony's. Or each side would just prod the process along until it worked.

Her head hurt. She needed to find her brother. Briony sighed and rubbed Poes absently on the head for a long moment before the presence of the mountain cat registered. "Oh, thank the Old Ones!" Briony knelt and threw her arms around the mountain cat's neck. "I thought…" The worst. But here he was! His fur was matted with blood on one side, and both ears were ripped. A large cut crossed one eye. Briony ran her fingers through his fur. It was hard to tell in the dark, but though the wound was large, it seemed to be clean, and the blood was all old. Briony buried her head against his neck, and he nuzzled her back. Here, finally, was some hope amid all the destruction. She pulled away. "Can you help me, one last time? And then I promise I'll never ask anything of you, ever again."

The mountain cat blinked his good eye and swished his tail, which Briony chose to take as assent.

"I need you to help me find Jael."

Briony had never really been sure how exactly the mountain cat understood her. Poes stretched then took off at a slow lope through the undergrowth. Briony followed. Maybe something would go right, for once.

Poes led her due east, in the general direction of the lake, but not the normal way she would have gone. Jael must have been aiming for it but not known the path to take. Briony could feel her spirits rising. Poes was alive, her brother was as good as found, her family and Kishan were on their way to safety, and...

...and unless she did something, probably to cut the City off forever, it would fall into the Scarred's hands. But if she did that, she would never see Theo, never hold her...

Briony shook her head to clear it. Focus on the present. Jael.

Poes slowed to a stop. Ahead, Briony could see someone moving through the undergrowth, but their movements were jerky, mechanical. Scarred. Briony held her breath. Poes must have not wanted to get too close, and she couldn't blame him. They'd have to wait until the Scarred went on its way.

But it didn't, and after a moment, Briony could tell that there were two more, lower to the ground and harder to see. They were working on something on the ground, claws glittering in the moonlight.

Poes whimpered, almost silent, and Briony caught a flash of white-blond hair beneath the Scarred.

Her world froze for a moment, then tipped sideways. Briony shook her head again, forced herself to breathe. She dug her fingers into her palms. Why didn't he cry out? Was he already dead?

It didn't matter if he was or not. She couldn't leave him. But what could she do? She was no fighter like Theo, had no helpful magic like Kishan or Mardu. And she wouldn't order Poes to fight for her again, not after it had almost gotten him killed. Her healing skills wouldn't help Jael if she couldn't get to him.

All she had was her amulet, but what good was spirit talking here? She couldn't even control it.

Briony closed her eyes, fighting down the grim realization that there was nothing she could do, and that Jael would want her to go. She couldn't give up. She wouldn't give up. She'd almost given up, back at the cottage, when those Scarred had bore down on her and Brin. Kishan had saved her then, but he wouldn't now.

Thinking of Kishan gave her pause. His magic could do more than one thing. It healed, and it protected. Briony opened her eyes, looking down at the pale blue glow of the amulet. And she remembered visiting Rissa and watching the blue glow of the box as she Sent letters. Both magics were blue. Did that mean that they were the same? Did that mean that she could speak, and that she could send?

That she could connect?

Slowly, Briony rose. She peered through the undergrowth. The Fractured plants the Scarred had set up were nearby. She wrapped her hand around the amulet. Everyone else knew spells to do what they wanted them to do. Maybe Briony would have learned them too, if she'd gone to the Academy. But it was too late for that now. She'd just have to rely on hope.

Send, she thought. *Connect.* She focused on one of the Fractured plants, then on the nearest Scarred.

She wasn't sure what she'd been expecting. A flash, maybe—the plant suddenly closer to the Scarred, sent to a new position. Nothing was happening. Jael was lost.

But then she noticed the plant was moving. It crept across the ground, reaching its tendrils out. Slowly, so slowly. But the Scarred did not notice it, and eventually, it was close enough.

The Scarred almost seemed to stumble into its embrace.

One of the Scarred heard the cry of its companion and took a few steps into the dark, perhaps looking for an enemy. It found one, though not the one it expected.

The last Scarred was not so easily ensnared. It whipped something off its belt and pointed it at the plant. A blast of fire scorched it, reduced it to ashes. And then the Scarred went back to the task at hand.

Briony had hoped that Jael would react, that he would throw off his lone attacker, but he didn't move, despite the evened odds.

What now? Briony took another deep breath. Could she ask Poes to go after just this one? But Poes was injured, and the Scarred was on guard, occasionally pausing in its work to look around.

Poes growled, raising his hackles. Briony followed his gaze, expecting to see the moonlight glint off more horrible masks, but all she could see was a single, steady set of eyes, glowing low through the darkness.

Old Ones. A Fracture. What kind she couldn't tell, but surely no natural animal would stand so close to the unnatural death of the Scarred.

But still...Briony's grip tightened on the amulet. She stared into the eyes of the Fracture. *Connect.*

The eyes blinked. Briony kept up eye contact. *Connect.*

The Scarred heard the Fracture coming. It took one look at it and fled into the night, the Fracture on its tail, so fast that Briony still was not sure what exactly it had been trying to be. As screams filled the air, she darted forward and grabbed Jael under the arms. He was so much lighter than she had expected.

She made it a long way back to town before exhaustion finally set in. When had she last slept? What time was it? Poes stared out at the forest as Briony knelt beside Jael on the ground, trying to use the moonlight to see how he was. Her hands shook as she felt for his pulse.

His wrist was slick with blood. But, thank the Old Ones, there was a heartbeat.

Briony wiped at her eyes. "Jael," she said, but could barely hear herself. She swallowed, then tried again. "Jay. Wake up. Please."

Still nothing. Briony pressed her hands against her mouth and took a deep breath. She needed to be calm, methodical. Heartbeat, so alive. His chest was moving, so breathing. Briony ran her hands around his head, neck, chest, checking for injuries. The blood seemed to be confined to a single arm. Numerous small cuts, all bleeding, decorated the arm. *They'd been carving him up.* There was also a lump on the back of his head, but nothing that indicated there'd been any real damage. Had they hit him? Or had Jael hit his own head when they fired a tube at him, and then they'd just taken advantage?

It didn't matter. Nothing seemed immediately life-threatening. Briony carefully rolled him onto his side.

Jael awoke with a start, jolting upright, and Briony had to duck a swing of his arm. "Jay! It's me."

"Bree?" Jael took several deep breaths, as if he was trying to calm himself down. "Old Ones. What happened?" The hand of his good arm went to the cuts on the other, but then Jael jerked it back.

"I don't know. Look, I sent the children with Kishan. You need to catch up with them." Briony hauled herself to her feet, then offered her brother a hand. "Kishan'll be able to deal with your arm better than I can. Just get out of here, all right?"

Jael stared at her hand, then at her. "What?" Old Ones, was he concussed? Briony hadn't thought he was, but she couldn't send him on his own if so, and it was hard to check in the dark.

"I said—"

"No, I heard you." Jael waved her hand away and clambered to his feet. Briony watched his movements closely, but they seemed natural enough. "You can't expect me—"

"I can't believe you'd come after me!" Jael flinched enough at her tone of voice that she could see it in the moonlight. "You have four children for whom you are the only parent and you risk all that? What in the world were you thinking?" Briony took his good arm and spun him south. "Now, I don't want to hear another word. You go after Kishan, and you stay with your children, and I will be along shortly, but you are not to wait for me. Do you hear me, Jay? You keep going, and you keep going until all of you are safe, and you do not come back for me."

Jael stared at her. "But, Bree—if I don't look out for you, who will?"

Theo. Briony shook her head to clear the thought. Theo was in the City and, if Briony did this right, she would stay there. "I'll be fine. Go."

Her brother took a few steps before turning back. "Are you meeting Mardu?" he asked, sounding hopeful.

Mardu. Another person who was lost out here in these woods. "Yes," she lied. "We've got a plan. You should see his magic, Jay. He took out three Scarred with a single spell." She laid a hand on Poes. "Plus, I have Poes to keep me safe." She was talking too much. It had to be obvious.

But maybe the facade was enough for Jael. He nodded and went, slowly fading into the undergrowth, until even the reflection of the moonlight on his hair disappeared.

Briony swallowed. So what if it was just her and Poes? She had something she needed to do. If she looked in the direction of the lake, she could swear that something was slowly fading into existence. Surely that was the outline of a tower, and that, another. She set her shoulders, straightened her bag, and set off again.

THEOSOPHY

"SOLVENT," Theosophy said quietly.

Solvent moved to stand beside Theosophy again. The dean seemed not to notice.

"What's going on?" Solvent whispered, eyes searching her face. "Theo, what are you thinking?"

"I think I can save the world, but you have to free me."

"You're going through, aren't you? To your other lover?"

Theosophy nodded.

"She makes you happy," Solvent said.

"It's not that. She gave me hope for the world."

Solvent smiled, a little sadly. "And for yourself. Don't discount that."

Solvent knelt by Theosophy's side, pulled a dagger, and cut the ropes. Theosophy shot to her feet. The dean turned and shouted, raising the musket again. Theosophy dove behind the dimensional modulator. Her injured shoulder flared and she collapsed to the ground. A flash and a bang, and Theosophy ducked. It took her a moment to realize she was unhurt. But Solvent stood, tottering, looking down at her stomach, where blood welled, then gushed.

"No," Theosophy shouted, staggering to her feet.

Solvent swayed into the dean, pushing her down, and they fell together. The dean's head hit the edge of the dimensional modulator. Crystals flared and her whole body jerked uncontrollably. Solvent held on. She looked up at Theosophy and said, "I love you."

Theosophy felt her eyes prickling. When was the last time she had cried? She leaned down, grabbed the musket out of the dean's unresisting hand, and kissed Solvent one last time. Then she turned away, found the spot where the trees were most visible, and jumped.

CHAPTER THIRTY-TWO
BRIONY

POES STAYED BY her side as Briony stalked through the forest. She'd found one of the Scarred's tubes—though she didn't know who had dropped it and suspected she didn't want to know why—and had brought it along. It was heavy, though not as heavy as it looked, and had a variety of levers on it that Briony hadn't the faintest idea what they did. But it was a weapon, and she'd take that. If nothing else, she could swing it like a club.

It was getting harder to see in the direction of the lake the farther she went from it, but she was sure the City was coming back. Theo must have not been able to stop it, if she'd even tried. Briony tried not to think about that too hard. She couldn't blame Theo if Theo hadn't. It must be terrible, being trapped in there with monsters. Theo didn't know the Scarred.

So it would be up to Briony to save her—them. Those poor people deserved better than to think they were escaping one set of monsters only to find another waiting for them.

And whatever she did, she'd find a way to reverse it, so that when the Scarred were gone they could get out. She'd go to the Academy, despite Carys's and Kishan's misgivings. She'd make them help. The Academy would want something, too—obviously did, judging from Mardu's interest—but they wouldn't kill everyone in the City to get it, just because they could.

Would they?

Briony waved the thought away and buried her fingers in Poes's fur. First things first.

The sky was lightening, but she had realized that it was from the incoming Scarred, not because this horrible night was ending. Whatever she did, she would need to do it before they arrived. Was it an invasion force, specifically for the City? Or just the Scarred sweeping in from the border intent on doing—whatever? As far as Briony knew, there'd been no attempts at diplomacy, no sent demands.

She reached the familiar edge of the forest no closer to any answers. The Scarred had the anchor illuminated. Thin strands of something—magic, maybe?—stretched from each surrounding post to the center, main one, the one with the carving on top. There they combined into one larger strand which shot off in the direction of the lake and the City.

They'd made the connection. They were pulling it back.

Briony balled her hands into fists. Right. It was now or never.

Despite the action at the anchor, there weren't actually any Scarred present. Had they gone into the forest to meet the City? Were they just out of sight behind one of the ruins of her former home?

It didn't much matter. She'd take what she could get. "Stay, Poes," she said, and stepped out of the trees.

Nothing happened, so Briony hurried over to the anchor. What now? Was it safe to enter? She stuck the end of the tube into the circle of posts and, when it remained much the same, followed, creeping low to the ground to avoid the strands. Maybe she could disrupt the strands somehow.

She raised the tube up into the strand closest to her. Maybe disrupting a strand, or a few, would halt the process. Or maybe she could reflect the strand back at its originating post, which might cause some useful trouble.

But the strand just sliced right through the tube. Briony stared at the half that dropped onto the dirt next to her. It steamed slightly, and the end was cleanly cut, as if the metal had provided no resistance at all. So much for that idea.

There was a yell from behind her. Had she set off some sort of alarm? She could hear the rhythmic footsteps of the Scarred approaching. Briony scurried out of the circle of posts and laid flat on the ground behind a pile of rubble. Apparently just in time—she could hear the Scarred reach the circle and converse, though too quietly for her to hear what they were saying.

Silence fell. How long until they went away? Some of the rubble must still be smoldering, and Briony could feel the heat starting to sear the hair on her arm closest to it.

There was a shout. Crap. Briony had left the tube piece, and it hadn't been small.

It wouldn't take long for them to find her. The forest was too far away to retreat to, and it was across open ground anyway. All right, fine. Briony stood, pointed the remains of the tube in the proper direction, and pulled the levers in what seemed like a logical manner.

The resulting explosion knocked her head over heels. There were several cries from the direction of the anchor, some of which might have been in pain, if the Scarred believed in such a concept, though it was hard to tell around the ringing in her ears.

Briony pushed herself back upright. The Scarred at the anchor had scattered, and she'd managed to knock the center post slightly out of alignment, so that the flow along the strands occasionally flickered like they might break. But they were holding for now.

It wouldn't take the Scarred long to regroup. Briony took up the remains of the tube and ran back, sliding under the strands. She pressed her back against the center post and pushed, though she didn't expect much. After all, how many times had she and Jael played among and over these posts? How many times had her nieces and nephews? How many times had the children of her family over the last several centuries?

The post didn't move. Briony grunted in annoyance and spun, pointing the tube at it again. She flicked the levers.

Nothing happened.

Great. She could see the Scarred regrouping out of the corner of her eye, so she was running out of time. Thus far none seemed to be pointing anything at her, but that was probably because they were worried about hitting the anchor. They'd come up with something else soon enough.

Dropping the useless tube on the ground, Briony wrapped her hand around her amulet. She placed the other on the post. It vibrated beneath her touch. *Send*, she thought, focusing on the edge of the forest. *Send.*

But the post went nowhere. In fact, it shocked her. Briony snatched her hand back and cursed the Old Ones and her ancestors for making something that was unbreakable. They were going to be their own downfall.

The Scarred were getting closer. What was she going to do? Brute force wasn't going to work, her magic wasn't going to work. She pulled the bag off her back and started digging into it, throwing the contents across the ground beside her. Food, clothes. Some medical supplies. Useless, useless, useless.

A hiss from behind her. Briony looked over her shoulder to find one of the Scarred ducking beneath the strands and creeping closer. Fuck. She returned to the bag. More clothes. A waterskin. Her notebooks.

Tucked in the very bottom was a smaller sack Briony didn't recognize. She pulled it out. A piece of paper fluttered to the ground. *Just in case. —Mardu*

Inside was a purple ribbon, weird and slick to the touch. Old Ones, now she really owed him, the ass.

There was a sharp pain on her cheek and she found herself lying on the ground, staring up at the Scarred looming over her, sharp claws bearing down at her face. Briony screamed.

The Scarred was knocked to one side, a blur of fur following him. Poes.

"No," Briony murmured to herself. She rolled up. "No, no, no!"

But he had bought her time. Briony wrapped the ribbon around the post, grabbed both ends, and pulled.

The post beneath her cracked and the strands wobbled. But they stayed.

Briony wiped at her face. Her hand came back wet and bloody. Curse the Old Ones, all that foresight and they couldn't build in some sort of failsafe in case the anchor fell into enemy hands? She should have read that stupid procedure closer. She should have figured out a way to bring it with her.

Regrets wouldn't help her now. She tossed the ribbon away, pushed on the post above the crack. The forsaken thing still held. Briony could see Poes weaving in and out of the other posts, keeping the Scarred at bay, though not without painful consequence.

She was running out of time. And ideas.

Briony stood, carefully avoiding the strands, and stared down at the carving on the top of the post. The strands all convened on top of the carving before shooting off toward the City.

This symbol had been all over that procedure back at the lake. It was tied to whatever had been done to hide the City away.

And there'd been that slip of paper: *Ealadgast has volunteered to—*

Briony had thought he—or she—had volunteered to guard the anchor. But what if guarding it had been more than just keeping the physical anchor safe? What if…?

Briony took a deep breath. Raising her left hand, she held it above the strands, over the symbol. Before she could regret it, she brought her hand down.

The pain seared through her hand. There was a noise like something ceasing to be, and everything went white.

When Briony could see again, she was several feet back toward the forest. She rolled onto her knees, clutching her hand against her chest, and looked back toward the anchor. Or where the anchor had been. Several of the outer posts lay on their sides, though a few were gone completely. The center post was nothing more than a pile of rubble. The strands were finally, blessedly, gone.

The destruction did not seem to extend beyond the edge of the anchor, however. A full dozen Scarred were bearing down on her. Briony took a deep breath, trying to calm her nerves. She'd done it. The City would be safe, at least from the Scarred, and maybe even from the monsters. Her family was safe, on the move south, where they'd be able to get help and protection.

And Theo, well, Theo was out of her reach. It was a shame to die without ever holding her, but Briony had done the best she could.

Surely that was all anyone could ask out of this life.

Poes jumped in front of her, raising his hackles and growling at the approaching Scarred.

"No," Briony said. "Poes, go!"

The mountain cat turned and blinked his eyes at her. He padded over, nudged her toward the forest with his head.

"No." Her voice came out garbled around something in her throat.

Poes nudged her again, harder. Briony pushed up to her feet. "Poes…"

He hissed at her, then turned back to the Scarred. He showed his teeth. And then he charged into their midst.

With a sob, Briony turned and fled into the safety of the trees.

BRIONY HADN'T MADE it very far before a bright green light flashed above the trees from the direction of the lake. Still cradling her injured hand, she slid to a stop. Had the Scarred reestablished the connection with the City? No, no—not after Poes had sacrificed himself to save her.

Had she been too late?

She should get away from here. But if the City had come back, if the Scarred would have access to it—she needed to know that, so she could tell someone, so she could try and do something about it.

She hurried through the undergrowth, heedless of Fractured plants or other dangers. But as she went, she realized the flash had been closer than the lake. Briony slowed. If not the City, what had it been?

She rounded a tree and stopped completely. Ahead of her, through the low light of the forest, she could see a person. But they didn't move with the mechanical precision of a Scarred. In fact, they moved fluidly and gracefully, like Briony imagined a warrior would. Light glinted off some kind of long blade in the person's right hand, but the weapon hung limp, as if unnoticed. The person was looking around them, staring up at the sky, reaching out to the trees like they'd never seen them before.

Briony crept forward. If she wasn't mistaken, that profile was very familiar, though she'd only seen it through a blue glow before.

She slid to a stop. "Theo?" She pinched herself hard, then looked up again. It was Theo, really Theo. Old Ones. It was a miracle. The City loomed overhead, still just an echo, a mirage over the water. But Theo!

Theo looked directly at her and said her name.

It suddenly seemed like too much. To have Theo really here, after all that hoping. Briony forced herself to take a step forward, then another. The distance between them closed, and still Theo was there. Watching her, smiling at her.

And then she was less than an arm's length away.

Briony reached her uninjured hand out slowly, disbelievingly. Theo took her hand. She was warm and Briony could feel the calluses on her palm. Blood caked a wound on Theo's shoulder, and she smelled like a privy. Old Ones. She was really there.

"I don't understand," Briony said. "Did I—is the City coming back?"

"No," Theo said. Her voice sounded different in person, fuller. She looked up at the City over the lake. "It's...stuck. You did that, I think."

"Then...how are you here?" Briony gave Theo's hand a squeeze. Still there. Still real.

"The dimensional modulator started working, and I jumped through before it was done. I meant to come through and break the...anchor, did you call it? But something went wrong and I was trapped between the dimensions. I still don't know how I got out."

Briony looked down at their intertwined hands. "I think maybe that was me, too. But I'm glad you did."

Theo gave her hand a squeeze, and met her eyes. "Me too. Being here with you...it's amazing. But I can't stay. I have to get back."

"Back...?" Briony looked around. The day was finally starting to break, but it was still fairly dark in the forest. She couldn't see anything that was out of place, anything that would denote a passage into the City. "How?"

"The way I..." Theo turned and looked behind her. Briony looked over her shoulder, but could see only trees. "Oh." She turned back to Briony, tears in her eyes.

Briony brought Theo's hand to her lips. "Oh, Theo," she whispered. "I'm so sorry."

Theo shook her head. "I guess...the dean said the Rift would close if the City phased all the way back in, and with it stuck halfway, it's mostly closed. The monsters should be a lot fewer now. They can manage without me. Life will be better. I just...without the monsters, I don't know what I'm here for. I never thought I'd live this long."

"Speaking of that..." Briony looked back toward where her home, her town, had been. Surely the Scarred would come to investigate the light, just like she had, if they weren't already looking for her. "We shouldn't stay here. You're injured, and so am I. We need to get someplace safe."

"We." Theo smiled and wiped at her eyes. "You know, I like the sound of that."

THEOSOPHY

THEOSOPHY WENT to take a step, and hesitated, her hand still in Briony's. Briony leaned forward. Theosophy found herself drawn toward her. Their lips met. Briony's mouth was warm, and she met the strength of Theosophy's kiss with equal passion. It felt wonderful.

Theosophy pulled back at last, looking down into Briony's eyes with something like awe. Was this what it was like, letting oneself live? Theosophy thought she could get used to it eventually. She wouldn't stop trying to get home, but really, the City was in good hands now. Solvent and Lever were dead—and she needed time to mourn them—but the Scarred and Dean Prosody had been stopped, Synthesis knew at least some of what the stakes had been, and he and Astrolabe, Cosmogony, and Paradigm were still there. Maybe she could let them take care of things for a while and just...be here with Briony.

She thought she might even be happy.

Briony pulled back and smiled at her. "Let's go."

Theosophy took her hand and let herself be pulled along.

ACKNOWLEDGEMENTS

First, Kit would like to thank Siri for not strangling her during the writing process, and Siri wishes to return the sentiments with equal warmth.

Thanks to KD, Erin, Arvin, Kit's mother Ann, and Carolyn for their very helpful critiques and edits, which have not only made this book much better but also caught some embarrassing problems.

Thanks and love to our families for not killing us for being overly stressed or even for ignoring them for hours on end while typing madly, talking to someone in a different country, and researching all sorts of strange things.

Thanks and smooches to our friends at the Spork Room who stroked our egos by being so interested in the "sekrit project."

Siri would also like to thank her in-person critique group and Chris Baty, founder of National Novel Writing Month, both of whom made this happen.

And thank you to *you*, you beautiful person, for reading our book! We would love you *even more* if you would leave us a review on Amazon or Goodreads.

ABOUT THE AUTHORS

Kit Campbell

It is a little known fact that Kit was raised in the wild by a marauding gang of octopuses. It wasn't until she was 25 that she was discovered by a traveling National Geographic scientist and brought back to civilization. This is sometimes apparent in the way that she attempts to escape through tubes when startled.

Her transition to normalcy has been slow, but scientists predict that she will have mastered basics such as fork use sometime in the next year. More complex skills, such as proper grocery store etiquette, may be forever outside her reach.

Kit can be found cavorting about the web at http://kitcampbellbooks.com.

Other books by Kit Campbell:

Hidden Worlds
(Turtleduck Press, 2010)
Margery Phillips finds a magic door and then manages to screw everything up. Fantasy adventure.

Shards
(Turtleduck Press, 2013)
Eva Martinez just wants to figure out what to do with her life. Instead she gets embroiled in a millennia-old conflict. Mythic urban fantasy romance.

Kit also has stories in each of Turtleduck Press's anthologies, which you can find under Siri's bio.

Siri Paulson

Siri Paulson writes all over the fantasy and science fiction spectrum, including (so far) secondary-world fantasy, urban fantasy, steampunk, Gothic, historical paranormal, and YA with spaceships. She is also the chief editor at Turtleduck Press (http://turtleduckpress.com/). By day, she edits non-fiction for the government.

Siri grew up in Alberta, Canada, but now lives in an old house in Toronto. Her other current passion is contra dance, a social/folk dance done to live Celtic and roots music. Her favourite places in the world are the Canadian Rocky Mountains and a little valley in Norway.

She occasionally blogs at https://siripaulson.wordpress.com/ and tweets at http://twitter.com/Siri_Paulson.

Siri has edited and contributed stories to a series of anthologies put out by Turtleduck Press:

Winter's Night: A Turtleduck Press Anthology (2011)
Speculative fiction stories of winter.

Seasons Eternal: Stories of a World Frozen in Time (2012)
Imagine a world where seasons never change.

The Best of Turtleduck Press, Vol. I (2013)
A collection of the best short fiction from Turtleduck Press's first three years.

Under Her Protection: Stories of Women to the Rescue (2014)
Women kicking butt and taking names.